DRIVEN

Leipfold Mysteries

DRIVEN

Leipfold Mysteries

Dane Cobain

Encircle Publications, LLC
Farmington, Maine U.S.A.

Editor: Cynthia Brackett-Vincent
Book design: Eddie Vincent
Cover design by Christoper Wait
Cover images © Getty Images

Published by: Encircle Publications, LLC
PO Box 187
Farmington, ME 04938

Visit: http://encirclepub.com

Sign up for Encircle Publications newsletter and specials
http://eepurl.com/cs8taP

Printed in U.S.A.

A Note on the Text

MAILE AND LEIPFOLD live in a London that's similar to, but not identical to, our own. It's a London where the villains are straight from the pages of a comic book, where the heroes are unusual (but normal) people struggling to do the best they can in the knowledge that life doesn't always turn out like it does in storybooks.

Because of this, not all of the city's geography is one hundred percent accurate. If you walk along Balcombe Street, you won't be able to follow it down an alleyway, up the stairs and into Leipfold's office. You won't be able to visit Cholmondeley at the Old Vic, either.

Likewise, all of the characters are creatures of the imagination. Any similarities with real people—living or dead, fictional or otherwise—are purely coincidental. Except for the bit about Justin Bieber.

Autonomous cars already exist, and trial runs are taking place around the world. But there's work to be done before they become a common sight on British or American roads.

If you ever find yourself falling through a rabbit hole and resurfacing in Leipfold's London, be sure to buy him an orange juice from me. And if he's riding Camilla, give her a pat on the handlebars.

Chapter One:
Donna Takes a Walk

DONNA THOMPSON turned the volume up on her iPhone, tightened her scarf, and started to walk a little faster. It was a Tuesday, and Tuesdays were the worst day for tips. Tony's had been empty all day.

It was also night-time. After cashing up and waving goodbye to Tony, the eponymous boss who'd sunk his life savings into the place, she'd walked out of the café and started out on the long journey home.

She lit a cigarette, looked both ways, and crossed the road. The streetlights shone down and made monsters in the shadows. She tugged nervously at a lock of her hair. Her fringe hung down to her eyes. Her face itched with the concealer that helped to hide the bags that grew when she worked too many late shifts. The deception was completed by layers of eyeshadow and mascara and a thin line of eyeliner that made her look like a faux-Egyptian pharaoh queen.

Meanwhile, the cold air chafed at her lips, accentuating their pink tint and wearing away at her Carmex. She finished her cigarette and threw it into the gutter, then reapplied her lip balm without breaking her stride. It was a twenty-minute walk to the station. While her boots kept her warm and dry, the soles of her feet were perpetually blistered from walking across the café's tiled floor.

A black cab motored past her. Donna thought about flagging it down but ignored the urge. She barely had enough to live on as it was, and luxuries were for other people. Besides, she knew she looked pretty good, a blue-eyed brunette with a reddish tinge and a hanging fringe, a size ten dress, and decent legs that were covered with a thick pair of grey leggings. She wasn't a ten, but she thought she could pass for a seven or an eight if the lighting was good, and anything could happen in a sketchy area like this one. Like her mother had always told her, there were some bad people out there. And some of those people drove taxis.

It was a cold, quiet night, too cold to stand around, with hardly any traffic and no other pedestrians in sight. Donna shivered and thrust her hands into her pockets then continued to walk along the deserted street. It started to rain, and Donna realised just how impractical her clothes were. She was still a quarter mile from the station, and she had to walk back to her apartment once she reached her stop.

She shivered as the rain started to gather momentum. She thought about waiting it out and decided against it. *Better to press on, surely.* At least that way she'd be able to dry off once she got home. The water had started to soak through her clothes and into her bones, and her hair was already tangled and matted, a far cry from the comfortable bun she'd tied it in when she left the house that morning.

Her phone rang.

With the water still pelting down and tearing at her eyes like a harpy, she willed herself to forget it. But her FOMO was kicking in and the lure of the vibrating device was too much to ignore, so she crouched in a narrow archway outside a house on Wentworth Road and pulled it out of her pocket to glance at the screen. It was an unknown number and it caught her at a bad time, so she ignored it and packed her phone back away in her pocket.

Instead, she stepped back out into the rain and hit a right at the traffic lights. She didn't notice the black sedan that was inching slowly along the road, a good hundred yards or so behind her.

Donna walked along in a world of her own, mindlessly thinking about the hum of the wind in her ears, the smell of fresh rain in the middle of winter, and the slick sound of tyres on grit. She reached a T-junction and looked to her left and then her right. Then she froze, illuminated by headlights.

The black sedan had skidded off course and was heading towards the pavement. By the time she realised what was happening, it was already too late. Donna tried to dodge out of the way, but the vehicle clipped her side and sent her tumbling through the air.

She died the second her head hit the asphalt.

Chapter Two:
Meanwhile...

SOMEWHERE ON THE OTHER SIDE of the city, private investigator James Leipfold was sitting in his office, hunched over his desk with a copy of *The Tribune* in one hand and a black biro in the other.

Leipfold thrived on challenges, even if they were the intellectual challenges of Mr. A. Phelps, junior reporter and crossword compiler at *The Tribune*. There was little else for him to do. He had the kind of mind that rebelled when left to its own devices. He needed something to focus on, something to niggle away at him, something to dwell on in the shower or in the early hours of the morning.

That evening, he was dwelling on eleven across. It was an anagram, and Leipfold hated anagrams. Clues were fine, and cryptic clues were even better, but anagrams were for people who dealt in words. Leipfold dealt in problems, not words. That was a job for journalists and other hacks. Leipfold hated journalists because he never knew where he stood with them. They took his words and turned them against him.

Not that anyone, journalist or not, had talked to Leipfold lately. His last major coverage had been a couple of years ago after the case of the crippled hipster. Now in his forties with a receding hairline and a criminal record, Leipfold was hardly a catch. Couple that with his thin face and his stocky shoulders, his worry lines and his eternal frown, and it was easy to see why the ladies passed him by. His male friends, meanwhile, were mostly on the force or in the slammer, and either way they didn't have much time for a cheeky pint at the Rose & Crown.

Not that Leipfold drank anymore, either. Drink was a demon that he'd lived with for over a decade, but he'd been sober for the last four years and he meant to keep it that way.

He turned his attention back to the crossword. Eleven across: *Go near fresh fruit.*

He wrote "orange" in the little boxes and turned his attention to nineteen down.

* * *

Tom Townsend was at The Ledbury, the upper-class eatery at the Grosvenor House Hotel on prestigious Park Lane, enjoying dinner with a stunner of a woman who was all dark brown eyes and sparkling smile. The starter was so-so, but the main course, grilled kipper with mustard butter, was delicious.

He stared at the woman as he wiped his lips and reached for the wine. Her mobile phone rang. She glanced at the screen and then excused herself as she rose from the table to answer it. She was gone for five minutes. Five long, uncomfortable minutes for Tom Townsend, who took out his own phone and started to fiddle with it.

When the woman came back, her hands were sweating and her face was flushed, but if her date noticed, he pretended not to. He smiled as she sat back down at the table. "Where were we?" he asked.

The woman smiled back at him and reached across the table to cup his hands in hers. "You were telling me how much you want me," she said. "And I was telling you how much I want to be in your production."

Tom laughed. "Yeah? I'm sure we can come to an agreement. Are you sure you're ready?"

"Tom, I was born ready. Just give me a chance and I'll prove it."

He paused mid-bite to look at her. She *looked* the part, but she was untested, a wild card. Business was business and pleasure was pleasure, but he was thinking with his crotch and not his wallet, again.

"Please, Tom," she said. "I'll do anything."

He smirked and put his fork down on the plate. "Anything?" he asked.

***

Leipfold had finished his crossword, but his brain still craved something to keep it occupied. In years gone by, he would've reached for the bottle, but the bottle had let him down too often. With no booze and no crossword, he felt like he was out of options.

He picked up the paper and tossed it onto his desk. Then he stretched his arms, stood up slowly and began to pace around the room.

After ten minutes had passed, he paused and looked around. The office was dingy and shabby looking, but it felt more like a home than his apartment. His eyes wandered lazily over the cheap plastic kettle and his mismatched mugs, past the faulty intercom and the hooks on the back of the door and then further along to where two potted plants sat sadly on a bookshelf beside a bunch of old textbooks. His cool, grey eyes settled on the only part of the office he was proud of, the sign he'd bought when he first went into business.

It read James Leipfold: Private Detective.

He smiled softly, remembering the first time he walked into the place. After the accident and his subsequent imprisonment, it'd been hard to find a job. He had a record, a past and the kind of face that put prospective employers on edge. Even when he managed to land something, it didn't last. Back in the army, he had a reputation for mouthing off to his superiors. As a civilian, he took no shit from anyone.

Leipfold walked over to the door and grabbed his jacket. He pulled it over his shoulders, turned off the lights and walked out of the office, locking the door behind him.

***

Meanwhile, Maile O'Hara was at home with four cans of Relentless and a controller. With her work done for the night, she'd powered down her laptop and kicked back with a console. Her housemate thought she was crazy to spend so much time on it. They didn't see eye to eye on a lot of things, but they both paid their rent on time and they'd settled into a comfortable routine. Kat cooked dinner more often than not, and Maile made it up to her by offering a sympathetic ear.

There was a knock on her door. Maile cursed and, without taking her eyes off the screen, shouted, "Come in!"

The door opened and Kat walked into the room. She perched on the end of Maile's bed, crossed her legs and stared pointedly at her housemate until she paused the game and dropped her controller.

Maile turned to look at Kat, who was staring at her with an eyebrow raised. "What?" she demanded.

Kat was actually a Kathleen, at least on her passport, but everyone shortened her name and she was just fine with that. Half a dozen years older than her housemate, Kat was an ambitious woman in her early thirties. She worked for a recruitment company, but she hated her job and wanted to change it—like most of her colleagues.

That evening, while Maile was relaxing in her Pikachu pyjamas, Kat was dressed up for a night on the town. She'd straightened her hair and climbed into a pair of skinny jeans, then donned a black blouse and a leather jacket. She was wearing makeup but not too much, just enough to highlight her features and to subtly draw strangers' gazes to her eyes and lips.

She smiled at Maile and said, "Xbox again? There must be a better way to spend the night."

"It's better than getting loaded on white wine and listening to shitty music," Maile replied. "Besides, I hate people. They give me a headache."

Kat looked at her. "Is that why you carry pepper spray in your handbag?" she asked.

Maile laughed. "Hell no," she said. "It's an old habit. Better safe than sorry, right? There are some fucked up people out there. That's why I do computers. Computers are predictable. You know where you stand."

"Yeah," Kat said. "And you can turn them off when you're done with them. Anyway, listen. I'm going out with the girls. You coming?"

Maile shook her head. "I'm good," she said. "But tell them I said hi."

"Come out tonight," Kat insisted. "You can tell them yourself."

Maile shook her head again, this time with more enthusiasm. Her fringe fell across her face and she brushed it haphazardly away. "I can't," she said. "I'm busy."

Kat sighed theatrically and headed off to her room to finish getting ready.

Maile picked up her controller and unpaused the game. Then she turned the volume up.

***

While Kat and her friends were getting loaded on white wine and listening to shitty music, Donna Thompson lay bleeding in the road as a gaggle of pasty-faced onlookers waited for an ambulance to arrive. Someone had covered Donna with a towel to keep her dry, but she was unresponsive when people tried to talk to her.

The rain was still hammering down, and a small stream of Donna's blood was already melting away across the surface of the road. On the other side of the street, a solitary car or two passed by before the ambulance arrived. A police car pulled up soon after and the two vehicles blocked off the road. The paramedics spilled out and rushed towards the body while the cops moved the onlookers back and started to take down names and addresses.

On the other side of the city, a black sedan was cruising beneath the streetlights. It had a big dent in the front and the engine was whining like an injured animal. It wound its way through the backstreets towards its final destination.

The city was half asleep, for now at least, and the heavy rain kept most people indoors. There were nearly nine million people in the city, and most of them, like James Leipfold, Tom Townsend and Maile O'Hara, were hiding from the elements and hoping for some sunshine in the morning.

For Donna Thompson, it was the end of the line. For the rest of the city, life was only just beginning.

Chapter Three:
The Old Vic

DETECTIVE INSPECTOR JACK CHOLMONDELEY was running late for work. He hated being late, but he'd overslept and the traffic was worse than usual.

The night before, he'd had a dream about retirement. Even though it was a dozen years in the future, it was a prospect that seemed both too near and too far away. He woke up at quarter past seven, which was later than he'd slept for as long as he could remember. His wife, Mary, was fast asleep at his side. She was a couple of years younger than him, but she was also semi-retired and self-employed, so she usually got out of bed just in time to give Jack a quick kiss before he straightened his tie, picked up his briefcase and walked out the door.

On that day, they got up at the same time and Cholmondeley dressed in a hurry while Mary brushed her teeth in the bathroom. He pulled a jacket on over his shirt, hastily threaded a belt through his trousers and walked out the door with a slice of toast in his hand. A fastidious man, he held it in a napkin and took care not to drop it on his clothes. In Cholmondeley's experience, image was everything, and he couldn't lead his men if they were laughing behind his back at a stain on his suit.

Cholmondeley unlocked his car and settled into the driver's seat, checked his pinstripe tie in the rear-view mirror and then buckled up tight before easing the Beemer out of the driveway. He made up some time by taking a couple of shortcuts, but by the time he reached the station he was eight minutes late and counting.

He checked his pockets for his phone and wallet, then grabbed his keys and got out of the car. He locked it and made his way to the front of the precinct. There'd been a time many moons ago when he used to jog the hundred yards from the car park to the station's entrance. Cholmondeley still had the same enthusiasm, but he wasn't as fit as he used to be. His days on the beat were long gone, and he was fine with that.

The cops called the station the Old Vic, although there were few on the service who remembered why. Officially, the building, with its high-ceilings, its whitewashed walls and its red-brick façade, was called the Metropolitan Municipal Building. But to the old-timers, the veterans who remembered what policing was like before the Internet came along and forced them to diversify, it would always be the Old Vic. It was named after the queen who cut the cord to open it.

Cholmondeley's phone buzzed in his pocket as he entered the station, but he ignored it. It was probably the wife, asking him to pick up some food on his way back home. He had neither the time nor the inclination to talk to her.

Instead, he walked into the office and discovered a shitstorm. He didn't take a break until the early afternoon.

***

"He's got five more minutes," Sergeant Gary Mogford said. "If he's not here then, we start without him."

Mogford had requisitioned one of the meeting rooms after forming a team as soon as the call came in. That was at four o'clock in the morning, and now his patience was wearing thin. He was ready to start the meeting, and he'd waited long enough to lead one. True, it looked like an open and shut case, but there were formalities to observe, loose ends to tie up. Mogford knew it was the little details, like punctuality and efficiency, that could earn him his next promotion.

Sergeant Gary Mogford was around Leipfold's age, a man who was so devoted to his job that it had cost him his wife and kids. His unremarkable face was lined with perpetual worry, and his baggy eyes betrayed the long-term lack of sleep that every senior cop was forced to wear like a badge of honour. His uniform looked as tired as he did. It had seen a lot of action, like its owner.

Mogford and Cholmondeley had a love-hate relationship, and Mogford didn't give a damn whether his boss was there or not. He was just about to start the briefing without him when the door opened and Cholmondeley ambled into the room with a hot cup of coffee and a scowl on his face.

"Nice of you to make it, sir," Mogford said, as his superior settled into a vacant seat at the front of the room.

Cholmondeley stared at him, took a swig of his coffee and said, "Get on with it."

Mogford cleared his throat and looked uncomfortably around the room. There were a half-dozen officers present, mostly fresh faces from the day shift who'd been drafted in to replace the tired team who'd dealt with the initial call.

"Okay, folks," he said, clearing his throat and taking his place at the head of the task force. "Listen up. At approximately three fifteen this morning, emergency services received a phone call to report an accident on Wentworth Road. Paramedics responded immediately, but the victim was pronounced dead at the scene. At this early stage, she's believed to be a young woman in her early to mid-twenties, and she appears to be the victim of a hit and run. Any questions so far?"

The room was silent, but Mogford waited a couple of seconds before continuing. The atmosphere was neither tense nor electric. It was tired and uninspired.

"Okay," Mogford continued. "Good. Now there's no sign of a vehicle, but officers spotted chipped black paint at the scene, so that's something for us to go on. The damn thing is out there, somewhere. And so is the scumbag that hit her and left her to die."

"Who called it in?" Cholmondeley asked.

"We don't know," Mogford replied. Cholmondeley glared at him, but he shrugged his shoulders. "You know how it is, boss. The operator tried to get a name, but the caller hung up. Could've been the perp for all we know."

"Perhaps," Cholmondeley murmured. "What else have you got? Anything on CCTV?"

"On it already, boss," Mogford continued. "But I wouldn't hold your breath. Most of the shops have cameras inside, but most of them aren't active. Either way, there's not much on the road where the victim was found."

Cholmondeley cursed and shook his head. "Any ID?" he asked.

"We found a purse with a driving license in the name of Donna Thompson. Looks like a match, but we'll get someone to formally identify her. Next of kin is Eleanor Thompson, her mother. I spoke to her this morning, but she was babbling. You know how it is, sir."

Cholmondeley nodded. He knew how it was, all right. He was glad he didn't have to face that part of the job anymore. But still, he wanted to see her.

"Bring her in," he said.

"Will do," Mogford replied. He waited to see if his boss wanted anything else before continuing with the briefing. It took over an hour, partly because Cholmondeley kept interrupting him.

After the briefing, Cholmondeley left the room and stalked off towards his office. Half of the team followed him out. It was always the same when he started a shift. There was always something to talk to him about, an idea to run past him or an old case to be reopened. Gary Mogford made his way out of the room alone. He stopped at the canteen for a coffee and took one last look at the case notes before heading out.

Some briefing, Mogford thought. *The old man talked more than I did.*

***

Cholmondeley was on his third cup of coffee by the time he'd caught up with his emails and finished reading the notes on the Thompson case. Mogford could be a nightmare to work with, but he was good at his job and his briefing and the subsequent notes were as comprehensive as anyone could ask for. And yet there was just something about the guy that grated on him, a feeling like he didn't belong.

The first order of business was to put out an APW for a black sedan with visible damage. It was a shot in the dark, but it was still a shot worth taking. Judging from the tracks at the scene, Donna had been struck by a large car with wide axles. Its big wheels had left marks on the road from where the vehicle skidded after the moment of impact.

It was unlikely that the car itself had emerged unscathed, not after a collision like that. The chipped black paint at the crime scene supported this theory, and Cholmondeley thought it was a good enough hunch to act on.

After that, he made preparations to visit the crime scene. The victim's body had already been removed by the coroner's office but Cholmondeley had seen the photos and it was pretty obvious what had happened. Unless he was very much mistaken, Donna Thompson had died upon impact.

At the crime scene, he knew he'd be able to get a handle on things. It all seemed simple enough. He just needed to get his hands on the driver, and then they'd be able to wrap up the case and push for a prosecution. But first he needed to catch the guy, and to catch the guy he needed to get a feel for the lay of the land. With any luck, they'd have a lead on the car by the time he got back to the station.

His train of thought was interrupted by a knock at the door. He looked up and called, "Come in."

The door opened and Constable Groves shuffled in with a fresh cup of coffee. She looked alert and awake, just like she usually did. Cholmondeley smiled as Groves set the drink down on his desk, closed the door behind her and stood to attention.

Constable Groves was one of Cholmondeley's newest additions, a plain-faced but able recruit who'd served as a PCSO before joining the police force. She styled herself conservatively, an effect which was emphasised by her uniform. She was of average height and build with average brown eyes and average brown hair. Her only concession to her personality was a sparkling silver wedding ring on her left hand. She hovered nervously as she waited for Cholmondeley to acknowledge her. He nodded and asked her what she wanted.

"Sir," Groves said. "I wondered if I could have a word with you."

"Of course," Cholmondeley replied. "My door is always open." He gestured for her to take a seat. "Would this have anything to do with the conversation we had a couple of weeks ago?"

Constable Groves sat down and said, "Yes, sir. Could you have a word with them? They're making it hard for me to do my job."

"Our job is always hard," Cholmondeley said. "But I'll have a word with them. You know how it is. Some of the lads get out of hand at times, but there's no malice in it. Boys will be boys."

"They treat me like dirt just because I'm new and I'm a woman," she said. "They give me all the dirty jobs and force me to change my shifts. They say things behind my back. Sometimes they say them to my face. How am I supposed to get anything done?"

"Rise above it," Cholmondeley replied. "Like I said, I'll have a word with them. In the meantime, don't let it bother you. Focus on proving you're a better copper than they'll ever be."

"You think so, sir?"

Cholmondeley paused and thought for a moment. "I think you have the potential," he said. "But the rest is up to you. Will that be all?"

Constable Groves pursed her lips and looked across at him. "No, sir," she said. "There's something else. You've got a visitor. We brought Donna Thompson's mother in and she's ready to talk to you."

***

Cholmondeley sighed and went over his notes again. Then he drained his coffee and looked across at the woman he'd been interviewing for the last half hour.

"So let me get this straight," he said. "You don't speak to your daughter because she's—"

"A spoilt little bitch with a sense of entitlement," Mrs. Thompson supplied.

Cholmondeley sighed again. "Of course," he said. He paused. "Forgive me, Mrs. Thompson, but this is, after all, a police investigation. Your daughter is dead. Given the circumstances, I'm surprised you're not upset."

The old woman glared at him. "Perhaps I didn't make myself clear," she said. "I'm sad that she's dead. Donna is—or *was*—my daughter, after all. I wouldn't wish death on anyone. But I fail to see what that has to do with my daughter's personality."

"The two of you didn't get on?"

"You could say that," Mrs. Thompson replied. "Donna has always been independent. She left home when she was eighteen. Said she wanted to make it on her own. She used to do it all the time. Trouble is, one time she left and never came back."

"And you never thought to report her disappearance?"

"Why would I do that?" Eleanor Thompson snapped. "I knew she was safe, or as safe as she wanted to be. She called me from time to time, but I never asked her where she was. I never cared. The girl was as good as dead to me."

Cholmondeley winced at her choice of words. "But now she *is* dead, Mrs. Thompson," he said. "And we've brought you here to help us to find out what happened to her."

"I know. Mr. Mogford told me all about it."

"*Sergeant* Mogford," Cholmondeley corrected. "He filled me in on what you talked about, but I want to hear the truth from you, not from him. We need to determine what happened to your daughter."

"I thought it was an accident."

"As far as we know, it is," Cholmondeley said. "But we'd like to make sure of it. Can you think of anyone who had a reason to harm your daughter?"

Mrs. Thompson thought for a moment and then shook her head. "I'm sorry," she said. "I can't. Like I said, I barely knew her. It was probably just an accident."

Cholmondeley stared at her for a moment. "Perhaps you're right, Mrs. Thompson," he said. "But it can't hurt to check these things."

Then, for the benefit of the tape, he added, "Interview terminated at twelve fifteen p.m."

Chapter Four:
Office Hours

LEIPFOLD HAD A PROBLEM. He was running out of money and resources, and business wasn't going so well. If it didn't turn around in the next three months, he'd lose his beloved bike or have to default on the office. Or maybe he'd lose his apartment, a tiny, one-bedroom bedsit in Brixton. He spent as little time in the place as possible.

Leipfold didn't have a home, and he hadn't had one since he joined the army. Now that his parents were dead and his own place felt like a coffin, he preferred to spend his time in the office. Not that the office was much bigger. He had the first floor in a poky little block behind Marylebone Station, a grotty little place with no access from the main road. Visitors to 19a Balcombe Street had to meander down an alleyway to find the entrance to the building.

He thought back to his last case, a relatively simple investigation into a jealous husband-to-be's fiancée. He'd tracked her around the city for the best part of two weeks before delivering a final report which left her in the clear, as he'd suspected all along. Leipfold had been able to document her every move, but the husband-to-be was unconvinced and had refused to pay his fees. So Leipfold did what he did best, digging up a little more dirt and threatening to blow the lid on the guy's cocaine habit. He'd paid up quickly enough after that.

His lack of budget was a worry. It was a chicken and egg situation; he needed the work to make a hire, and he needed to hire to be able to do the work. He knew how to carry out an old-fashioned investigation, but he didn't have the know-how to keep up with the constant flow of new technology that was changing the world around him. Leipfold could just about handle simple electronics, but navigating the complex world of servers and cybersecurity was beyond him.

And so Leipfold found himself looking for help with no way to pay for it. He did the only thing he could think of and advertised for an intern. After all, it cost him nothing to bait the hook. If nobody bit, then whatever. He'd call in a few favours instead.

Leipfold clicked a few buttons to post his ad, then sat back and finished his coffee before getting started on the next phase of his investigation.

***

Leipfold woke up at his desk again. It was a bad habit that he'd picked up during his drinking days and had never quite grown out of. It was usually more convenient to stay at work than to face the grim streets of the city. When he was a younger man, he'd enjoyed wandering around, especially at night. But these days, the prospect was daunting. He had enemies, and it wasn't the ones he knew about that scared him. He feared the ones he'd pissed off with his investigations, usually by exposing secrets that their owners thought were dead and buried. He'd worked for hundreds of clients, and almost every investigation left someone with a grudge or a thirst for vengeance. A weaker man might have lost his mind.

But Leipfold hadn't.

He wiped the crust from his eyes and pulled himself to his feet. Then he washed his face in the adjoining bathroom, smoothed his clothes as best as he could and nipped out to get the day's papers. The headlines were typical, and typical of their publications. New Fears Growing Over Post-Brexit Britain. Reality TV Star Bares All for Charity. Deadly Earthquake in Myanmar: Two Brits Feared Dead. It paid to know what was happening in Leipfold's line of work, but it grew tiresome to read the same stories over and over again with just the names and the details changed.

Leipfold thought that the worst crimes of all were the international crimes—the wars, the genocides and the atrocities in the global game of life. They were followed by the stories in the national news, companies embezzling from investors, and murders over drugs and money. Then came the local news, which usually focused on charity events and pensioners. He paid less attention to that stuff.

On that day, nothing stood out. A spate of break-ins, a criminal hobo with a habit, a piece on an upcoming charity bash to raise money for injured ex-cops, and a fatal hit-and-run just a mile or so away from his office. It had been a slow news day.

Leipfold reached the end of the paper and flipped back through to the crossword. It took him nine minutes to finish it. As he filled out the last clue and scribbled down the date and time beside it, he realised he'd arrived at a decision. With precious little work around and with no new cases on the horizon, he needed something else to keep him busy. And after finishing the crossword, he thought he had an idea.

It's about time I saw some action, he thought.

***

The sun was out by the time that Leipfold arrived at the scene of the accident, but the weather was still cold enough to make him wish he'd worn a warmer jacket. The articles that he'd read had been brief when it came to detail, but he didn't have any trouble finding the location. The collision had taken place on a busy thoroughfare just a short drive away from the office. He arrived on the back of Camilla, his trusty motorcycle, and parked it in a space between a Jeep and a dark blue Mercedes.

The police had been and gone, and the traffic was coursing inexorably along the road. In the daytime, with better driving conditions than the night before, it was as busy as ever, although some of the motorists turned their rubber necks around to take in the yellow tape at the side of the road. None of the would-be mourners had known the victim. To them, she was just another casualty in the war for safer roads.

Leipfold took it all in from a distance and began the long search for evidence by going from door to door. He picked the doors like he picked out the answers to his crossword puzzles. He was mainly looking for CCTV cameras, and they were only fitted to the bigger houses and the local businesses. Most conversations followed a pattern.

"Good afternoon," Leipfold would say. "My name is James Leipfold, and I'm looking into the accident that happened here last night. I was just wondering whether you have any CCTV cameras on your property."

"Go to hell."

"I have money," Leipfold would lie, and he'd either be invited inside or told, with a look of regret, that there was no such equipment on the property.

He hadn't been expecting to find anything, but he was pleasantly surprised after a quick chat with an elderly couple who'd hired a security firm to set up some cameras. It was easy to see why they'd bothered. They were the last of a dying breed, the rare upper class, people who'd been born into money and had continued to earn it. They had two cars in the driveway and their garden shouted opulence. They didn't invite him inside, but Leipfold glimpsed artwork on the walls and an expensive pair of Louboutins tucked carefully into an upcycled shoe rack. They had money all right.

And Leipfold had nothing, no money and no footage. But he did know that the Poplars of The Old Moat House on Wentworth Road had a home security system. And that they'd give him the footage if he could make them an offer.

***

Cholmondeley was looking curiously at the tyre marks when Leipfold arrived at the scene. The detective coughed and Cholmondeley looked up at him. They stared at each other for a couple of seconds and then Leipfold laughed and broke the silence.

"Jack Cholmondeley," he said. "You old bastard. How the devil are you?"

"Leipfold," the policeman grunted. He didn't look pleased to see him. He nodded a terse acknowledgement before turning back to look at the tyre marks. "How long has it been?"

"Too long," Leipfold said. "I bet I can guess why you're here."

"You'd win that bet, so I'm not going to take it," Cholmondeley said. "You're here for the same reason, I assume?"

Leipfold nodded. "I read about it in the paper," he said.

"Looks like a pretty standard case to me," Cholmondeley said. "What brought you out of that shit-heap office of yours?"

"Is the station any better?" Leipfold asked. "At least I don't have to work with idiots."

"Is that so?" Cholmondeley mused. "And who are you working with now, I wonder?"

Leipfold said nothing, taking the opportunity to duck under the police tape to get a closer look at the tyre tracks. Cholmondeley made no attempt to stop him. He knew from experience that trying to stop James Leipfold was like trying to stop a dog from digging up a bone.

"So what do you make of the case?" Cholmondeley asked. "I've got my best men working on it. Right now, my priority is finding the driver."

"You won't find the driver," Leipfold replied. "You should focus your search on the car."

"It's the same thing."

"Is it?" Leipfold murmured. "I wonder."

He spun around and looked at Cholmondeley like he'd never seen the man before. "As you're here, Jack," Leipfold said, "I need a favour."

"Why should I help you?" Cholmondeley asked. Leipfold hunkered down to take a closer look at the tyre tracks and then took out his mobile phone to snap a couple of photos.

"For old times' sake," Leipfold replied. "My business has gone to shit and I need a favour from an old friend. I'm not being paid for this job. I'm just doing it to survive. When I prove that this was no accident, the press will pick up on it. And when the press picks up on it, business will go through the roof. Until then, I've got nothing better to do than to start my own investigation. I'll keep you in the loop if I find anything. What do you say?"

Cholmondeley looked shrewdly across at him. "Sounds like wishful thinking to me," he said. "It's not like you to ask for help."

"Don't get any funny ideas, Jack," Leipfold said. "It's just the once, and it's not like I've never helped you out before."

"Well that's true," Cholmondeley replied. "How did you know I'd be here?"

"I didn't."

Cholmondeley grinned. "Hell," he said, "what's the favour?"

"I need you to pay a visit to The Old Moat House on Wentworth Road," Leipfold replied. "Talk to the couple there. They have some footage I want to look at. I think your boys will want to see it, too."

Cholmondeley grunted and picked up his phone to call Mogford at the Vic. While his attention was elsewhere, Leipfold stepped outside the police tape and walked over to the flowers that the public had piled at the roadside. One or two of them had names on them, and a couple more included a scribbled prayer or a message of hope and condolence.

Leipfold read through them and took a step back to snap a photograph. Then he turned back to look at the flowers. His eyes alighted on a small bunch of lilies. They were partially hidden, but Leipfold brushed the other flowers aside and picked the lilies up by the stems. Then he read the message that was attached to them.

It simply said *I'm sorry.* Leipfold took a photograph of each side of the card, being careful not to touch it, as well as photos of the flowers themselves and their place amongst the rest of the displays. Then he walked back over to where Cholmondeley was finishing off his phone call.

"Now," the policeman said. "Where were we?"

But Leipfold just smiled and said nothing.

***

Leipfold was idling at the lights when his mobile phone beeped. He reached into his pocket, glanced down at the screen and read the incoming message from Jack Cholmondeley. *I've got the footage. Will send you a copy after we've processed it.*

Leipfold smiled and put the phone back in his pocket. *So far, so good,* he thought.

The lights turned amber. He revved the engine before hitting two rights and a left as he looped his way back to the office on Balcombe Street. As he approached it, he idled the bike to a standstill and then flipped up his visor, removed his helmet, locked up the bike and walked towards the door.

A young woman was waiting outside.

She didn't look like a typical client. She was insubstantial for a start, too thin by half and in need of a healthy dinner. She had messy black hair down to her shoulders with at least a half-dozen piercings across her face. She was wearing a tight-fitting leather jacket, a little like the one that Leipfold wore when he cruised the streets on the back of Camilla, and he could just make out the tip of an angel's wing, tattooed across her skin and peeking out above her collar.

"Hello," Leipfold said, uncertainly.

"Nice bike!" the stranger replied.

"She's called Camilla," he told her. "Don't ask me why."

"Good name." She scrunched up her face and leaned in to get a good look at him. "You're James Leipfold, aren't you?" she asked.

"So what if I am?" Leipfold replied.

"I'm here about the ad you posted," his visitor said. "You know, for an intern. My name's Maile O'Hara. I do computers and stuff, and I think I can probably help you."

Leipfold looked her up and down, all five and a half feet of her if you counted the boots she was wearing. He said, "I think you've come to the wrong place."

"I don't think so," she said. She looked him up and down again. "You *are* James Leipfold. I know all about you. You served time and now you work for yourself because no one else will employ you. But you're not a bad guy."

Leipfold did a double take. Then he laughed. "How do you know all this?"

"Like I told you," Maile said, "I'm good with computers."

Leipfold looked her up and down again, then stepped around her to slip his key into the lock. He opened the door to the building and ushered Maile inside.

"Come on in," he said. "Show me what you can do."

Chapter Five:
A Little Detective Work

IT WAS AN UNORTHODOX INTERVIEW, but Leipfold was an unorthodox employer. He didn't know what to ask and Maile didn't know how to answer him.

He looked over at her appraisingly. Maile was in her mid-twenties, an alternative girl with a dozen tattoos. She was wearing a T-shirt and a sweater, as well as a pair of black jeans with a chain through the loops of her belt. Her hair was short and swept across her face. She was carrying a small black handbag with a yellow smiley face on it and wearing black plimsolls on her feet, black bands around her wrist and black nail varnish on her fingertips.

Leipfold, meanwhile, was a typical bloke, relatively short and somewhat stocky. He had short, ginger hair and steely blue eyes. The worry lines on his forehead stretched all the way up to his scalp, where his hair had already started to recede. So far, Maile hadn't seen him smile. He just frowned at her while absentmindedly clicking the button of a pen in his breast pocket. After a long silence, Leipfold removed the pen, opened up his notebook and tried to figure out what to ask the woman who wanted to work with him.

"So," he said, looking across at her. He'd offered her a seat in reception on one of the plastic chairs that he'd saved from a skip outside St. Martin's. Leipfold stayed on his feet and loomed over her. It put him in a position of power, but Maile didn't seem rattled. "Who died?"

"You got a problem with the way I look?"

"No," Leipfold said. He coughed and pretended to write something down inside his notebook. "Okay then, next question. Why do you want the job?"

"It's a challenge," she replied. "Isn't that enough?"

Leipfold smiled. "Perhaps," he said. "And you can work for free? For now, at least?"

"Sure," Maile replied. "Buy me a sandwich and find me a space for my computer. You do that and I'm yours."

"I see," Leipfold murmured. He was impressed by her spark and vivacity and won over by how she was willing to work for nothing. "If all goes well, we'll bring in some new business and I can put you on the payroll. In the meantime, you've got yourself a deal. The sandwiches are on me. Now listen up. I need help with something."

"Well, yeah," Maile said. "If you didn't, I wouldn't be here. What do you need?"

Leipfold grunted and gestured for her to follow him to his computer. He pulled up the photos he'd taken of the flowers at the crash site.

"Your first task," he explained, "will be to follow up with these. Find out who sent them and how they paid."

"That's it?" Maile laughed. "That's easy. I'll get right on it."

"Great," Leipfold said. "Consider the task a test. Get it done, then send me the results and head home. If you're good enough, you start tomorrow."

"Sure thing," she replied.

"Well, go on then. What are you waiting for?"

Maile grinned. "The Wi-Fi password," she said.

***

"I'll try my best, darling," Detective Inspector Jack Cholmondeley said, "but I can't make any promises."

Cholmondeley barely listened to his wife's reply. He only called her in the first place because she'd left a voicemail saying she urgently needed to speak to him. It turned out to be about what he wanted for dinner. That would have been the end of the conversation, but she wasn't happy because it took him six hours to get back to her. After twenty minutes on the line, she was still rambling on and on.

But Cholmondeley had a job to do. He made the usual sympathetic noises and ended the call with a brisk "love you" before putting the phone down. He wheeled around in his chair and almost had a coronary. Sergeant Gary Mogford was standing just inside the door, watching him with wry amusement.

"All right, boss?" he said.

"Mogford," Cholmondeley growled, ignoring the look on his subordinate's face. "How can I help you?"

"You can't," he replied, handing his boss a coffee in a Help for Heroes mug. "But maybe I can help you. Constable Groves is back from the crime scene with the footage you asked for."

Cholmondeley grunted his approval. "Is it any good?"

"Not sure, boss. Couldn't say. Haven't seen it. There's a hell of a lot of it and we'll need someone to process it. To see if we can't find something useful."

"I have someone in mind," Cholmondeley replied.

"Sir?"

"I'll fill you in later. So where's the footage?"

"It's in the Cloud," Mogford said.

"The what?"

"It's been uploaded to the Internet," Mogford explained.

"Is that safe?"

Mogford shrugged. "It must be," he said. "The order came down from above. It's part of an effort to boost collaboration between stations. Something about miscommunication costing lives."

"But if it's on the Internet, can't everyone see it?" Cholmondeley asked. "Like the bastards we're trying to catch in the first place, for instance?"

"God no," Mogford said. "It's encrypted and password-protected, all of that stuff. But you can log in with your badge number. I'll send you the link so you can check it out. Groves has already had a look. She thinks she's found the car, but..."

Cholmondeley looked up as the inspector trailed off. "But what?" he asked.

Mogford shrugged. "It's weird, boss. She said there was no one behind the wheel."

Cholmondeley stared at him, and Mogford took the hint and pulled up the footage on his laptop computer. The new recruits liked to joke about Mogford's computer because it looked so fragile and delicate when he picked it up or typed away at it with his pudgy hands. When he was sitting at his desk, he hit the keys so hard that it shook, and yet he'd never mastered the art of typing with more than two fingers.

They watched the footage and then Mogford put it on a loop so they could look at it again and again. He put the machine down on a nearby table and looked at his superior officer.

"What do you think?" Mogford asked.

"Hmm," Cholmondeley said. With the footage right there in front of him, it really did look like the black sedan had no one in the driver's seat. "Let me look at it again."

He watched it again and then again, and then he ordered Mogford to show him the two minutes before and the two minutes after. They watched it together in silence. There was no need for them to replay it.

"There was another car," Cholmondeley said. "See if you can run the plates and find out who the driver was. It looked like a black cab, so check the register."

"I'll see what I can do," Mogford replied. "Even if it *is* a cab, we can't do much without the plates. There are twenty-one thousand registered cabs in the city, guv. Or there were, last time I checked."

"I'll get Constable Cohen to ring every rank in the bloody city if I have to," Cholmondeley said. "And who was that at the end of it?"

"Who, sir?"

"Rewind it," he ordered. Mogford quickly did so, and they both stared intently at the screen. The last three seconds told a story of their own.

"There's someone there," Cholmondeley whispered. "A man, by the looks of it. Show me the rest of the footage. I want everything you've got. We need to find out who that is and what they saw."

***

When the CCTV footage fell into Leipfold's inbox, he clicked the download link and called Maile over to take a look at it. She perched herself awkwardly behind his shoulder while they waited for the attachment to download.

"You need to get high speed in here," Maile said. "We'll be here all day."

Leipfold just grunted, and Maile resisted the urge to wander back over to her desk beside the door. She hated inactivity, and she could see from the download speed that they'd be waiting at least six minutes for it to finish. Six minutes was enough time for her to do a little more digging on the Thompson case, but instead she spent it sitting behind Leipfold in silence, biting her fingernails as he waited for the file to open.

When it did, her heart sank. She could see from the first few frames that the angle of the shot wasn't great. Worse, there was no timestamp, which meant that they'd have to check through the footage until they found what they were looking for.

"Where did you even get this?" Maile asked.

Leipfold shrugged. "From an old friend," he replied. "Someone who's just as determined to solve this case as I am."

"So it's a race? I'm down with that."

"It's not a race," Leipfold said. "Cholmondeley isn't convinced there was even a crime, but I disagree. The silly old fool thinks it was some sort of accident. I'm trying to find out what *really* happened so that the case stays open until they find out who did it."

"So, you think Donna was murdered?" Maile asked.

"Donna?" Leipfold asked, glancing across at her.

"Yeah, Donna," Maile replied. "You know, Donna Thompson. The victim?"

"How did you know her name?" Leipfold asked. "It hasn't been released yet. I've been through all the coverage I can find and it was withheld from every single article. So how did you find it out?"

"I have my sources," Maile said. "You can find anything online if you know where to look."

Leipfold smiled. "You're pretty good," he said. "If I had the cash, I'd keep you on."

"If I needed cash, I wouldn't be here," Maile replied. "I've got something else for you, too. I did a little research on the flowers at the crash site. Found a florist who remembers the order."

"Jesus," Leipfold said. "There must be a hundred of the damn things in the city."

"A couple hundred at least," Maile replied. "More, if you count the petrol stations and supermarkets that sell cheap flowers to guilty husbands. But I ruled them out pretty quickly. The photo you took told a story to anyone who was ready to listen. The flowers were wrapped up and tied together with a little ribbon. Definitely not your typical low-end stuff."

"So you called all two hundred florists?" Leipfold asked. He was looking at her in the same way that a scientist looks at a new species.

"Hell no," Maile replied. "I did a little detective work. I cropped the photo and shared the image on a couple of forums, which helped. I got a few leads on the bouquet. You saw the black lily in the middle, right?"

"Of course," Leipfold said, though he hadn't.

"They're rare," Maile explained. "They're called calla lilies. Most places don't stock them. I was able to find a couple of places that did, so I sent a few emails."

"Why didn't you call?" Leipfold asked.

Maile blushed. "I don't talk on the phone," she said.

Leipfold stared at her for a moment. "Interesting," he said. "Good work. File a report and I'll read it this evening."

"I've already emailed it over," Maile replied. "Send me the CCTV footage and I'll see what I can do with it."

Leipfold did as he was told and then watched curiously as Maile made her way back over to her desk. He called her name and asked her to put the kettle on, then printed off a copy of her report.

***

Maile was starting to see the footage on the inside of her lids when she closed her eyes. Despite the lack of a timestamp, it hadn't been difficult to spot Donna Thompson as she made her way home from work. The streets were deserted, eerily derelict of both pedestrians and motorists, so Maile could skip through until she'd isolated the footage and done her best to improve its quality.

She was more familiar with cyber-spying and deep research than with the ins and outs of video software, but she did much better than Leipfold would have done. It wasn't perfect, but Maile did what she could, enhancing the grainy footage by zooming in, sharpening the image and playing with the contrast. She also ran it through an algorithm so she could focus on the specific frames that she wanted to see.

Her throat tightened as she watched Donna's final minutes on the computer screen. She came into shot at the end of the Poplars's driveway, two-thirds of the way down Wentworth Road. Maile watched as Donna paused for a moment, pulled something from her pocket, replaced it and then bowed her head as she walked off again into the wind and rain. Less than thirty seconds later, a black sedan came into view. It was only in the shot for a dozen frames, but Maile could see enough. There was no driver, and the car seemed to be cruising comfortably along with a mind of its own.

Maile analysed each of the frames in detail, trying to make sense of it all. The car was behaving like a car *should* behave. It wasn't driving erratically. If it wasn't for the corpse in the morgue, she could've passed it off as a glitch or a trick of the light. And then there was the research she'd carried out on the victim. Leipfold hadn't asked her to, but Maile had always liked taking the initiative. Besides, she was curious. That was why she was sitting in the dingy little office in the first place.

She tried to focus on the task in hand: emailing Leipfold a copy of her findings. He'd disappeared again and asked her to send him regular updates. They'd talk it over when he got back, but he'd asked her to email him as soon as she had something.

Okay, she'd written. *It looks like Donna Thompson was an actress. In fact, she was due to star in a play called* Driven. *Its opening night is tomorrow. Do you want me to book tickets? I also found a couple of her old blog posts. Looks like she was a party girl. If she was murdered, maybe she got in with the wrong crowd and it snowballed from there. And then there's the CCTV footage…*

Maile stopped writing for a second to replay the frames from start to finish. She honed in on the footage of Donna as she walked past The Old Moat House. She paused it, rewound it and watched it again. Then she realised what she was looking at. Someone had called Donna, a couple of minutes before the accident. And Donna had looked at her phone, saw who it was and decided not to answer it.

Who was calling you? Maile wondered, staring at Donna's final moments in the footage. *And why didn't you want to answer?*

***

Leipfold was sitting in what his old sergeant used to call "an undisclosed location," checking his emails while some civilian with a sanctimonious attitude was lecturing her audience about God and the Twelve Principles. Leipfold wasn't paying much attention, but he felt better just for being there. And besides, it wasn't like he'd taken time off work. He'd taken his laptop along and hooked it up to the Wi-Fi.

He popped open his emails and scrolled through them, deleting the usual spam from Russian brides and horny matures before reading Maile's update on the Thompson case. He opened the attachment to check that it worked, skimmed through the first couple of pages with mounting interest and then skipped back to the email itself.

Leipfold read Maile's overview and laughed into his coffee, then hurriedly hushed as he felt the eyes of the room turn to look at him. He read her email again and then forwarded it to the anonymous address that Cholmondeley used. He added a comment of his own.

Thanks for the footage, Leipfold wrote. *You sly old dog. Looks like we're making breakthroughs on our end, too. I'll keep you posted and let you know when I've got something. There's a reward if I solve the case, right?*

He chuckled again, drained the rest of his coffee, crushed the cup and then tossed it in the trash. He couldn't resist adding a final line to the email before he hit the send button: *Have you figured out who called Donna Thompson yet?*

Leipfold laughed again. This time, the facilitator picked up on it. She turned his way, a troubled frown upon her brow.

"Did I say something amusing, Mr. Leipfold?" she asked. "Perhaps you should talk about *your* struggle for a change."

The detective shook his head, told the woman he was fine and walked out of the room. He had a job to do.

***

Leipfold's email was the last thing Cholmondeley read before leaving the office and going home to Mary, who'd promised him a fish supper. She said she'd even allow him a pint of bitter, as long as he promised to brush his teeth before he kissed her.

He whistled softly under his breath and sat back in his chair. Then he shut down his computer and started to think about the question that Leipfold had asked him. *Have you figured out who called Donna Thompson yet?*

Cholmondeley picked up his phone and called Constable Cohen at reception. Mogford had already left, but he was due back on shift in the early hours. Cholmondeley asked Cohen to pass on a message and waited for him to find a pen and paper.

"Tell Mogford to find the phone," Cholmondeley said. "Looks like the Thompson girl rejected a call on her walk home, but she had nothing on her person when we found her. We're going to need to find that phone. Let's see if we can figure out who was trying to get hold of her."

Constable Cohen repeated the message and bade Cholmondeley goodnight before putting the phone down. The Detective Inspector barely heard him. He was already thinking about Mary—and the fish supper he hoped was still waiting.

Chapter Six:
Eleanor Thompson Has a Visitor

DAWN ROSE LAZILY the following day, and Leipfold was woken by a blood-red sun cresting slowly over the horizon. He'd started rising at dawn back in the army and it was a habit, like many he'd picked up while in uniform, that had stuck with him long after his discharge. As was his custom, Leipfold rose with the sun and leaned out of the window to take in the sights and smells of the city. It was where he'd been born and raised, but there was something about the place that made him feel like an intruder in his own neighbourhood. Everything changed so quickly that he couldn't keep up with it. The streets he used to walk along were still the same streets, but they were also different.

The people had changed, too. As Leipfold was getting dressed, he thought about the people he'd met throughout the years. At forty-four years old, Leipfold wasn't as young as he used to be, but he was still in pretty good shape, especially since kicking the booze. He wouldn't have swapped places with anyone for all the money in the world. But he sometimes wondered whether those old acquaintances ever thought of him and what they'd think of him now if they knew about his plans for the evening.

Even if they did, Leipfold reflected, *they'd picture me passed out in some dive bar or waking up in a police cell.*

But that was the old Leipfold. The new Leipfold browsed through his wardrobe until he found what he was looking for, an old black suit with a bow tie. He couldn't remember the last time he'd tried it on, but a quick check of the pockets revealed a couple of receipts that helped to place it at the wedding of a distant relative whose name he'd long forgotten. That had been six years ago, and he'd put a little weight on since. The tuxedo still fit him, but it was tight. He'd have to take a light lunch if he wanted to wear it that evening.

Leipfold was planning on taking in a little culture. He'd booked a pair of tickets for the opening night of *Driven* and was surprised to find he was looking forward to it. It had been a long, long time since he'd been to the theatre, and even longer since he'd gone *anywhere* with a beautiful young woman on his arm. True, Maile wasn't exactly a model, but she was a pretty girl with intelligent eyes and that was the best that Leipfold could hope for.

He frowned as he inspected his reflection in the mirror. Then his expression returned to its usual neutral while he packed his suit into its carrier and got ready to head to work. It was shaping up to be a busy day.

***

After dropping his suit at the office, Leipfold's first destination was the Thompson house. Maile was still working on an address for the victim, but she'd come up trumps by finding Eleanor Thompson, the victim's mother, in an online database.

"She probably doesn't know she's on here," she'd said. "People usually don't."

And so, armed with the woman's address and his customary lack of charm, James Leipfold made his way across the city to a small suburban street. It was home to a curious mix of classes and incomes with beautiful townhouses on one side of the road and terraced communes and high-rise flats on the other. Eleanor Thompson lived on the more affluent side of the road in a small bungalow with a tidy garden and off-street parking.

Leipfold paused to take a couple of snaps on his mobile phone before wandering up the driveway and ringing the old-fashioned doorbell. It echoed in the hallway and was followed by a shuffling sound and a soft click as Mrs. Thompson popped the latch. The door opened a couple of inches and then jammed. Leipfold guessed, correctly, that the old woman had a chain in place on the other side.

"What do you want?" Mrs. Thompson asked.

Eleanor Thompson was pushing sixty, but she looked good for her age and clearly took care of herself. She was wearing a pair of white trousers and a blue shirt with a plain jacket on top. The colour had mostly faded from her hair and had started to thin out at the scalp. Her skin was clear and her face was positively radiant. She looked like she'd just got back from a holiday.

"Hello, Mrs. Thompson," Leipfold replied, jamming his foot in the door. "My name's James Leipfold. May I come in?"

"Like hell," Mrs. Thompson growled. "Get your foot out of my door before I call the police."

"I'm with the police," Leipfold lied.

"The police? I doubt it. Show me your badge."

Leipfold frowned. "I, uh…left it at the station."

"Rubbish," Mrs. Thompson said. "Who are you really, and what do you want?"

"I'm looking into the death of your daughter," Leipfold explained. "I'm a private investigator. The papers say your daughter's death was an accident, but I don't believe them. Call me crazy, but I've got a suspicious nose and some time on my hands. I was hoping you could answer a couple of questions."

"You're crazy, Mr. Leipfold. You didn't know my daughter. I did."

"What do you mean?" he asked.

"I knew my daughter better than you ever could," Mrs. Thompson said. "Oh, it wasn't an accident. I'm sure of that. But she wasn't murdered, either."

Leipfold just stared at her with his shrewd, grey eyes. Experience had taught him that at times like these, it was better to stay silent, especially if the silence was uncomfortable. It forced people to say something to fill it. Mrs. Thompson didn't let him down.

"Do I have to spell it out for you, Mr. Leipfold? My daughter wasn't murdered. She killed herself."

"Is that right?" Leipfold asked. "And where were you when this happened?"

"I was at home," she said. "Alone. Now please, remove your foot from my door. I'm in mourning. I wish to be left alone."

Leipfold hummed to himself as he left Eleanor Thompson's place. He had the information he needed, at least from her. Besides, he'd enjoyed to-ing and fro-ing with the cantankerous old woman. She reminded him of himself, and she posed the first challenge he'd come across since taking the case. Not much of a challenge, but a challenge nonetheless.

When he got back to the office, Maile was sitting in her usual place by the door. She greeted him with a pleasant smile and a quick update on the case.

"I paid a visit to the flower shop," she said. "Had a good chat with the woman who owns it. The order was placed on their website, but they can't access their records to give us a name. It's all encrypted."

Leipfold sighed. "Okay," he said. "Keep digging."

"I might be able to break the encryption if you give me some time," Maile said. "It's not exactly legal, but…"

"I'm not a copper, Maile," Leipfold reminded her. "I don't care how you do it."

"Yes sir." Maile grinned. "This is turning out to be my kind of job."

***

The clock ticked another hour away. Maile went back to work while Leipfold wandered over to his desk. He downed a cup of coffee and picked his way through the daily papers, but they contained nothing to pique his interest and the Thompson case had already been relegated to the seventeenth page. He spent a little time catching up with his emails, made himself another coffee and sat down to do the crossword.

But someone had already done it. Every square of the complex cryptic crossword had been filled in with a delicate hand. Leipfold stared at it for a second and then scowled and looked over at Maile. She grinned and flashed him a thumbs up. He didn't return it.

Leipfold walked over and slammed the paper on her desk. "Let me guess," she said. "You're mad because I finished the crossword."

"Something like that," Leipfold replied. "Mad. Impressed. Slightly put out. Take your pick. I don't like people messing with my routine."

"Then you're not going to like this," Maile said. "Because you might need to head back out again. I pulled a few strings and figured out who our anonymous shopper was. The flowers, remember?"

"I remember," Leipfold said. "Go on."

"The florist gave me a login to the database."

"And?"

"I'm getting there," Maile said. "The data was encrypted, but it was running old software and I found a few tools to make some sense of it. I didn't have to do much to decode it. Eleanor Thompson bought the calla lilies the morning after her daughter died."

Leipfold thought for a moment. "I went to see her this morning," he said. "Strange woman."

"Did she say anything about the flowers?" Maile asked.

"No," Leipfold replied. "And she didn't seem too sorry, either. I wonder what it all means."

Chapter Seven:
An Interview

DETECTIVE INSPECTOR JACK CHOLMONDELEY and Sergeant Gary Mogford were going over the case together when Mogford's phone rang and he excused himself to take the call. Cholmondeley was grateful for the break. The stress of the job was starting to get to him.

Mogford came back a couple of minutes later. "Groves and Hyneman have got the phone," he said. "Seems suspicious to me, sir."

"In what way?" Cholmondeley asked, leaning back in his chair.

"It was nowhere near the crash site, sir," Mogford explained. "It was handed in at the station by a member of the public."

"Did you get a name?"

"No, sir," Mogford said. "It's been a busy day. The guy handed it to Constable Cohen and ran off before anyone had a chance to take his details. But at least we know where he found it."

"Where he *says* he found it," Cholmondeley replied, a stickler for detail as always. "Get me the footage from the CCTV. I want to see what he looked like."

"Will do, sir. He told reception he found it by the post office."

"That's almost a mile away," Cholmondeley murmured. "How did it get so far from the scene of the accident?"

"That's what we're trying to figure out," Mogford said.

"The Superintendent isn't going to like this," Cholmondeley murmured. He sighed. "There's no chain of command. How can we even be sure that it's the victim's phone?"

"We'll get the tech team on it," Mogford said. "But we can be pretty sure that it's hers. She's still logged into a couple of apps and the photographs are consistent with what we know about the victim."

"And how do we know that it wasn't tampered with before it was handed in?"

Mogford shrugged. "I suppose we don't, sir. Leave it to the tech boys. If there's anything to find, they'll find it. They've already sent over a message that they pulled from voicemail."

"Very good," Cholmondeley said. "See if you can find the chap who brought it in. I want a word with him."

"Already on it," Mogford replied. "In the meantime, sir, there's someone here that you might want to talk to. A man called Adrian Ford spoke to Constable Cohen on reception. He says he saw the victim on the night of the accident."

***

Mr. Ford turned out to be a weasel-faced man with hairy arms and a bald head, bad psoriasis, and lobster-like skin that was blistered and peeling. While Cholmondeley was talking to him, he found it hard to concentrate because the guy kept on scratching and picking at his head, examining his fingernails and flicking the dead skin onto the floor.

Cholmondeley introduced himself with his name and rank and asked the man what he could do for him.

"Right," Ford said. "Well it's like this, see. I saw the girl in the paper. The girl who was hit by the car. The papers are saying it was an accident, but it wasn't. I was there. I saw it."

"You were there?" Cholmondeley repeated. He looked the man up and down.

"I was indeed," Ford replied. "I'm a taxi driver, see. If you check with HQ, they'll confirm I was on duty. All of our vehicles have built-in GPS and telematics so they can keep an eye on us. It'll show you exactly where I was that night."

"Did you have a passenger?" Cholmondeley asked.

"I didn't," Ford said. "I was trying to find another fare. That's why I remember the girl. I thought she was going to flag me down but she just carried on walking. I felt bad for her, out in the rain like that."

Cholmondeley nodded and took down a couple of notes. Then he gestured for Mr. Ford to continue.

"The paper said it was an accident," he said. "Bollocks to that. I saw the car hit her. It all happened in my rear-view mirror."

"Did you get a good look at the driver?" Cholmondeley asked. He sat forward in his chair, his pen and paper forgotten. In the background, the digital recording spun on.

"Well, that's just it," Ford said. "There wasn't one."

"There wasn't one?" Cholmondeley repeated. His expression remained deadpan. Two days earlier, the claim might have seemed preposterous, but the CCTV footage gave Ford's testimony some gravitas. And then he remembered the black cab that they'd seen. The tech team had been unable to sharpen the picture enough to get the plates from it, but he was willing to bet that it would have been a match to the vehicle that Ford was in.

Not that he'd admit that—not yet. He reminded himself of rule number one of police work: everyone's a suspect.

"That's what I said, isn't it?" Adrian Ford crossed his arms defiantly and looked Cholmondeley dead in the eye. "Look, I know it sounds crazy. But that doesn't make it a lie. There was no one behind the wheel. I'll swear by it. I'll take a polygraph."

"We might hold you to that," Cholmondeley said.

"Be my guest." The man sighed. "Look, I've been driving these roads for most of my life. I could get across the city with my eyes closed. When I tell you that there wasn't a driver, I know exactly what it sounds like. But I also know that my eyes don't lie. I saw what I saw."

"Interesting," Cholmondeley murmured. "Of course, we only have your word for it."

"Excuse me?"

"Well who's to say that your story is true?" Cholmondeley asked. He smiled at the man. "You must understand, it's my job to ask questions. What if, for example, you mowed the girl down yourself and came here to try to cover it up?"

"I told you," Ford said. "Check the telematics."

"But can you prove that it was you behind the wheel?"

"I don't have time for this," Ford growled. "I came here to help. You have to listen to me. I saw how it happened. The damn car drove itself straight into the back of her. Sent her flying through the air like a rag doll."

"Even if that's true," Cholmondeley replied, "why didn't you talk to us sooner? Why didn't you call for an ambulance?"

Ford stared across the table at him. He was on edge, deeply concerned about this new line of questioning and intimidated by the high, white walls of the interview room. He shivered.

"I was on shift," Ford said. "Making money. Paying the bills. Okay, there was no one in the cab, but I didn't want to write the rest of the night off. She was dead. You could tell she was. No one survives an impact like that. And besides…"

"Besides what?" Cholmondeley asked.

"There was someone walking down the street behind her," he said. "When the girl was hit, he ran over to her. I figured he was going to call it in."

Cholmondeley sat up like he'd been shot in the spine by a pellet gun. He remembered the man in the CCTV footage, a chap who'd been too grainy to make out properly and whose identity was still unknown. He opened the door to the interview room, stuck his head out into the corridor and bellowed for Constable Groves. When she came scuttling across the station towards him, he told her to fetch a sketch artist as quickly as possible. Then he came back into the room and sat down again.

"What did this man look like?" Cholmondeley asked. "Think you could describe him?"

***

Jack Cholmondeley was thinking of something else entirely when the CCTV footage from reception filtered through and he was able to take a look at it. He didn't recognise the person who brought the phone in, but that didn't mean much. The quality of the footage wasn't great, but it was good enough to make out the basics.

The guy was wearing a black suit and carrying a satchel, and he produced the phone from an inside pocket and dropped it on the desk.

He had short black hair, light stubble, and a pair of sunglasses hanging from his breast pocket. Cholmondeley asked Groves to pull a few stills from the footage and to follow up with the reception staff, but he didn't have much hope of tracking the guy down. Not that he thought it would matter.

Cholmondeley was watching the footage for a third time when his thoughts were interrupted by a knock at the door. He answered it reluctantly and was greeted by a sweaty-faced Sergeant Mogford, who declined his invitation to enter the office and spoke to him through the doorway from the corridor.

"Can't stop to chat, sir," he said. "Lots to do."

"Likewise," Cholmondeley said, his mind drifting to his plans for the evening. Mary had booked some tickets to a play he'd never heard of, and Jack had gloomily agreed to go with her. It wasn't his sort of thing—he preferred the television—but he felt like he owed it to her. A policeman's wife had a lonely life, and a night at the theatre seemed like a small price to pay to keep her happy. "What have you got for me?"

Mogford shrugged. "It's the Thompson girl," he explained. "I don't understand why we're still investigating. It's an open and shut case, an accident. Why bother tying up resources?"

"It's an open case," Cholmondeley said. "There's no shut about it. Until we confirm what happened that night, I want you to assume the worst and hope for the best. Either way, we've got to find out."

"But, sir," Mogford protested. "It's obvious. It was an accident, or maybe a suicide. The silly girl was probably drunk and walked out into the middle of the road."

"Suicide?" Cholmondeley murmured. "I wonder. If it was a suicide, why not do it at home? And if it was an accident, why hasn't the driver come forward?"

"Beats me," Mogford said.

"Besides," Cholmondeley continued, "there's this." He booted up a file on his computer. "The tech boys found it. Looks like they recovered some of the data after all."

Cholmondeley hit the play button, and Mogford walked into the room and closed the door behind him. The quality of the recording was terrible, and even with post-processing it was difficult to listen to.

Mogford could just about hear a woman's voice over the sound of the snowy static. It was distorted, but it was good enough to tell who it was and what they were saying.

It was Eleanor Thompson, and it sounded like she'd been recorded against her knowledge. They could hear the muffled sound of traffic, and every now and then a door opened or closed. Eleanor's voice was low, like she was in a public place and she didn't want to be overheard. But there was no mistaking it.

She was angry. No, more than that. She was furious. And Cholmondeley wanted to know why.

Chapter Eight:
A Rocky Relationship

JACK CHOLMONDELEY was having a busy day.

He hadn't had a break since he pulled into the car park outside the Vic and hit the keys to lock the Beemer. Mogford had caught up with him before he entered the red brick building, and his time had been taken up ever since with meeting after interminable meeting.

That was why he was in a bad mood when Constable Groves came to collect him and to lead him into one of the poky interview rooms.

"What is it?" he snapped.

"Sorry to bother you, sir," Groves said, flinching a little. "Sergeant Mogford and I are going to see Tony Barlow. He owns the café that Donna Thompson used to work at. We wondered if you wanted to tag along."

Cholmondeley didn't want to tag along, but he didn't want to admit it, either. He wanted a good, long sit down and perhaps an hour or two to catch up on his paperwork, but the fates had something else in mind. So instead of complaining, he said, "I'd love to."

That was how he found himself sitting in the passenger seat of a panda car with Mogford driving and Constable Groves in the back. It looked like some weird family outing, made stranger by the fact that Groves was the only one of the three in uniform.

Tony met them at the door and showed them inside. He spoke to them in public, sitting them down on a table beneath his logo and positioning himself with his back to the wall.

"Sorry about this," he said. "I'd take you out back but I'm short on staff at the moment and…well, you know. I like to keep an eye on things."

"Indeed," Mogford said. When they were still in the car, Cholmondeley had told him to take the lead on the interview. Mogford was pleased because he thought it showed that the old man had faith in him, and Jack Cholmondeley was pleased because he didn't have to do as much of the work. He could relax, somewhat, and watch as events proceeded.

"How can I help?" Tony asked. From the corner of his eye, he tracked the progress of a customer as she walked up to the till and placed an order for a bacon buttie.

"We're here to talk about Donna Thompson," Mogford said. "Does the name sound familiar?"

"It sure does," Tony said. "She works here."

Mogford whistled softly. He hated this part of the job. "I'm sorry to have to tell you this, Mr. Barlow," Mogford said. "She's dead. I'll understand if you need a moment or two to let it sink in."

"She's dead?" Tony looked surprised, but Cholmondeley noticed that he also looked a lot like the unidentifiable figure he'd seen walking down the road in the CCTV footage. "How?"

Constable Groves was nudged forward and she did her best to tell Tony what had happened after Donna left the cafeteria.

"That's awful," Tony said. "But what has this got to do with me?"

"Two questions," Mogford said. "First, can you think of anyone who might have wanted Donna dead?"

"No," he replied. "No one. She was a lovely girl. Never had any problems with her."

Mogford nodded at the man. "Very good," he said. "Second question. When was the last time you saw her?"

"When she left work that night," Tony said. "I was locking up when she went home."

Mogford nodded again, but Cholmondeley scowled across at him. "I think that's a lie," he said. "I think it was you in the CCTV footage. You saw her body."

Tony blanched. The colour drained from his face so quickly that it was as though an invisible bag of flour had exploded in the air above his head. "You *know* about that?" he asked.

"It's our job to know about it," Cholmondeley said. "So you don't deny it?"

"There doesn't seem much point," Tony admitted. "I was there all right."

"Why didn't you call it in?" Mogford asked.

"I, uh…" The man was starting to sweat, and Cholmondeley watched in fascination as his face appeared to crumple in on itself.

"You knelt down beside her," Cholmondeley said, casting his mind back to the grainy footage that had been secured from the crime scene.

"I did," Tony admitted.

"Why did you kneel down beside her?"

Tony looked uncomfortable. "I checked her pulse," he mumbled. "And then I took her wages. I'm sorry, sir. I figured it's not a theft if the person is dead. Besides, it was my money. I was just taking it back."

Cholmondeley stared at the man with a look that could have sliced through diamond.

***

Later that afternoon, Leipfold got ready for a repeat of the morning's performance. He didn't want to go, but Maile insisted that he needed to return to the Thompson house for a second interview. Leipfold thought it was a waste of time, but he agreed to do it anyway because he had nothing better to do, especially without the day's crossword to ponder. Besides, maybe she was right. Maybe he'd discover something that he hadn't learned the first time. But he doubted it.

The skies were clear, but the streets were bitterly cold as Leipfold wound his way towards Eleanor Thompson's house for the second time that day. He was feeling sorry for himself to begin with. Then he spotted the squad car parked on the kerb at the end of her driveway.

He weighed up his options and walked along the gravel path to Eleanor Thompson's front door. He knocked at it heavily and heard a murmur of voices from inside, the deep baritone of a man and the trembling falsetto of an elderly woman who smoked too many cigarettes. Then the door opened and Leipfold found himself staring into the gunmetal eyes of Eleanor Thompson.

"Oh," she said. "It's you. What do you want?"

"Just a quick word, Mrs. Thompson," Leipfold replied.

"I've already said what I have to say," she reminded him. "And right now I have company."

Leipfold grimaced. "Just tell me about the flowers and I'll be on my way."

"What flowers?"

"Mrs. Thompson, you're a terrible liar," Leipfold said. "I'm talking about the flowers at the crash site. The ones you didn't attach your name to."

Eleanor Thompson stared at him defiantly, held her head up high and then gracefully admitted defeat. She sighed and said, "I think you'd better come in."

Leipfold nodded and followed her into the house, observing from the state of the walls and the sweet smell of bleach and pine-fresh disinfectant that this was a woman who was living above her means, too poor to redecorate or refurbish. She was also a proud woman and one who kept a clean house. He followed her as she led the way into the chintzy living room. When he saw who her guest was, he wasn't surprised.

"We meet again, Jack," Leipfold said.

Cholmondeley pulled himself up from an armchair and reached over to shake his hand. Leipfold took it and the two men smiled awkwardly at each other.

"Afternoon, James," Cholmondeley replied. "Fancy seeing you here. How's the investigation going?"

"Not bad," Leipfold said. "I just stopped by to ask Mrs. Thompson a couple of questions about the flowers at the crash site. What about you?"

Cholmondeley smiled. "I wanted to talk to her about a voicemail message," he replied. "We found it on her daughter's mobile phone."

Eleanor Thompson coughed and lowered herself gently into her usual space on the sofa. "Gentlemen," she said. "You seem to have forgotten that I'm in the room with you."

***

"My daughter and I had a rocky relationship," Mrs. Thompson began. "We didn't always get on. You know how it is with kids."

Leipfold and Cholmondeley looked uneasily across at each other. Neither man had children and nor did they want them.

"Just tell us about the flowers," Leipfold said.

"What more do you want to know?" she asked. "That I sent some flowers to the crash site? I loved her in my way and I wanted to make it up to her. I felt bad about the message."

"The message?" Leipfold asked.

"The one on the voicemail," Cholmondeley supplied. "They had an argument. You've got some catching up to do."

"What was the argument about?"

"Donna wanted some money," Mrs. Thompson said. "Ha! As usual. I told her to go out and get a proper job. My daughter was spoiled as a child, but now that I'm retired, I just can't give her handouts willy-nilly whenever she gets herself into a sticky situation."

Leipfold and Cholmondeley exchanged another look but said nothing. It was an old tactic, but it worked. Mrs. Thompson had been brought up to be polite, and the uncomfortable silence was too much for her. She started to fill it.

"Donna always wanted to be an actress," she explained. "Ever since she was a little girl. I wanted her to go to university but she insisted on going to stage school. Oh, I helped her out enough to begin with. I even paid her tuition fees so she wouldn't be burdened with one of those dreadful loans. But I had my heart set on her studying law. I was hoping she'd eventually leave all that acting nonsense behind her, but no such luck. After she finished training for the stage, she went off the radar. I believe she was working in a cafeteria, if you can imagine that."

"Go on," Cholmondeley said, scribbling furiously away in his notebook. Leipfold, meanwhile, was recording the audio on his Dictaphone, which was tucked safely away in his jacket pocket.

"She came to visit one day, out of the blue," Mrs. Thompson said. "That must have been…let me see now…oh, maybe three or four weeks ago. She wanted money."

"How much did she want?" Leipfold asked.

"Ten grand," Mrs. Thompson replied. "She called it a loan, but we both knew what it was. Of course, I refused her. Then she said she'd disappear if I didn't pay her. Now, you can say what you like about our relationship, but Donna was still my daughter. I loved her very much, and that hurt. So I called her up to give her a piece of my mind. But she didn't answer, so I left her a message."

"And the flowers?" Cholmondeley prompted. "This is the first I've heard of them."

"I had some delivered to the crash site," Mrs. Thompson explained. "It was my way of making amends."

Cholmondeley looked satisfied. Leipfold had further questions, but the time wasn't right to ask them. Instead, he stayed stony-faced and silent. An idea began to form while Jack Cholmondeley was still jotting things down in his notebook.

***

After finishing up at the Thompson house, Leipfold and Cholmondeley caught up over a drink at The Rose & Crown. It was a proper boozer, a spit and sawdust public house full of men so old they made Leipfold look like a teenager. He asked for orange juice and Cholmondeley had a lemonade.

"Still on the wagon, then," Cholmondeley observed.

Leipfold shrugged. "Yeah," he said. "And you're on duty. I choose not to drink. You're just not allowed to."

"Fair point." Cholmondeley lifted his lemonade up to the light, looked at it and laughed. "So, what do you make of Eleanor Thompson?" he asked.

"Hard to tell," Leipfold said. "She's a strange woman."

"Did you pull your usual trick?" Cholmondeley asked. "Did you record it all?"

Leipfold winked and patted the phone inside his pocket. "Of course," he said.

"And you know it's not admissible in court."

"Yeah," Leipfold said. He patted his pocket again. "It's probably not even legal. Don't tell the cops, eh? It's just for my notes. It's harmless."

"Harmless, eh?" Cholmondeley shrugged. "Whatever. Send me a transcript if you can. Maybe she said something that we didn't pick up on. Maybe there's something there, something we can learn."

"Perhaps," Leipfold said. "Perhaps not. I've met her type before."

"Do you think she did it?"

"Do I think she did *what*?" Leipfold asked. "What are you boys calling it? A murder? An accident?"

"Officially, it's an accident," Cholmondeley said. "Until we prove otherwise. But between the two of us, I'm calling it murder. And if I had to put money down, I'd say the mother was behind it."

Leipfold coughed but said nothing, and Cholmondeley looked shrewdly across at him. "You don't believe me?"

"It's not that," Leipfold replied. "It's not that at all. But Eleanor Thompson? No, she didn't kill her daughter."

"But they hated each other."

"So what?" Leipfold said. "Love is stronger, more powerful." He paused to take a sip of his OJ. "How's Mary?" he asked.

"She's fine," Cholmondeley replied. "Still healthy, still happy."

"Good," Leipfold said.

They slipped into an awkward, morose silence, the sure sign of a small, sober group in a place that was built for drinking. Cholmondeley got up to go to the toilet while Leipfold passed the time by checking his emails and draining his OJ. When Cholmondeley returned, Leipfold hopped to his feet and grabbed his jacket.

"Can't stay," Leipfold explained. "I've got a job to do. Listen, it wasn't the mother. I'm sure of it. But it wasn't an accident, either. I'll look into it."

"And I'll do the same," Cholmondeley said, setting his glass down on the table. "It was good to see you, James. Let the best man win."

Chapter Nine:
A Night at the Theatre

THAT NIGHT, at the theatre on Jermyn Street, Maile wore a stunning sleeveless red dress that showed off her tattoos. She made up her face with a little rouge and a lot of eyeliner. Leipfold was suited and booted, but he still looked scruffy and out of place. They didn't talk much except for at the bar, where Maile had a beer and Leipfold had a Diet Coke. Then they headed off to find their seats.

The show, *Driven*, was about an immigrant girl who fell in love with an older man, a tragicomedy with too many one-liners, too much farcical humour and no real plot to speak of. In the final act, the heroine fell for someone more suitable, a pizza deliveryman who told her, "Life is a lie that you buy from the newspapers."

Leipfold *hated* it, but Maile disagreed with him.

"You're just pissed off because you're overdressed," she said. "Look at you, in your suit and tie."

"What does smart casual even mean?" Leipfold murmured. "And while we're at it, what's *that*?

Maile followed his outstretched finger to a stranger with a bushy moustache. He was sitting three rows in front of them and drinking a fruit smoothie from a plastic bottle.

"It's a hipster," Maile said. "A hipster in a cravat."

"And a monocle," Leipfold added. He sighed. "I hate the theatre," he said.

"Who cares?" Maile replied. "We've got a job to do."

***

They finished their drinks in the foyer. Maile was leading the way to the dressing rooms when Leipfold stopped abruptly.

"What's wrong?" Maile asked. Leipfold shushed her and grimaced as an older man in a funeral suit walked over and shook him by the hand.

"Fancy seeing you again," Cholmondeley said, clapping Leipfold on the shoulder. The policeman looked strange out of uniform. Mary was standing there beside him in a lilac dress that made her look ten years younger. Leipfold noticed that she too was overdressed.

"How are you doing, Jack?" Leipfold asked. He watched the policeman's face as his eyes tracked left. His pupils dilated a little as he spotted Maile and realised that the two of them had come together.

"I'm grand, thanks," Cholmondeley replied. "Who's the lucky lady?"

"This is…"

"Hi, I'm Maile," she interrupted, stepping forward to offer Cholmondeley her hand. "Nice to meet you. I'm Mr. Leipfold's assistant."

The old man was taken aback. Mary laughed and said, "You'll have to excuse my husband. He's a little slow today. They've been keeping him busy at work."

"I'm sure they have," Leipfold replied. "Good to see you again, Mary."

"James," she said.

Leipfold took the hint. "Well," he said, "it was good to see you both. Look after yourselves, you hear?"

***

A quarter of an hour later, the milling crowd had all but dispersed and Leipfold and Maile found themselves talking to the show's lead actress. She had a forgettable face but was still somehow beautiful, with olive skin and long brown hair. She was tall—too tall—but she pulled it off with an air of easy confidence.

"Thanks for coming out," she said. "What did you think of the show?"

"It was—"

"Wonderful," Maile interrupted. "We loved it. Didn't we, boss?"

"I suppose we did," Leipfold said.

"Excellent," the actress replied. "We all worked so hard on it. Come with me if you'd like. I can introduce you to Tom, the director."

Leipfold shrugged politely and said, "I'm afraid we didn't come here to discuss the show, Miss…"

"Rieirson," she said. "Marie Rieirson at your service. You don't want to talk about the show? That's a new one. Most people want to tell me what they thought of it, even if they thought it was awful."

"It *was* awful," Leipfold murmured.

"What?"

"Forget it," Leipfold said. "I was hoping you could answer a couple of questions."

"Sure thing."

"It's about Donna Thompson."

Marie's face darkened and her smoky eyes flicked from Leipfold to Maile and back to Leipfold. "I think you'd better follow me," she said.

***

"So," Leipfold said, once the three of them were sitting in her dressing room and Marie was giving him her full attention. "You knew Donna Thompson."

Marie stared at him for a second. Then her jaw dropped. "*Knew*? Has something happened to her?"

"She's dead," Leipfold said. "I'm sorry. I thought you knew. Did you not notice she was missing?"

"Of course," Marie replied. "I took her role, after all. But…oh my goodness, is that what happened? Tom Townsend, the director, he told us that she'd handed in her notice. I just thought that she couldn't cut it. I was glad that she'd left. But this…this is awful."

Leipfold nodded and made a mental note to follow up with Tom Townsend. He wondered why the man had lied to her—or whether he even knew the truth himself.

"I'm sorry," he said. "My name's James Leipfold and I'm a private investigator. I want to find out what happened."

"What about the police?"

"What about them?" Leipfold laughed. "Half of them can't tie their shoelaces. But for what it's worth, the police are already looking into it. Think of me as a second pair of eyes."

"A second pair of eyes that I don't have to talk to if I don't want to?" Marie asked, crossing her arms. "I know my rights."

"You don't *have* to talk to us," Maile said before her boss had a chance to reply. "But you should if you have a heart. We just want to know what happened."

"Why should I care? I never liked the girl."

"Doesn't matter," Leipfold replied.

Marie sighed. She peered across at Leipfold, uncrossed her arms and said, "Fine. How can I help?"

"Let me get straight to the point," Leipfold replied. "See, you have a motive. With Donna gone, you were the natural choice to take over her role."

"Are you accusing me, Mr. Leipfold?"

Leipfold shook his head. "No," he said. "I'm not. But I'd still like to be able to rule you out. All I want to know is where you were on Monday night."

Marie looked confused, but she did her best to answer. "I was having dinner with Tom," she explained. "You know, the director. He said the part was mine if I learned the lines in time."

"You mean you were offered the role before Donna died?"

"Of course," Marie replied. "Tom said he'd had enough of her. I told him if he wanted me to do it, I'd do it. As a favour."

"I see," Leipfold said. "And can anyone confirm that?"

"You could try the restaurant," Marie replied. "The Ledbury. Ask if they remember Tom Townsend."

"I will," Leipfold said. Marie seemed relieved, but the conversation wasn't over. Leipfold had one last question. "Why did you want to speak to us in private as soon as I mentioned her name?" he asked.

"That one's easy, Mr. Leipfold. Donna's name was mud around here. I know it's awful, but I'm glad she's gone. It's horrible that she died, of course. But really, we'll all be better off without her."

"Motive," Leipfold murmured.

"I have an alibi," Marie reminded him. "Now if you don't mind, I need to get out of here. Good luck with your investigation."

Chapter Ten:
A New Case

MAILE AND LEIPFOLD arrived on Park Lane as The Ledbury, the high-end eatery at the Grosvenor House Hotel, was winding down for the night. They ordered a couple of drinks from the bar and waited for the punters to finish their dinners. It was a typical Thursday evening.

Leipfold put the drinks on his credit card and started chatting to the barman, who turned out to be all too happy to talk to them.

"How can I help?" he asked.

"I wanted to ask a couple of questions," Leipfold said.

"Can you ask them while I work the bar? I just called last orders." The barman paused to wipe the sweat from his forehead with the sleeve of his shirt. "I *hate* closing time," he murmured. "It's a lonely place when you're alone here."

"I'll make it quick," Leipfold said. "I'm trying to see if my friends were here on Monday night."

"I was on shift," the bartender replied. "So maybe I can help." He leaned towards Leipfold and lowered his voice. "What are you, some kind of cop?"

"I'm a private investigator," Leipfold said.

"Jesus," the bartender replied. "Did you fall out of a movie?"

Leipfold laughed. "There aren't many of us left," he admitted. "I guess I'm the last of a dying breed."

Maile pulled up a photo of Marie Rieirson from DrivenThePlay .com and handed her tablet to the barman. "Do you recognise this woman?" she asked. "We think she was here with a guy called Tom Townsend."

The barman glanced at the picture and pinched the screen to zoom in on it. Then he handed the tablet back to Maile.

"Yeah," he said. "I remember her. Tom Townsend, huh? He was here, too. He was a big tipper."

"Do you remember anything unusual about them?"

The barman laughed. "I get it," he said. "He's your boyfriend, right? That's why you're checking up on him."

"Hell no," Maile replied. "I've never even met him."

"Townsend was looking around all night," the man explained. "His head wasn't in the game. A woman like that deserves your full attention."

"What else can you tell us?" Leipfold asked.

"Not much," the man replied. "But there *was* one other thing."

Leipfold leaned closer. "What's that then?" he asked.

"Townsend's date got up from the table in the middle of her meal to take a call. It might not be much, but it's something. She was gone for about five minutes."

Leipfold nodded and thanked the man, then started to walk away.

"Hey!" the barman shouted. "What about a tip?"

Leipfold laughed and finished his drink, then walked out of The Ledbury. Maile reached into her purse and gave the man a fiver.

***

It was the following morning, and Jack Cholmondeley was sitting at his desk and trying to warm up after a short walk in the winter sun. It was a Friday. While most people were looking forward to the weekend and making plans to see their friends and family, Cholmondeley was facing hours of unpaid overtime.

It had been three long, hard days since Donna Thompson had been found in the middle of the road. Cholmondeley promised himself he'd give it a couple more days before turning the case over to Sergeant Mogford and, eventually, the coroner. If they couldn't track down the owner of the car—which was looking increasingly likely—then they wouldn't have much choice. They'd have to file it as an accident.

Cholmondeley didn't want that to happen.

He checked his calendar and then made his way to one of the meeting rooms where he had an appointment to honour. Constable Groves had tracked down the guy who'd dropped Donna's phone off and he'd agreed to come in for an interview.

After introducing himself and explaining the importance of the situation, Cholmondeley cut to the chase. "I'm going to ask you a couple of questions and then you can get out of here," he said. "First off, for the record, could you please state your name and occupation?"

"Sure," the visitor said. "My name's Eddie Burns and I'm a carpenter."

"Are you an Edward or an Edmund?"

"Just an Eddie," Eddie said.

"Thanks, Mr. Burns," Cholmondeley replied. "Do you mind if I call you Eddie?"

"Call me whatever you like."

"Great," Cholmondeley said. "And could you tell me how you found the phone?"

"That's easy enough," Eddie replied. "I was on my way back from a job and thought I'd stop off for a bite to eat. I saw the phone while I was parking up, just lying there in the grass. I like to think I'm a decent bloke, so I decided to pick it up and drop it in."

"So you didn't know whose phone it was?"

"Nope," he said. "It didn't occur to me to check. Why? What's with all the questions?"

Cholmondeley sighed. "The device in question is part of an active investigation," Cholmondeley explained. "A woman is dead, and you were the lucky one to find her phone. I want you to think as hard as you can. Tell me everything you can about where you found it."

"She's dead?" Burns asked. Cholmondeley had been watching for the man's reaction, but his shock seemed genuine and the cop was willing to believe it. His mouth hung open for a moment as he processed it. He frowned. "I'm sorry to hear that."

"I was hoping you might be able to give me some further information," Cholmondeley said.

"All I know is I found it outside the chippy at the dodgy end of Wentworth Road."

Cholmondeley had passed the place a thousand times over the years and he could picture it in his mind's eye. He made a note to send a team over there and then nodded at the man. "You did the right thing, son," he said, glancing discretely at his wristwatch. "I'd like to take your fingerprints before you leave if that's okay."

"Go ahead."

"Great," Cholmondeley said. "Constable Groves will see to that once we're done here. There's one other thing I'd like to know."

"What's that?"

"When you gave us the phone, why didn't you stick around?" Cholmondeley asked. "It took time and resources to track you down."

"Well, gee," Eddie said. "Sorry about that. I was in a rush. Like I said, I was on my lunch break when I found it. Lunch was over and I had a job to get to. My bills don't pay themselves. I wish they would."

Cholmondeley smiled and stood up. "Me too," he said, thinking about Mary and their credit card bills. "Thanks for your time, Mr. Burns. I'll let you know if we need anything else from you."

***

Meanwhile, at Leipfold's office, there was a visitor. The woman identified herself as Doreen Fisher. Maile guessed she was in her seventies. Mrs. Fisher didn't have an appointment, but business was slow and so they squeezed her in. Maile took her duffel coat and brought her a cup of tea and a plate of biscuits while Leipfold sat her down in their makeshift reception area and promised he'd be right with her.

Five minutes later, when he'd finished checking his emails and the woman had settled in, Leipfold sat down beside her and asked how he could be of service.

"I need your help, Mr. Leipfold," she said. "I saw your ad in *The Tribune*. You're just the sort of man I'm looking for."

Leipfold grinned in spite of himself. Even though money was short, he'd refused to cancel his adverts. It looked like he was about to witness that "return on investment" thing that his accountant liked to talk about. Good. He'd been thinking about selling Camilla. He still might have to unless a new client came in through the door. "What seems to be the problem?" he asked.

"I want my money back," the woman said. "I was taken in,

hoodwinked. By one of those whatjamicallits from the Internet. A slammer."

"A scammer?" Maile asked.

"That's the one," she replied. "They swindled me out of my savings with some cock and bull story."

"A Nigerian prince?" Maile guessed.

"Oh!" the woman exclaimed. "He emailed you too?"

"No," Maile said, "but please continue." Leipfold flashed her a brief glance and she blushed a little.

"Well, where do I begin?" the woman said. "It all started with an email. I don't use the computer much—not with *my* eyes—but I log on every now and then to keep up with the grandkids. The first email must have been two or three weeks ago. It was a Wednesday. I remember that because on Wednesdays—"

Leipfold coughed politely, apologised and said, "Go on."

"They said I'd inherited a sum of money," Mrs. Fisher continued. "Now, I may be old, but I'm not stupid. I thought something seemed fishy, but he seemed to know a lot about me. He asked after our Trev, for example, and said he'd talked to Mr. Jennings at the bank."

"Interesting," Maile murmured.

"Anyway," the woman continued, "I was asked to pay a processing fee before the money could be moved. So, like a fool, I paid it. I was told to wait three days for it to transfer. So I waited. When nothing arrived, I sent him an email, and then another one, and then a dozen more after that. Nothing."

"And you want us to find out what happened to your money?" Leipfold asked.

"Damn straight," Mrs. Fisher replied. "And I want you to get it back for me. How else am I supposed to pay you?"

There was an awkward pause while Leipfold thought about what she'd said. Then he asked, "Does that mean what I think it means? You want me to take your case without paying a retainer?"

"I don't know what that means," Mrs. Fisher said. "Look, I'm not asking you to do this for free. I'm asking you—*begging* you—to get my money back. If you manage it, you'll get a commission. And if you fail, well, you'll only have yourself to blame for it."

Leipfold thought about it again. "Mrs. Fisher," he said, "I can't help you." Then he looked over at his assistant. "Luckily," he continued. "I know someone who can."

***

Leipfold went back to his computer while Maile talked to Mrs. Fisher, but he was still listening to the conversation. Back when he was a kid, he'd learned to multitask by reading books while watching television, and it was easy enough for him to carry out a little research while eavesdropping.

Maile, meanwhile, was in her element. She asked for a copy of the email and the old lady dutifully provided a printout from her oversized handbag. Maile asked her to forward a digital copy when she got home, then took the piece of paper and read through it. Then, she read through it again and laid it flat on the table in front of her.

"Hang on a second," Maile said. She jogged over to her desk to grab a highlighter, then sat back down and started scoring through different words and sentences. She stopped as suddenly as she started and held the paper up in front of her eyes. She squinted.

"So what do you think?"

"You're right," Maile said. "Interesting. I count at least a dozen personal references that—if they're true, at least—suggest that the sender knows you. Plus, the spelling and grammar are impeccable."

"And that's unusual?"

"Mmmhmm," Maile said. "It's more uncommon than you'd think. Especially in emails like these. They usually deliberately add mistakes to make them look less legitimate. It's a sort of idiot filter. Most people would recognise the email as untrustworthy, but the ones who don't are more likely to fall for the next stages of the scam. Send something deliberately bogus and only an idiot would fall for it. Not that you're an idiot."

Mrs. Fisher sighed impatiently and asked, "What does that mean for me?"

"It means that this isn't a typical scammer," Maile said. "Mrs. Fisher, it's likely that this email was written by someone you know in real life.

58

Possibly a friend or a relative. Can you think of anyone who might be capable of this?"

The old woman shook her head. "I'm afraid not," she said. "And besides, I'm not exactly made of money. I just saved away for a rainy day. No one even knew I had it."

"Someone must have known," Maile said, "or you wouldn't be here." She offered the old lady another cup of tea, which Mrs. Fisher gratefully accepted. Maile looked expectantly over at Leipfold, who glanced across from his screen and met her gaze. Leipfold scowled at her and mumbled something, but he took the hint and started clattering about in the open kitchen.

Meanwhile, Maile handed Mrs. Fisher a pen and paper and started running through the list of what she needed.

"We'll start with the email itself," she said. She leaned over and scribbled something down on the pad, then tore it out and handed it over. "This is my email address. Find the email they sent and any subsequent communication between the two of you and forward it over to me."

"Got it," Mrs. Fisher said, scribbling a few notes down.

"While you're at it, I want you to give me a copy of your contacts," Maile continued. "But I'm also going to need you to write a list of everyone who has your email address. I want you to think about forms you've filled out, mailing lists you've joined, anything that springs to mind where you gave someone your email address. It might not be someone from your address book."

"I'll certainly try my best," the woman said. "But it won't be easy."

"Nothing ever is," Maile murmured. "Oh, there's one other thing. I want you to think about what I already asked you. Do you know anyone that might be capable of doing something like this?"

"No," Mrs. Fisher said, shaking her head. "I'm sorry, I really am."

"That's okay," Maile replied. "Just think about it. That's all I ask. If any names come up, write them down and send them over."

"And what will you do?" Mrs. Fisher asked.

Maile grinned and reached for a biscuit. "I'll do what I do best," she said. "Just leave it with me."

Chapter Eleven:
Milton Keynes

LEIPFOLD WAS GETTING READY to leave the office. He'd completed the day's crossword in record time, but he couldn't take all of the credit. He liked to think Maile was just a spectator because it was Leipfold holding the pencil, but in reality they'd been working as a team.

With the last clue filled out and the pencil and paper packed away, Leipfold grabbed his jacket and left Maile in the office while he went to follow up on a lead. With Maile's help, and a little stalking on some social networks, he'd been able to track down Tom Townsend's rehearsal space in Shoreditch.

He arrived at the space around lunchtime, just in time to catch a gaggle of actors lurking outside, smoking cigarettes and half-heartedly learning lines. Leipfold edged past without making eye contact and found himself inside a converted warehouse. From outside, it looked abandoned, but the inside was a labyrinthine mess of creativity from potteries and studios to rehearsal spaces for musicians, small rooms for bohemian business meetings and even a makeshift auditorium.

Leipfold found Tom Townsend in the auditorium. He identified him on sight thanks to a photo from the production's website. But the photo didn't do him justice, and Leipfold was surprised by just how tall he was. At five foot six, Leipfold was shorter than average. He'd been the shortest in his unit back in the army days. Tom Townsend was at least six foot three, and maybe a little taller.

"Mr. Townsend?" Leipfold asked.

Townsend, who'd been fiddling with his phone while holding a sheaf of paper between his arms, stood up a little straighter and looked at him.

"Yes?" he said. "And you are?"

"My name's James Leipfold. I'm a private detective. I was wondering if I could ask you a couple of questions."

"No," Townsend said. "Sorry." He glanced at the door and started to walk towards it.

Leipfold followed him and kept talking, even though Townsend had his back to him. "I promise it'll only take a minute."

"I can't help you, sir," Tom Townsend said. His legs were longer and he could walk a little faster, but Leipfold was keeping up by sticking to his tail in a half-run. "My mother told me never to talk to strangers."

"Please, Mr. Townsend. It's important!"

Tom Townsend spun around and Leipfold almost walked into the back of him. "I don't want to talk to you, Mr. Lightfoot."

"Leipfold," he corrected.

"Whatever. It's not important. I'm not going to talk to you. Please, just let me go. I have work to do."

Leipfold acquiesced, but only because he had no choice. Tom Townsend scuttled off and Leipfold spotted a group of the director's cronies heading towards him. He frowned at them and tried to find his way back out of the labyrinth.

***

Cholmondeley spent the evening in Milton Keynes, hopping on a train after work and heading to a fancy ballroom in an upmarket hotel. Mary was with him and they were both dressed up in their finery, Cholmondeley in his uniform and Mary in a navy-blue ball gown. She'd treated herself to a haircut and painted her fingernails to match her dress, and she was wearing a touch of foundation and a subtle shade of lipstick.

"You look wonderful, dear," Cholmondeley told her as they piled into the back of a taxi at the train station. He meant it, too. Mary was on the wrong side of fifty and already in early retirement, but she scrubbed up nicely when she wanted to impress. And that, as Cholmondeley had explained to her a dozen times during the train journey, was exactly what the trip to Milton Keynes was all about.

It was the night of an annual charity ball that was held to raise money for the families of coppers who'd laid down their lives in the line of duty. It was a big event and anyone who was anyone would be there. They always were.

Inside, they found themselves seated at a table with the wife of a police commissioner and a retired superintendent. Mary and Cholmondeley introduced themselves and were soon drinking glasses of Chardonnay and tucking into the five courses that the waiters brought over to their table.

During the auction, Cholmondeley put in a couple of low bids that he couldn't afford, just to impress his superiors. He'd open up the bidding and then sit back and relax as people with more money than sense paid through the nose. He wished them all the best for it. Everyone knew what the auction was about. Nobody wanted the signed football shirts, the champagne hampers and the music memorabilia. They just needed an excuse to open their wallets for a good cause.

The last item of the night rolled around, and Cholmondeley dutifully sat forwards and raised his hand. But someone else started up the bidding and Cholmondeley's heart leapt up into his mouth as he saw who it was.

Is that…? he thought. *No, it can't be.*

But it was. Cholmondeley's eyes weren't as sharp as they'd been when he'd first joined the police force, but he could still see better than most and he knew exactly who he was looking at. James Leipfold was there, starting off the bidding in the same suit he'd been wearing at the theatre the night before.

"I'll be damned," Cholmondeley murmured. "I guess he has a heart after all."

He turned his attention back to the auction and noticed two disturbing things at the exact same moment. The first was that everyone had turned to look at him. The second was that his hand was still in the air.

"Sold!" the auctioneer boomed, his amplified voice echoing around the room, a sound that Cholmondeley would remember forever.

He poured himself another glass of Chardonnay and tried to sink into the ground. He avoided his wife's eyes and stared into the glass, wondering gloomily what he'd bought and how much he'd agreed to pay for it.

***

"But don't you think it's a bit...y'know..."

"Suspicious?" Leipfold asked. "No, I don't."

"But come on, boss," Maile said. "You're telling me that the theatre guy refused to speak to you and you don't think it's unusual?"

It was the following day, a Saturday, but Maile and Leipfold were still in the office. There were crosswords to solve and cases to investigate, and neither of them had anything better to do. If he hadn't been working, Leipfold would have spent the day at home, rereading his battered Shakespeare folios and watching repeats on TV. Maile would have stayed in bed with her laptop, throwing code around.

"Lots of people refuse to talk to me," Leipfold said. "I don't take it personally. And I don't think it's suspicious."

"But you think there's something suspicious about the case, right?" Maile asked. "I mean, what if it really was an accident?"

"I doubt that," Leipfold replied. "I doubt that very much. Donna Thompson was murdered. I'm sure of it. I just wish we knew who was behind the wheel of the car. If we can find them, we solve the case."

"If there was anyone behind the wheel in the first place," Maile murmured.

Leipfold glanced across at her. "What do you mean?" he asked.

"It's probably nothing," Maile said, twirling a loop of her hair and avoiding Leipfold's steely eyes. "It's just that not all cars need a driver."

"I'm not sure I understand."

"Technology moves fast," Maile said. "Faster than you'd ever believe. A lot of companies have driverless cars. Google has one, and so does Tesla. Most of the major manufacturers are developing their own models. And there are plenty of hobbyists doing the same thing. It's usually illegal, of course, but you'd be surprised at how easy it is to teach a car to drive itself."

"So?"

"So maybe we're looking at this the wrong way," Maile replied. "I was working on the basis that someone was crouching down behind the wheel. That would explain why you couldn't see them in the footage."

"That's one theory," Leipfold said.

"But what if there's another explanation?" Maile continued. "What if there was no one in the car at all? What if it was just following orders? Orders contained within its programming? Orders that told it to kill Donna Thompson?"

Leipfold considered this for a moment and then shook his head. "It seems unlikely," he said. "Too far-fetched. There must be a simpler explanation."

"It would explain why no one found the driver," Maile said. "And that's not all. I checked online and these cars are more common than you might think. I found a club for enthusiasts and a half-dozen reports of recent sightings."

"Good work," Leipfold said. The more he thought about it, the more convinced he was that she was on to something. "Get me the details of that car club. I want contact info and a member list. And look into those rumours as well. See if you can find out where the cars were spotted and if any of them were black sedans."

"Sure thing," Maile said. She flashed Leipfold a winning grin. "I'm on it."

Chapter Twelve:
Bateman's Motors

MAILE WORKED FAST while Leipfold pored over the papers. She printed out her report just after midday, then grabbed the stack of paper and plopped it down on Leipfold's desk. He waved his hand impatiently and asked her to give him an overview.

"Okay," Maile said, dragging a chair over so she could sit down beside him. "I found reports of five different autonomous cars over the last two weeks, but only one of them was a black sedan. They're pretty rare and they're not exactly road legal, but a couple of people have them anyway. To be honest, I'm surprised I didn't find more of them. A lot of these guys are using open source scripts to develop their own."

"I get it," Leipfold said. "Nerds need flashy cars just like everyone else."

"No one says nerds anymore, boss," Maile replied. "We're not nerds. We're geeks. But yeah, you're right. And a lot of them have the cash to follow through."

Leipfold shrugged and thought about how quickly the world changed. He didn't know it as well as he had when he was eighteen and taking his first tentative steps into adulthood. It scared him.

"What else have you got?" he asked.

"That's just it." Maile grinned, leaning forward in her chair and glancing through the stack of paper. "There's only one place you'll find a black, self-driving sedan. Bateman's Motors in Clapham."

Leipfold flashed her a rare smile, grabbed the keys to his motorbike and left the office without another word.

"Damn it," Maile mumbled, shuffling back to her desk to eat her lunch while she half-heartedly manned the silent telephone. "Finally something cool comes along and he doesn't take me with him. Go figure."

***

Leipfold slowed to a stop outside Bateman's Motors, parked his bike and removed his helmet. Then he stalked purposefully towards the reception office. It was a hot mess, but it offered everything a motorist might need, from a garage and repair shop to a hire lot and a sales floor for a couple dozen used cars. Leipfold thought that if there was anywhere he might find a black, self-driving sedan, this place was as good as any. But he was going to need a little help to find it.

Bateman was working the front desk. The guy looked like he was about to have a heart attack. Greg Bateman was in his late thirties, but he looked at least ten years older. He was a skinhead in a sharp suit with more meat than a butcher's window. Leipfold waited for him to finish a phone call and then introduced himself.

"Leipfold, huh?" Bateman murmured. "The name's Greg Bateman. Put it there." He held out a fleshy paw and Leipfold took it. Bateman's handshake felt honest, and Leipfold distrusted it immediately. He remembered one of Jack Cholmondeley's old sayings. *Never trust a used car dealer.* A simple saying, but one that had served him well over the years. It had even influenced his decision to drive a motorbike.

"Nice to meet you, Mr. Bateman," Leipfold replied. "I've got a little business to send your way."

"You have? What kind of business?"

"We'll get to that," Leipfold said. "But first, I was hoping to ask you a couple of questions."

"Fire away," Bateman replied. "I'll do what I can."

Leipfold smiled. "I'm looking for a specific type of vehicle," he said. "It's an autonomous black sedan. I hear you might be able to help me."

Bateman froze, then fixed Leipfold with a look of intense concentration.

"Yeah," he said, choosing his words like a chess player picking his moves. "I might be able to help you. You understand, of course, that there's a lot of paperwork involved with a vehicle like this? A lot of laws and regulations."

"I understand," Leipfold replied. "Thing is, I don't think you have much choice. That car is part of an active case."

Greg Bateman laughed uncertainly, then stopped when he realised Leipfold wasn't joking. "You a cop?" he asked.

"I'm a private investigator," Leipfold replied. "Can we talk?"

Bateman frowned and shook his head. Then he logged out of the computer, took the phone off the hook and led Leipfold into his office, just off to the side of the showroom. He locked the door behind them, showed Leipfold to a small sofa, drew the blinds and then sat down behind his desk.

"This better be good, Mr. Leipfold," he said.

***

James Leipfold and Greg Bateman spent so long talking that their stomachs started to rumble. Leipfold told him what he knew about the Thompson case and Bateman listened with growing interest. They went over the scene of the crime. Leipfold supplied as many details as he could, including what little they knew of the car. Bateman's face fell as Leipfold's story continued. By the end of it, he sat slumped, defeated, with his face in his hands. Leipfold waited for him to say something.

"This isn't good," Bateman said. "This isn't good at all. I know the car that you're talking about. I own it."

"Can I see it?"

"Could be a problem," Bateman said. "The last guy who hired it had an accident. Nothing too serious. Said he hit a fox when he had it on manual."

Leipfold's eyes lit up. "A fox, huh? So where's the car now?"

"It's in for repairs," Bateman said. "Should be back in a couple of hours."

Leipfold sighed, thinking about the potential evidence that was being removed from the car at that very moment. He asked Bateman if it he could call off the repairs, but the salesman shook his head.

"Can't help you there, mate," he said. "It's already on the way back. I sent one of the lads out with it. You know, to keep an eye on it. It's an expensive piece of kit."

"Hold it here when it gets back," Leipfold replied. "I'll want to take a look at it. Do you remember the name of the man who caused the damage?"

Bateman scowled. "Of course," he said. "How could I forget? The guy was called Tom Townsend."

***

After their meeting, Leipfold hopped on Camilla and drove back to the warehouse where he'd first met Tom Townsend. This time, he lurked outside, trying his best to look nonchalant. Unlike Townsend, Leipfold couldn't act, but it was London and no one gave a damn. Townsend didn't even look around when he left the building.

Leipfold chained his bike to a nearby railing and followed Tom Townsend on foot. He had his head down and his eyes on a mobile phone screen, so it wasn't difficult to avoid being spotted. Nevertheless, he kept his distance as Townsend wormed through the streets towards his apartment. Leipfold had a hunch that he wouldn't walk far, and he was right. After eight minutes by Leipfold's watch, Tom Townsend turned into a cul-de-sac and walked up to a white front door.

Leipfold approached him while he was fumbling with his keys.

"Afternoon, Mr. Townsend," he said. "Let me guess, just nipping home for a bite to eat?"

Tom Townsend looked confused for a moment. Then, exasperation took over and his eyes narrowed.

"You again," he said. "How did you find me?"

"It was a guess," Leipfold admitted. "But an educated one. You live for your work. I figured you'd have a place nearby so you could spend as much time in that warehouse of yours as possible. After that, I just had to follow you."

Townsend stared at him. He sighed and turned back to the door, flipping the latch with his key. He tried to close the door in Leipfold's face, but the detective used the same trick he'd used at Eleanor

Thompson's place and didn't even wince when the wood banged against the side of his foot.

"Not so fast," Leipfold said. "I want a word with you."

"Move your foot," Townsend replied.

"Not a chance. I want to talk to you about self-driving cars, Mr. Townsend. Self-driving cars and Donna Thompson."

Leipfold had expected a reaction and he got one, but if he'd been hoping to be asked inside then he was sorely disappointed. Townsend pushed past Leipfold and stepped back onto the street, closing the door behind him.

"Let's walk and talk," Tom Townsend said. "What do you want to know?"

"Let's start with the car," Leipfold replied. "The self-driving sedan. Why did you hire it?"

"I hired it because I could," Townsend said. "The car guy gave me a discount. Still more expensive than a taxi, but totally worth it. I was taking someone to dinner and I wanted to impress her. It worked."

"Marie Rieirson?"

"Oh," Townsend said. "You know her."

"We've met," Leipfold replied. "So the two of you are dating?"

"Sort of," Townsend replied. "But I don't see how that's any of your business."

"You're right. My business is with the car." Leipfold glanced across at him as their feet pounded the pavement. "Mr. Townsend, are you aware of the damage to the vehicle? I believe Greg Bateman—the, uh, car guy—charged you for some repair work. What happened?"

"That's easy," Townsend replied. "Nothing happened. The guy's a shyster. That vehicle was in good shape last time I saw it. It even had a full tank."

"And when was the last time you saw it?"

"Outside the restaurant," Townsend said. "Ask the staff. Marie and I got out of the car and sent it back to Bateman's place when we were done with it."

Leipfold thought back to Maile's reports. "Aren't those cars supposed to have someone behind the wheel at all times?" he asked. "You know, just in case?"

Tom laughed. "Yeah," he said evasively. "About that…"

***

Back at Bateman's Motors, Leipfold was eyeing up the black sedan. Greg Bateman had given him a brief overview of the way that the machine worked, but Leipfold was an old-fashioned guy and he didn't retain much of it. He nodded along while Bateman talked about GPS, 4G and real-time computing, knowing all along that he'd drive it in manual on the way back to the office.

"Be careful with it," Bateman said. Leipfold grunted and signed the paperwork while the salesman fetched the keys.

"Of course," Leipfold replied. "I give you my word. And you do the same with Camilla."

"It's a deal," Bateman said. "You sure you want to go through with this? You could get a better price at another dealership."

"I could," Leipfold admitted. "But you'll be doing me a favour. I'll sell you the bike, even though you're fleecing me, and you'll lend me that car of yours."

"You want to buy the car?" Bateman paused for a moment. "I'm sorry, it's not for sale."

"I don't want to buy it," Leipfold replied. "I want to borrow it. Just for a day or so."

"And the motorbike?"

"I need the money," Leipfold explained. "I love Camilla, but I can't afford to run her. She gulps down petrol like there's no tomorrow and my insurance is about to go up. Then there's cash flow and my debt installments. Legal fees. Overdue invoices. Final demands from the taxman. It's her or the business. I choose the business."

"Makes sense." The car dealer thought for a moment. His brow furrowed. "Okay," he said. "It's a deal."

"You just take care of Camilla," Leipfold growled. "Don't sell her unless you get a good offer. One day, I'll buy her back from you."

"I'll do what I can," Bateman replied. "But I'm a businessman, Mr. Leipfold. If the right offer comes along, I'll take it."

"Understood."

Leipfold shook Bateman's hand and left him to it, then pulled on his biker gloves to hide his prints and climbed into the driver's seat of the sedan. Then he threaded through the streets towards his office. He hadn't driven a car since his accident, but now he was back behind the wheel and scooting through the streets of London. He knew he'd miss Camilla and that he'd got a bum deal for her, but he also knew that if he could crack this case then business would boom and he'd be able to buy her back again.

He parked the sedan outside the office and hurried inside to talk to Maile, who was eating sushi and tapping away at her laptop. She didn't look up when he entered the office.

"I've got a job for you," he said. "It's a fun one. I've got the car, and I need you to take a look at it. Figure out how it works, what it does and what bearing it has on the case. I'm convinced that there's something to find, and I want you to be the one to find it."

"Sure thing, boss," Maile replied.

"You've got two hours," Leipfold said. "And then I'm calling Jack Cholmondeley. It can't hurt for him to owe us a favour. Besides, I'm not going to withhold evidence from the boys in blue. Find out as much as you can. Check its fail-safes and that sort of thing. I understand it's programmed to avoid accidents, so why did it mow down Donna Thompson?"

"Got it. Are you sure it's the right vehicle?"

"Pretty sure," Leipfold said. "Now we just need to find out who programmed it to kill."

"That's not going to be easy," Maile replied. "I can't promise I'm going to find anything."

Leipfold shrugged. "Two hours," he said. "Get going."

***

Maile had the car and Bateman had the motorbike, so Leipfold took the tube to Marie Rieirson's place. Maile had found her address online and jotted it down inside his Moleskine.

It was dark by the time he arrived, although it was only early evening. Leipfold wore a jumper beneath his coat, but the wind still bit at his fingers and chafed every time he reached into his pocket to check his phone. Marie Rieirson lived on a busy main road, like the road Donna Thompson died on, but Leipfold found her address with ease.

The front garden was wild and overgrown, but the façade of the house was in good shape and looked almost inviting. There was no light from the front of the house, but Leipfold could see the dull glow of an interior light from somewhere deeper inside. He hesitated for a second to take stock of the place, then strolled up to the door and rang the bell.

It echoed throughout the house, bouncing off the walls and the woodwork like an alarm in a multi-storey car park. Leipfold waited and then waited some more, but no one came to answer. He looked for movement on the other side of the curtains, but the house was suspiciously still. Leipfold didn't like it. He had a bad feeling about it, and he'd learned long ago to trust his instincts.

Leipfold swallowed his worries and rang the bell again, but still nothing. He followed the wall to where it met a wooden fence, then scrambled up and over it and fell gracelessly to the ground on the other side. He found himself in Marie's back garden, a cluttered affair with too much wildlife. Leipfold disentangled himself from the bush he'd landed in and made his way across the patio towards the back door.

He cupped his hands against the glass and pressed his face against the door, but he couldn't see much. He knocked again and waited for a response, but he wasn't expecting one and so he wasn't disappointed when nobody answered.

So he turned to the artillery, pulling out his pocket knife and using one of the attachments to pop the lock. It was a model that Leipfold was unfamiliar with, but the principle was the same and he was inside the house within a minute. On the other side of the glass, in the darkness of the living room, Leipfold could sense something, a pervasive atmosphere that sent his primal fight or flight reflex into overdrive. It was the same thing he felt in a danger zone, when the birds went silent before a sniper shot rang out through the dust-ridden air. He hadn't felt that feeling for a long time, but he recognised it like an old, old friend.

The hit of adrenaline was more comforting than any bottle and Leipfold felt a new strength running through him that he hadn't felt since his twenties, maybe not even since his days in the army.

This is living, he thought. He wondered what Cholmondeley would think if he knew where he was and what he was doing, and he quickly dismissed the thought and filed it away as one to come back to in the future. He was breaking and entering, and he knew he was breaking and entering, but he also didn't give a shit. That's where he differed from Jack Cholmondeley. He had no interest in the law; it was just a means to an end. He preferred the hunt for the truth, and he knew from experience that the law had a habit of getting in the way of that. Law or not, he wanted answers. Whether the evidence would stand up in a courtroom was a different matter entirely, and something that he left for the police force to worry about. There was no client here, no obligation to Lady Justice. Leipfold just wanted an answer, and maybe a front-page story in *The Tribune.*

Leipfold stalked through the house, holding the knife in his hand just in case. *A dull knife is better than no knife at all,* he thought. He used his phone as a flashlight until he found the light switches and then roamed from room to room in search of the house's occupant. But she was nowhere to be found.

His night was about to get a hell of a lot worse. Leipfold thought he was being clever by taking the back way out and relocking the door behind him, but no such luck. He hopped the fence again and landed straight in the waiting arms of Constable Hyneman.

Chapter Thirteen:
Jailed

JAMES LEIPFOLD wasn't happy. He'd thought he was done with jail cells. Yet there he was, cooped up all over again. He scowled, leaned back against the wall and went over the events of the night before.

Constable Hyneman had cuffed and cautioned him on suspicion of breaking and entering, then bundled him into the back of a police car. They'd driven back to the station, and Hyneman had booked Leipfold in and left him to stew it out. After an hour or so, he was visited by Sergeant Gary Mogford, who was wearing his uniform and who had a grim expression on his stubborn face.

"You're in trouble now," he said, cutting straight to the chase. "The guvnor can't help you now. No special treatment for you."

Leipfold shrugged and said, "I don't expect it. But I do expect two things. First off, I'd like a lawyer. I know my rights and I'm entitled to legal support. I'd also like to make my phone call."

Mogford growled, but he had no choice. He summoned Constable Groves and asked her to escort Leipfold through the booking process and out to the phones in the waiting room. She stood a respectful distance away while he put in a call to the office.

Maile answered on the third ring and she didn't seem too surprised when Leipfold told her where he was. She listened as he recounted his adventures and then faithfully obeyed his instructions when he asked her for an update.

"Well," she said, "the car has gone, just like you wanted. Some old copper came to pick it up. I told him what you told me to say and kept Greg Bateman out of it, but it's not going to look good if they start asking questions. What did they pick you up for?"

"Breaking and entering," Leipfold said. "It's nothing. Happens all the time in this line of work. Did you learn anything about the car?"

"Of course, boss. I'll tell you about it when you get out. When are they going to release you?"

A dozen feet away, Constable Groves caught Leipfold's eye and tapped her watch. He winked at her.

"Soon," Leipfold said. "I'm working on it."

***

A couple more hours passed. Leipfold spent the time thinking about the Thompson case and how Donna met her end beneath the wheels of a car with no one in it.

When the door to the cell opened up again, Detective Inspector Jack Cholmondeley was on the other side of it. He grinned ruefully and instructed his men to lead Leipfold through to an interrogation room. There, Leipfold was introduced to his public defender, a man whose name he immediately forgot.

Leipfold and Cholmondeley shook hands like gentlemen and had a quick, off-the-record chat before Constable Groves walked in and started up the recorder. They talked about the charity ball and the ongoing investigation. Cholmondeley said he no longer believed that Donna's death was an accident, but he played fast and loose with the details. He didn't mention the car, even though they both knew he had it, and he was quick to reiterate that they weren't there to talk about Donna Thompson. They were there to talk about what Leipfold had been doing inside Marie Rieirson's flat.

"But don't you see?" Leipfold protested. "The two are interlinked. You must have looked at Marie as a possible suspect."

"One of my men spoke to her," Cholmondeley said. "But that's about it. Why would Marie be a suspect?"

"She had motive," Leipfold replied. "With Donna Thompson out of the way, she got a starring role in Townsend's play."

"Strange reason to kill someone," Cholmondeley said. "Is that the best you've got?"

"I don't suspect her of being a murderer," Leipfold said. "But she's connected to the case somehow. That's why I went to her house. I wanted to talk to her."

"And yet you didn't ring the bell like a normal person," Cholmondeley replied.

"I did ring the bell," Leipfold said. "But no one answered. So I went round the back to look inside."

Jack Cholmondeley smiled sadly. "I'd like to believe you, James," he said. "I really would. I *do* believe you, as it goes. But I can't let you out of here just yet. We need to ask a few more questions and get you to sign a statement."

Leipfold looked across at his solicitor, who nodded his assent. "Okay," he said.

The questions continued. Leipfold slowly told Cholmondeley everything he knew about the Thompson case, leaving out none of the details. He had to tell the truth because it was the only way to explain how he'd ended up at the Rieirson house.

"I had a feeling that something was wrong," Leipfold explained.

"Something *was* wrong," Cholmondeley replied. "Marie Rieirson is missing. That's why Constable Hyneman was at the scene and why we brought you here in the first place. We've been trying to trace the girl."

"Missing?" Leipfold echoed, sitting to attention. "You've got to let me out of here. I can help you to look for her."

"Not so fast, old friend," Cholmondeley said. "The paperwork, remember? Sergeant Mogford will take you through it."

Cholmondeley stood up slowly, grunting as he rose. He walked over to the door and then turned back to look at Leipfold.

"By the way," he added, smiling with his eyes but not his lips. "Thanks for the tip about the car. We'll take a good look at it. You leave the Thompson case to us."

***

Leipfold got back to the office in the early afternoon and was surprised to find that the place was empty. He walked over to his planner and checked the date. It was only six days since Donna Thompson had died.

And yet, his office—his debt-ridden, inefficient office, which cost him more money than it made him—felt empty because Maile wasn't there.

He grimaced. He'd always hated Sundays, ever since his parents used to take him to church with the neighbours' kids. He tried to remember their names, but it was all so long ago. Now, as he reluctantly approached middle age, he still hated Sundays, but at least it explained why Maile wasn't in the office. It meant he had to boil the kettle himself.

Once he'd brewed a coffee—in a record seventeen seconds from when he dropped the first sweetener to when he launched the spoon into the sink—he grabbed the Sunday papers and sat down at his desk. He started to fill out the crosswords, noting as he did so the subtle nuances between the different writers. They gave him his daily fix in a dose that picked him up in the morning and kept him going in the afternoon.

He wondered where Marie Rieirson was and debated visiting her house again. Then he remembered spending the night in a police cell and his hands wandered automatically down towards the third drawer on the left, the special drawer with the special lock where he kept his special bottle of whiskey. It had survived the crash and served as a constant reminder of why he still stuck to coffee and orange juice.

Leipfold couldn't remember where the key was, so he picked the lock with his army knife—which the police had kindly returned to him—and pulled the bottle from the desk. It was an old, old bottle and the level of the liquid had decreased over time thanks to evaporation and inhalation. Leipfold liked to open it from time to time to give it a sniff. It was the real deal, with a kick that made his eyes water.

He went through the motions, opening up the bottle and pouring out a measure. He sniffed it again. Then he poured the liquid back into the bottle. He put the bottle back into the drawer and locked it. Then he sighed, put his head in his hands and wondered what in the hell had happened to Marie Rieirson.

Chapter Fourteen:
Missing

THE FOLLOWING MORNING, Leipfold woke at his desk with a parched throat and a dodgy stomach. It was almost as bad as a hangover, but it had nothing to do with alcohol. Leipfold had a stress headache and stomach pains. His liver, lungs and digestive system were at war with him, and he still didn't have any answers for the Thompson case. All he had was a good idea of where to go next, but that was enough.

Leipfold's phone went off, but he ignored it. His head was pounding and he needed water and coffee before he'd be ready to talk to anyone. He checked his watch. It read 7:17a.m., which meant he had a good hour and a half before Maile arrived at the office. He planned to take advantage of that fact to get some work done.

The phone rang again. Leipfold cursed and answered the call. "James Leipfold speaking," he said. "How can I help?"

"Stay away from the Thompson case." The caller on the other end of the line was using a vocoder, and Leipfold knew without needing a comparison that it was the same one he'd heard on the recording. He checked his phone, but the caller's number was withheld as he'd expected it would be.

"Who am I talking to?" Leipfold asked.

"A friend," the caller replied. "You don't need to know who I am. You just need to trust me. Stay away from the case."

"Why?"

"Do you like breathing, Mr. Leipfold?" the caller asked. "And more to the point, would you like to keep on doing it?"

"Is that a threat?" Leipfold asked.

"I prefer to think of it as a warning." There was a pause on the other end of the line. "Call it what you like. Just stay away from the case."

"Right," Leipfold said.

"I mean it, Mr. Leipfold," the caller said. "Stay away from the case. If you don't, you'll be sorry. We wouldn't want you to have an accident like poor little Donna Thompson. Remember, I've got my eye on you. I've got my eye on your assistant, too. It'd be a shame if something happened to her."

"It won't."

"Well, that's up to you," the caller said. "It depends on whether you listen to my warning. Remember what I said, Mr. Leipfold. Stay off the case."

The caller cut the call and Leipfold put the phone down on his desk. He massaged his temples and felt the sweat that had started to bead there. Then he picked his phone up again and sent Maile a message to tell her to be on the lookout.

***

Maile got to work at ten past nine, a full ten minutes after her official start time. But then, as she pointed out to Leipfold, she didn't have a contract. She could pick her own damn hours.

"You're lucky I came in at all," Maile said. "I could be racking up a kill streak right now."

"Games?" Leipfold guessed. "I always found reality exciting enough."

"Games are an extension of reality," Maile insisted.

"Whatever," Leipfold said. "What have you got for me? We're due a catch-up."

"You were at the police station," Maile reminded him. "And I was playing Xbox."

"Racking up kill streaks?"

"Right," Maile said. "And catching up with Mayhem. He's an Internet friend, never met the guy. But we have a few things in common."

"Oh yeah?" Leipfold said. "Like what?"

"Hacking. Programming. Cybersecurity." Maile shrugged. "That sort of thing."

"Another nerd?"

"I already told you," Maile said. "No one says nerd anymore. Besides, you might want to be a little nicer. I got him to take a look at the car with me. Hooked up a video feed and sent him a link to the specs. It's not as good as flying over here in person, but…"

"You did all that, huh?" Leipfold's steely eyes gave nothing away. Maile couldn't tell if he was angry or amused. "I don't remember telling you to get someone else involved."

"Mayhem is a good guy," Maile said. "Limited social skills, perhaps, but he's loyal. He said he wouldn't talk and I believed him."

"Does Mayhem have a name?"

"That *is* his name," Maile replied. "He helped me to do some digging. We found some tech specs and manuals. Some stuff about the programming language. Info on how the vehicle's AI makes its decisions. But it gave me a couple of ideas. Once I knew what I was doing, it was simple enough to modify the code. That's what the guys at the car club are all about. They don't just buy the cars and drive them. They learn to modify them, to create their own software to up their performance."

"And?"

"Well that's just it," Maile said. "See, it's not too difficult to fudge with the programming. Don't get me wrong. I don't think Eleanor Thompson would be up to it, but your average geek on the street? If they can code, they can code. Any one language is as good as another. I picked up the basics in an hour or so."

Maile paused to take a sip of water while Leipfold scribbled a few hasty lines in his notebook.

"Anyway," she continued. "Here's the crux of it. That car can be hacked, and it can be hacked remotely if you know what you're doing. I only had two hours and it was enough to bypass the programming and run my own routine on it. And get this, I almost killed Kat."

"You almost killed a cat?"

"Kat," Maile said. "My housemate, remember? I called her up and told her to get her ass down here. Then I made her stand in the middle of the road while I tried to kill her."

"That doesn't sound safe," Leipfold said.

"It wasn't," Maile replied. "But I proved my hypothesis. That car could easily be used as a murder weapon. It took me two hours to stop it from braking. In two days, I could've programmed it to hunt her down. Two weeks? I'd have that baby running MS-DOS."

Leipfold glanced over at her. "Bingo," he said. "Good work."

Maile beamed. "Now we just have to find out who reprogrammed it," she said.

"And why," Leipfold murmured, but Maile didn't hear him. She'd read her boss's mind and wandered off to fetch the paper and put the kettle on.

***

Maile checked her emails while Leipfold finished the crossword. Then, when he told her he wanted to talk to her, she wandered over to sit down on the edge of his desk.

"What's it about?" she asked. "The Thompson case?"

"Well, it's not like we've got much else on," Leipfold reminded her.

"There's the Fisher case," Maile said.

"Point taken," Leipfold replied. "But business is slow. Too slow, Maile. I'm worried."

"Give it time," she replied. "You do your thing and I'll do mine. You know, work a little magic. Get your website up and running, that sort of stuff. Maybe even start a blog."

"Do what you've got to do," Leipfold said. "But not the blog. We can't risk leaking information."

"Who said anything about that?" Maile asked. "You read the paper every day, right? Just talk to me about what you read in there. I'll write it up and stick it on the net. Search engines will find it, people will start talking and before you know it, the clients will be rolling in."

"Fine, fine," Leipfold said. "You do that. But don't let it distract you from the rest of your work. For now, I want to talk about the Thompson case."

And so Leipfold told her about the call he'd received, culminating with his conclusion that the two robotic voices from the phone and from the recording were one and the same.

"I've been trying to work out who it was," Leipfold said. "Best guess so far? Eleanor Thompson. That's what Cholmondeley thinks."

Maile shook her head. "I don't think it was her, boss. What kind of old woman knows how to use a voice changer?"

"How hard are they to use?" Leipfold asked. "Don't you just buy one, pick it up and use it? She's a smart woman. She could have figured it out."

"Maybe," Maile replied.

"But perhaps you're right," Leipfold said. "After all, what about the car? I doubt it was Eleanor Thompson, but *someone* interfered with it. The problem is, we need to figure out who. Can you do that?"

"I can try," Maile replied. "But no promises."

"Do it," Leipfold said. "I'll work on it as well. I've got a few questions of my own. What did they have to gain from it? And why go to all of that effort? Seems like an elaborate way to kill someone."

"Maybe they wanted to put on a show."

"Hmm," Leipfold murmured. "I wonder. Who do we know with a flair for the theatrical? And who would benefit if Donna was out of the way?"

***

Later that morning, Leipfold called the cop shop. He figured he owed his friend a favour.

"Let's get down to business," Leipfold said once the pleasantries were out of the way. "I'm guessing you know I haven't called you to ask after your health. How are things going with the Thompson case?"

"I can't talk to you about that, James," Cholmondeley said. "Not anymore."

"Are you sure about that, big man?" Leipfold laughed. "And what if I could help you?"

"What do you mean?"

"Well, it's like this," Leipfold said. "I'm not a lone wolf anymore. Remember Maile? She can use computers, and I don't just mean to make a spreadsheet. She can find things. She sees things that most people wouldn't see. She's a genius, even if sometimes it's a little…misapplied. A useful girl to have around in my line of work."

"I'll bet," Cholmondeley replied. "What do you want, James? Make it quick. Some of us have got a job to do."

So Leipfold told Cholmondeley, as best as he could, what Maile had explained to him about the car. As promised, when she'd finished her tests and wiped it clean, she'd parked it a couple of miles away and then anonymously reported it on the police helpline. Cholmondeley listened with steadily growing interest as Leipfold explained how it was theoretically possible for someone to reprogram the car. He whistled, softly, once his old friend had finished.

"That's quite the story," he said. "I'll get our tech guys to take a look to see if they can replicate the results."

"There's more," Leipfold said. "I received a call from someone who wanted to warn me off the case. Any idea who it might be from?"

"Your guess is as good as mine," Cholmondeley said. "Are you trying to find out if we have a suspect?"

"Don't need to," Leipfold replied. "I have one of my own. But listen, Jack. They threatened me. Me and my assistant."

"Did they threaten to kill you?"

Leipfold paused to think about it.

"No," he said, eventually. "But he did threaten to hurt us, and I believed him. Or her. Who knows? I need you to look into it, to see what you can find out. It could be connected to the case."

"Why should I do that?" Cholmondeley asked.

"It's your job," Leipfold replied. "And besides, you owe me one."

"I do?" Cholmondeley paused, weighing up his options. He sighed. "You scratch my back and I'll scratch yours, right, James? Okay, I'll look into it. There's something else as well. You told me about the car, so I'll tell you about Marie Rieirson."

"What about her?"

"Didn't you hear the news?" Cholmondeley asked. "She's officially been reported missing. We've opened up an investigation. Come to think of it, don't be surprised if some of my guys pay you another visit."

"Am I a suspect?"

"It's not your style," Cholmondeley said. "But it's not always up to me. Sergeant Mogford doesn't think much of you, for example. And I can't allow old times to influence policy. Either way, Rieirson is missing and I wouldn't be surprised if another body showed up."

"Who reported her missing?" Leipfold asked.

"She gave her name as Jayne Lipton. Do you know her?"

Leipfold shook his head and then remembered that Cholmondeley couldn't see him. "No," he said. "Can't say I've had the pleasure."

"Me neither," Cholmondeley replied. "Not yet. But we're hoping to get her to come to the station. I'll let you know how that goes. You'll keep me updated on your end, of course?"

"What's the matter?" Leipfold laughed. "Worried I'll solve the case before you?"

There was a pause. Leipfold could imagine Cholmondeley on the other end of the line, his face flushing like it always did when he was angry.

"That's not it at all," Cholmondeley lied. "I'm just worried, James. Worried about the case. We need to catch the bastard who's behind it before we find another body."

Chapter Fifteen:
A Meeting with Tom Townsend

LATER THAT AFTERNOON, Detective Inspector Jack Cholmondeley placed a call consisting of six words: a surname and an address. Leipfold knew the drill. They'd followed it before. After the call was over, they'd both pretend it never happened.

Leipfold checked his watch, surprised, and surmised that the boys in blue had already finished asking their questions, probably because they didn't know which questions to ask her. And so it was that James Leipfold found himself hopping on the tube again, lamenting the loss of Camilla while making his way to Shelden Street where Jayne Lipton lived.

Jayne answered the door after his second knock. She kept the chain on but she seemed happy enough to talk.

"I doubt I'll be much help," she warned him. "I've already told you everything I can."

"That's okay," Leipfold replied. "Although you haven't told me anything. I'm not with the police. I'm…well, I'm more what you'd call a consultant."

"Same thing," Jayne said.

Leipfold looked at her, curiously. She looked a little like Marie Rieirson—not overly so, but they had a similar style. Jayne was wearing a long-sleeved shirt and a pair of skinny jeans, and her auburn hair was tied back and hung loosely on her shoulder. Her eyes were dark and her expression was neutral. She gave nothing away.

"Can you tell me how you know Marie Rieirson?" Leipfold asked.

"Sure can," Jayne replied. "We used to live together. A friend of a friend introduced us when I first moved to London. She was looking for a housemate and I was looking for a house. I moved in a couple of days later."

"And you're the person who reported her missing?"

"Yeah," Jayne said. "She wasn't answering my calls. I went round to see if she was at home, but no one answered. I called her parents. They hadn't heard from her, either. We were worried, so I slept on it and ended up calling the police when there was still no sign of her."

"You did the right thing," Leipfold said. "And you have no idea where she might be?"

"If I did, I would've found her already."

"I thought as much," Leipfold said. "And what about Donna Thompson? Ever heard of her?"

Jayne seemed to consider the question for a moment, but she eventually shook her head and said, "Sorry, sir. I've never heard of her."

"It was a long shot," Leipfold replied. "But a shot worth taking all the same. Listen, Ms. Lipton, I don't want to take up any more of your time. I'm not even sure if this is connected to the case I'm supposed to be working on. But rest assured. We'll find your friend, whether I find her or whether the police beat me to it. Now, is there anything else you can tell me that might help me to track her down?"

"No," Jayne said. "Nothing."

"No friends? Anyone she might have confided in?"

"Well," Jayne murmured, "there is the one, I suppose. A guy called Tom Townsend. She used to work with him at the theatre. I always thought there was something going on between the two of them. Maybe they ran away together."

"Maybe," Leipfold replied. "But I doubt it."

***

Constable Groves had drawn the short straw, which was why she had the tedious job of watching the forensic team as they combed the car for clues. She understood what they did, of course. She just couldn't understand how they did it. As a relatively new member of the force, she didn't hold the same prejudices as Gary Mogford and Jack Cholmondeley, but she still viewed forensics as a strange mix of science and magic, some sort of hoodoo that they did to put the bad guys behind bars.

But that didn't stop her from watching them as they pored over the surfaces, dusting for prints, scouting for fibres and doing whatever the hell else they did so that they could take samples back to the lab.

Constable Groves nodded at one of the scientists as he withdrew from the vehicle. "How's it going?" she asked.

"Slowly," the man grunted.

"Anything promising?"

"Not really," he said. His voice was muffled by the mask he wore, but he made no effort to pull it aside. Groves wasn't surprised. The forensic team was notorious for following protocol. They knew that the slightest breach could come back to bite them in the ass and stop a bad guy from being brought to justice. "Couple of hairs and fibres."

"Enough for a DNA match?" Groves asked.

"Yeah," the man replied. "If we have a sample to compare it to. I can't promise we'll find anything, though. It'll take a couple of days to run it and we might not get a hit. We'll have to hope we have a suspect in the database."

"You'd better get a move on," Groves said. "Cholmondeley is impatient. He'll take it out on me if you take too long."

"Why?"

Groves shrugged her shoulders and looked over at the car again. "He just will," she said. "I think he sent me here to keep an eye on you. He—"

Constable Groves was interrupted by a shout from one of the scientists who was inspecting the car, and she was two and a half steps towards it when she was pulled back by the man she'd been talking to. His gloved hands were heavy on her arm. They pinched her like a vice as he yanked her backwards.

"Don't!" he commanded. "Not yet."

Groves nodded at the man who released his grip. The two of them edged slightly closer to the vehicle. A couple of new faces, still hidden behind masks and with their hair covered by lightweight nets, burst on to the scene and rushed over to the car.

"I can't see," Groves murmured.

"Me neither," the man whispered. Then he raised his voice and shouted, "Hey, what are we looking at?"

"I found something," someone replied.

Another man muscled his way forward, and Groves recognised him immediately as Sergeant Joe Riggs, the tall, broad-shouldered liaison between the crime lab and the rest of the station. He was a good-looking chap with chiselled features and fair hair that poked out from his hairnet. He nodded at Groves and approached the vehicle, where one of the scientists was holding something up to the light in a gloved hand.

"What is it?" Riggs asked. "What did you find?"

"We've got a ring," the man said. "Platinum, by the looks of it. With a diamond. An engagement band, perhaps?"

Riggs leaned in for a closer look. The tension in the air was electric, almost unbearable.

"So it is," Riggs said. "Bag it, tag it and get it back to the lab. And someone give Jack Cholmondeley a ring. No pun intended. He's going to want to know about this."

***

Leipfold was on the tube again, still mourning the loss of Camilla. He hadn't realised how much he relied on her until after he'd handed the keys to Greg Bateman. She was a part of his personality, like the strict habits he'd picked up in the army or the way he read the papers and completed the crosswords.

This time, he was looking for Tom Townsend. It was a Monday afternoon, so Leipfold had a good idea of where to find him. As long as he was either at home or in his studio, he knew exactly where to look. It didn't take long to track him down to the latter.

But Townsend wasn't alone. Leipfold had a habit of listening at doors before he opened them, another life-saving trick he'd picked up while on tour in Kuwait. Sometimes it paid off and sometimes it didn't. This time, it did.

He could hear Townsend's voice, as well as the voice of a woman. Leipfold recognised the husky tones of Eleanor Thompson, although her clipped, receptive voice had lost control and turned into the shrill song of a harpy. Townsend wasn't any better. He shouted right back at her. Leipfold could picture him, using his height advantage to tower over her like an angel of death.

Their voices were distorted through the wooden wall, but Leipfold could hear enough to make out odd snatches, like Townsend shouting "keep your voice down."

Then Mrs. Thompson said, "Make sure no one hears about that plan of yours."

Townsend mumbled something vague and then the two of them stopped talking. There was silence for a moment, followed by the sound of approaching footsteps. Leipfold barely had time to back through a nearby doorway—interrupting a pottery class—before Eleanor Thompson marched past. He watched her through the frosted glass in the classroom door, a shimmering blur of movement that was unmistakably her. It was in her walk, perhaps.

Leipfold opened the door again and peered out, catching the back of her head as she shuffled around the corner. She was talking to herself in a low voice. She didn't turn around to look at him.

Someone cleared their throat and Leipfold turned around. The pottery teacher, a man in a floppy black hat and clay-spattered jeans who had a long, matted beard and unkempt, ash grey hair, was staring at him, waiting for an explanation.

Leipfold smiled sheepishly and apologised, spent a couple of minutes learning about Delftware and then walked back out into the corridor. He knocked on Townsend's door, a relic of the old warehouse that was a work of art itself, and waited. When the door opened, Townsend didn't look surprised to see him.

"Mr. Leipfold," he said, shaking the detective's hand and gesturing for him to take a seat on a comfortable futon. It was a poky little room, barely big enough for the two men to fit in. "What can I do for you?"

"Perhaps you can help me," Leipfold replied. "We'll see. Marie Rieirson is missing."

"I know," Townsend said. "I've been trying to get hold of her. I haven't seen or heard from her since our second show. We had to reschedule the dates, and I'm *this* close to scrapping it altogether."

"What happened to 'the show must go on'?" Leipfold asked.

Townsend shrugged. "What would you do in my place?" he asked. "I've tried to find a replacement, but people are saying that the play is cursed. I've lost two leading ladies in a couple of weeks. Maybe they're right. It is cursed. Besides, even if I could find a replacement, we've lost half of the supporting cast. My reputation is ruined. What other option do I have? You haven't heard from Marie, have you?"

"Why would I have heard from her?" Leipfold asked. "Don't answer that. No, I haven't heard from her. No one has."

He paused for a moment and riffled through the pages of his notebook. He jotted something down and then looked sharply across at Tom Townsend.

"Are we done here?" Townsend asked.

"Why?" Leipfold replied. "Have you got somewhere that you need to be?"

"No," Townsend said. "Nowhere. I've got a clean calendar all day."

"I bet you have," Leipfold murmured. He stroked his chin thoughtfully, hiding the ghost of a smile as it inched across his face. He knew damn well he was taking up Townsend's time, and he was enjoying it. Besides, the man was a show-off. "So no meetings? No rehearsals?"

"None," Townsend said. "I'm here alone all day."

"Is that right?" Leipfold asked. "So you didn't happen to see Eleanor Thompson?"

"Nope," Townsend said. "I've never met the woman."

"I see."

Leipfold paused again and stared at him. Townsend crumpled uncomfortably and folded his arms defensively.

"She was here, you know," Leipfold said. "Right here. I saw her. I saw her, and I saw you. You talked to her."

"No way."

"Damn it, don't lie to me," Leipfold growled. He took a step closer, and even though Townsend was taller than him, he shrank back like a spider from the light. He backed away still further until he was trapped against the wall and then he flinched as Leipfold leaned in. "Tell me the truth."

"Okay, okay," Townsend protested. He brought his hands up to protect his face and tried to lean away from Leipfold. "I'll tell you. But understand that I've done nothing wrong. It's all Mrs. Thompson's fault. Perhaps you should talk to her instead of taking up my time. She wanted her daughter to have a *proper* job, whatever that is. She offered me a chunk of money if I turned Donna down for the role in *Driven*."

"The part that Marie Rieirson is playing?"

"That's the one," Townsend said. "But I did something bad, Mr. Leipfold. I took the woman's money and told her I'd do it, and then I kept it. And I kept Donna on, too. I know I shouldn't have, but I did. The girl could *act*, Mr. Leipfold. I had to keep her."

"And then she died," Leipfold said.

"And then she died," Townsend agreed. He seemed sad, but maybe not as sad as he ought to have been. Leipfold guessed, correctly, that Townsend hadn't really processed it.

Leipfold sighed. "Was there any animosity between the two of you?" he asked.

Townsend hesitated, picking his words with care. "Not exactly," he said, eventually. "See, Donna and I were an item for a while. I broke things off when they started to get too serious. Poor girl. But she didn't hold it against me."

Leipfold checked his notes again. "On the night of Donna's death, you were with Marie Rieirson, correct?"

"Correct," Townsend replied. "We were seeing each other too, but Donna didn't know about that."

Leipfold scribbled something else in his notebook and fixed Tom Townsend with a cynical stare.

"Are you sure about that?" he asked.

***

Maile was holding the fort back at the office. She hadn't worked there for long, but she'd already learned that when the doorbell rang it was the postman and when the telephone rang it was a salesman or a wrong number. Leipfold's office wasn't the busiest of places, but it had a frenetic energy of its own when he had his head down in a case. Despite being just around the corner from Marylebone Station, they didn't get many walk-ins. The entrance was on the edge of an alleyway and visitors had to buzz for entry and then climb a flight of stairs.

Leipfold and Maile shared the building with another office downstairs, but the place had been empty for a couple of months after the previous occupants, a graphic design firm, moved out into a building of their own. There was a story behind that, but Leipfold had never told her what it was.

Leipfold said he liked the peace and quiet, and Maile agreed with him. With Leipfold out and about, that left her with the run of the place, which meant she could listen to metal while carrying out an investigation of her own. The boss had left her in charge of the Fisher case, and Maile felt like it was her moral responsibility to get to the bottom of it, to reunite the woman with her money and to earn Leipfold a chunk of cash while she was at it.

Maile's first port of call was to check up on the email provider. The address was registered with a company she'd never heard of, Omegaserv, but she did a little digging and found a website and a couple of social media accounts. On their website, they proudly boasted eight million users and featured a quote from a guy called John Mayers, a name that she vaguely recognised. They also had a live chat app, which she logged into with a false name so she could ask a couple of questions.

The woman she talked to had a poor grasp of English and a good grasp of protocol, but Maile knew how to game the system. Through a combination of technical knowhow, duplicity and good, old-fashioned blagging, she convinced the woman to reset the account's credentials. Maile knew that if anyone found out, the woman could lose her job.

But hey, she thought, *survival of the fittest.*

With the login details in hand, she hopped into the inbox. It turned out to be a dummy account, created for the sole purpose of contacting Mrs. Fisher. Maile noted with growing interest that the account's owner, whoever they were, had read her frantic requests for her money back. They just hadn't bothered to reply.

She was also able to access a whole heap of personal information. While most of it looked spurious, including the name it was registered to, she managed to find a couple of references to the Channel Islands and a company called Fulwood Scientific. Familiar, as always, with the theory, Maile knew that most people allowed forms to complete themselves with the data they'd used elsewhere, which gave her a little hope that the information had slipped through unnoticed.

Maile updated her case notes and took a quick break to make a fresh cup of coffee before returning to her desk and cracking on with phase two. She knew she was easily distracted, but she could also apply herself when she wanted to. Resisting the urge to check her emails, Maile booted up a couple of search engines and started running different keywords. She used a piece of software that she'd developed herself. It ran different combinations of keywords and aggregated the results to pinpoint pages of interest. It was one of her favourite tricks, but for once, it failed to deliver. As far as the Internet was concerned, Fulwood Scientific didn't exist.

Which made Maile wonder what the hell it was doing in a scam artist's email account.

***

"So where are we at?" Maile asked. Leipfold was back in the office, and Maile was trying to distract the boss before he kicked her out so he could go wherever it was that he went when they weren't at work. Leipfold knew what she was doing, of course, but he humoured her. He needed her in a good mood. He had a little job for her, but it could wait until the morning.

"I'm assuming you're talking about the Thompson case," Leipfold said.

"Of course," Maile replied. "What's new?"

Leipfold pulled up his notes and said, "Well, let's see. First of all, I'm pretty sure we're ahead of the cops. It took them a while to treat the case as a murder, which we were pretty sure of from the start."

"But who did it?" Maile asked. "I mean, it's not like her mother could've hacked a car. Was it Tom Townsend? Greg Bateman?"

"Or, indeed, Marie Rieirson," Leipfold suggested. "I have my suspicions, but I'm not going to tell you who my money's on."

"Why not?"

"I don't want to bias the investigation." Leipfold shrugged. "And besides, it's only a theory. But it's a good theory, and I'll give you a little hint to help you out. The killer wasn't acting alone."

Maile whistled softly and cast her mind back over what they'd learned so far. "I think I've got it," she whispered. "There was a tech specialist. Am I right? Someone who reprogrammed the car to run Donna down? And then someone else who masterminded it?"

Leipfold grunted.

"If that's the case," Maile murmured, "then we can't rule out Eleanor Thompson. And what about Marie Rieirson? Where does she fit in?"

"I'm not sure," Leipfold replied. "That's what I'm trying to figure out. If you've got any ideas, now's the time to tell me."

"What if she was involved in Donna's death?" Maile asked. "If you're right and there are two people behind it, maybe something went wrong and they turned on each other."

"It's a thought," Leipfold admitted. "And there's also the possibility that Marie was the murderer and she's gone on the run."

"Is that what you think?"

"No," Leipfold replied. "But I can't know for sure until we find her."

Maile sighed and drained the rest of her coffee. "I guess I'd better get to work then," she said.

Chapter Sixteen:
Fieldwork

THERE WAS AN AIR OF EXCITEMENT at the police station, and Jack Cholmondeley was entertaining a rare smile as his team gathered for their morning meeting. He had good news to share. He waited impatiently for his staff to assemble so he could get the ball rolling.

When he couldn't wait any longer, he rapped his knuckles on the table and said, "Thanks for coming. How are you all doing today?"

There was a vague response from the ragtag group of policemen. A couple of them were left over from the night shift. While they weren't actively working the case, they did want to keep an eye on it. The rest were working mornings, and they'd barely had time to make a cup of coffee after clocking in before Cholmondeley ushered them all into the briefing room.

"I'll try to keep this quick," Cholmondeley said. "We've uncovered some new evidence in the Thompson case. Now, as some of you already know, we've been able to locate the vehicle. It's a self-driving model, which complicates things because it makes it hard to put someone behind the wheel at the time of impact."

"If anyone was behind the wheel at all," Mogford murmured.

"The car's with the tech guys at the moment," Cholmondeley continued. "But in the meantime, the specs are on the server. Unfortunately, the car was cleaned and repaired before we got to it, but I'm still hoping we'll find something. If this car killed Donna Thompson, there must be some trace of it. I'll keep you updated on that."

Cholmondeley paused to take a sip of coffee, then glared at Constable Groves when she dared to raise her hand.

"I'll take questions at the end," he growled. "Now, a piece of good news. We managed to retrieve some prints from the steering wheel, as well as the dashboard and one of the door handles. The prints on the wheel belong to Tom Townsend, who was good enough to provide us a sample."

"That bastard," Mogford murmured. "We've got him."

"It's not enough to convince a jury," Cholmondeley said. "We'll need to prove that he fiddled the software."

Constable Groves raised her hand again. "So what else have we got?" she asked.

"I said I'll take questions at the end," Cholmondeley reminded her. Groves was relatively new to the force, but he'd already taken a shine to her. She had enthusiasm by the bucketful and made a killer brew in times of crisis. "Now, let me see…"

Cholmondeley checked his notes and said, "The main lead we have so far is the second set of prints on the passenger side. Townsend told us that he picked Marie Rieirson up before going to the restaurant, so we'll need to get a sample from her to rule out a third party."

"And how are we going to print her?" Mogford asked. "It's not like we can just give her a ring and ask her to stop by on her way to work. She's missing, remember?"

"Easy," Cholmondeley replied. "Take Groves and pay her house a visit. Find something you can lift a clear print from. We're talking magazines. Hairbrushes. Bring me a damn door handle if you have to."

"What about a warrant?" Mogford asked.

Cholmondeley scowled moodily. "Fine," he said, "track down her parents or pay a visit to that theatre of Tom Townsend's. Get him to show you around and take a look at the changing rooms. Someone must have something she touched before she vanished, even if it's a bloody toilet seat. We'll take every print in the city if we have to."

"Yes, sir," Mogford said. "And what are you going to do?"

Cholmondeley smiled. "I'm getting to it," he said. "I haven't told you about the ring that forensics found."

***

At exactly the same time, several miles away and in less auspicious surroundings, James Leipfold was hosting a briefing of his own, and with a similar outcome.

"We've got a busy day ahead," he was saying, simultaneously looking through the papers while Maile checked her emails. "Or rather, *you've* got a busy day ahead. I need you to go over to Marie Rieirson's place and set up some cameras. Keep a low profile and don't let on that you're doing it, and make sure you stay on public property. The last thing we need is for you to get caught. I don't think I could call in another favour right now. The police will be keeping their eyes on me."

"It'll be fine," Maile said. "I don't get caught."

"You don't get caught because you do most of your work online," Leipfold reminded her. "This is different. This is *IRL*. Did I say that right?"

Maile laughed, slowly at first before throwing her head back and shaking so hard she chipped her tooth on her tongue piercing.

"What did I say?" Leipfold asked. His face was straight, but he had that tell-tale twinkle in the corner of his eye. Maile wasn't sure what he was thinking, but she managed to stop laughing for long enough to say "nothing" and to gesture for him to continue.

Leipfold shrugged. "Okay," he said. "I can't ask you to do anything you're uncomfortable with."

"It's nice to know you care, boss," Maile replied, "but I'll be fine. I'll get you your cameras, and I'll stay out of trouble while I'm at it. You forget I'm five foot five. I can blend in with a crowd if I cover my tatts and wear jeans and a jacket. But what are you hoping to get from it? And have you thought about the gear we'll need?"

"You need money?" Leipfold asked. He looked across at her as though she'd asked for a pay rise and then remembered he wasn't paying her to begin with. "The thing is, Maile, I—"

"You don't need money," Maile said, interrupting him. "You just need me. I've got everything I need back at home. Don't worry about that. But why? Why worry about Marie Rieirson? I thought we were trying to solve the Donna Thompson case."

"We are," Leipfold replied. He finished working through *The Tribune* and picked up the *Daily Mail*, scowling down at it and making a mental note to wash his hands once he was done with it. "It's the same case. As for what I'm hoping to get from it, I'm not so sure."

"Tom Townsend," Maile murmured. She tensed as she said the name and then sat down on the edge of Leipfold's desk as she pondered the implications. "You're expecting to see Tom Townsend."

But Leipfold just shrugged and turned another page of the paper. A couple of minutes later, he gave up on it and threw it into the wastebasket. Then he glanced at Maile's notes and picked up the phone to try to drum up a little bit of business.

***

Maile stopped by her flat to get changed before she set out again for a spot of fieldwork. Kat was at work, but she'd left Maile a note to say she'd be back late and to ask her to top up the electricity meter. The keycard was taped to the note and placed strategically on Maile's computer desk.

She chuckled to herself. She knew it hadn't been there in the morning because she'd logged on to check her emails. That meant that Kat had left after her, which probably meant that she'd overslept, which meant that she'd been running late and explained why she planned to stay a little longer at the office. Maile realised that she'd started to think like Leipfold, and it made her smile.

It took her twenty minutes to prepare herself. By the time she was ready to leave, she'd transformed from a bat into a butterfly. Her eyeliner was softer, her hair brushed straight and tied into a ponytail, and she was wearing black leggings and a charcoal dress with white Nikes and a plain handbag. Instead of her leather jacket, she topped the outfit off with a cardigan and a long coat that helped to hide her tattoos, and she'd removed almost all of her piercings. She examined herself in the mirror, applied a little lipstick and touched up her contours, then smiled with perverse satisfaction. She looked almost normal. While it wasn't the look she would usually have gone for, it would help her to blend in with the crowd.

"For a job like this, I need a little camouflage," she'd said to Leipfold, and she meant it. Her handbag contained all of the gadgets that she needed, but she'd be loitering around for a while and there's something about a short woman on her own that attracts unwanted attention. Maile knew a little jujitsu and she could look after herself when she needed to, but her job wasn't going to be any easier if little kids started to point at her and creepy guys with hygiene issues started asking for her number.

Maile hopped on the tube and made her way to the address that Leipfold had given her, then approached Marie Rierson's house on foot. She knew there was a problem when she turned the corner and saw a hive of activity outside one of the houses. She hoped that it was all just a coincidence, but it was a Tuesday and she'd always hated Tuesdays, so she wasn't surprised when she reached the address and discovered half a dozen policemen milling around outside of it.

She cursed her luck and continued to walk along the street. She found a bus stop forty yards down the road, so she slowed to a stop and sat down. She pulled her phone from her pocket and gave Leipfold a call, hoping for some further instructions. But the boss didn't answer, so she took a chance and acted on her initiative.

Maile got to her feet again and turned a corner, finding herself in a small city park that was bordered by trees and cast-iron railings, offering plenty of privacy beneath the eaves. She pulled up a spot on one of the benches and looked around suspiciously, but she was alone apart from a couple of cameras. Maile wasn't worried. She had her back to one, and the other was too far away to pick her up.

So Maile unpacked her bag and arranged her devices in a line beside her. She had everything she needed, from spy cameras and storage devices to waterproofs and old smartphones, which she'd stripped for parts so she could use their modems to power the cameras. They had enough storage to shoot for a couple of weeks, if the solar-powered battery packs held out, but only enough data to upload a frame every couple of minutes and a short, low-quality video whenever they detected motion. But that was enough. Maile had used the same setup before for a different purpose altogether, and she knew that the equipment would do the job. And, best of all, the cameras were tiny. She'd built them into empty cigarette packets, the perfect urban camouflage. Easy to hide, easy to position, and easy for people to overlook if they happened to see them.

It only took her a couple of minutes to assemble each device, but they were too delicate for her to handle more than one at a time. Instead, she had to stash them by the entrance to the park and make a couple of passes, stopping with the pretence of checking her mobile phone or tying her shoelaces so she could place a camera and move along. The cops outside Marie's place weren't paying much attention. On her penultimate trip, with camera number four, there was no one outside at all, although their vehicles were still parked on the kerb. She checked the feeds on her tablet and all were working, so she treated herself to a can of Monster.

Maile hid the last camera in the loose masonry of Marie's garden wall, aiming it squarely at her front door and the living room window to the right of it. She leant on the wall for thirty seconds or so, as if she were lost in thought and trying to decide what to do with her afternoon, then set off again.

She was just about to call Leipfold when she felt a heavy hand upon her shoulder. She whirled around, reaching for the pepper spray in her handbag, then caught sight of the panda-like uniform of the Metropolitan Police. Maile sighed and dropped her hand. She followed the policewoman back to the Rieirson place.

Chapter Seventeen:
Digging

CONSTABLE JENNY GROVES stayed silent as she led Maile back towards the house. At first, Maile thought they were heading inside. Then she thought that Groves was going to cuff her and put her in the back of a cop car. But she was wrong on both counts. The policewoman stopped a half-dozen steps away from Marie's driveway and pulled out her badge to identify herself.

"Don't worry," she said, "I'm not into the whole good cop, bad cop thing. I just want to ask you a couple of questions."

"I'm not worried," Maile said. She shifted slightly and tried to glance past Groves into the house. "What's up?"

Groves smiled and Maile found herself returning it. "We're investigating a crime here," she said. "I was wondering if you're local. Perhaps you saw something that could help us."

Maile thought for a moment, chewing absentmindedly at the nubs of her fingernails.

"Anything at all," Groves prompted, pulling Maile back to the here and now. "If it helps, we believe the victim to have been a young woman in her mid-twenties. Marie Rieirson. Ring any bells?"

Maile gasped softly and looked fixedly at Constable Groves. "Victim?" she asked.

"Damn," Groves replied. "I wasn't supposed to say that. Did you know her?"

Maile shook her head, which was only half a lie. "Past tense," she observed. "So she's dead, then? What happened?"

"This is strictly off the record, okay?" Groves said. Maile nodded. "We took a call from her cleaner. She said she found her employer's body at the foot of the stairs after letting herself in for her weekly visit." Groves paused. "Are you sure you don't know the victim?"

Maile looked past Groves and at the house, where a couple of men in uniform were securing the building so that forensics could go in. She watched as the front door opened and two policemen led a distraught young woman out of the building and into the back of a waiting car.

Then she glanced at her nails. "I've never heard of her before in my life," she lied.

Constable Groves looked at her suspiciously but let her go about her business. She handed Maile a card with her office number and email address and bid her farewell, but Maile was barely listening. She was busy thinking about Marie Rieirson and her cleaner and about how she'd headed home that morning before coming over. She cursed herself and wondered what might have happened if she'd arrived half an hour earlier.

Maybe I could've done something, Maile thought. *I could've seen something, saved her.* She had no reason to feel sorry for the woman, but that didn't stop her. *No one deserves to die.*

***

Maile couldn't wait until she got back to the office, so she called Leipfold and filled him in as quickly as she could. Then she headed underground. The tube seemed to take forever, and it was packed with sweaty passengers cradling suitcases between their legs or hanging from straps with their backpacks in other people's faces. She chewed thoughtfully at one of her fingernails and called Leipfold back as soon as she got some signal.

She was still on the phone to him as she climbed the stairs and let herself in. Leipfold had boiled the kettle and booted her computer so she wouldn't have to wait for it to load. It was a quirk that the two had developed within a couple of days. They didn't have much in common, but they *did* share a soft spot for efficiency.

Maile cut the call as she walked into the room, then took her coat off and hung it on the back of her chair. Leipfold glanced at her and said hello as she sat down and started to check her emails.

"I've got some good news," Leipfold said.

Maile grunted an acknowledgement.

"We've got another case," Leipfold explained. "It came in through the website. I met the client while you were gone and they already signed the contract. It's not much—just a couple hundred a week to begin with—but there's room for it to grow."

"What's the case?" Maile asked.

"Nothing too complicated," Leipfold replied. "It's for the CEO of an ad agency. Their creative director quit and took their biggest client with him, so they want us to dig up some dirt to help scupper his success. Shouldn't be too hard, especially with you on board."

"I'll take a look at it this evening," Maile said. "I want to check the cameras first. And then there's Tom Townsend."

"What about him?" Leipfold asked.

"I want to do a little more digging," Maile replied. "See what he's all about, you know?"

Leipfold shrugged. "And how are you going to do that?" he asked.

Maile laughed and opened a new tab on her laptop. "Ever heard of doxing?" she asked.

Leipfold *hadn't* heard of doxing, but it didn't take Maile long to bring him up to speed. It was a technique that she'd used before, something par for the course for a millennial like her with a passion for technology and a habit of poking her nose into other people's business.

"It takes its name from the same root word as 'documents,'" Maile explained, remembering Leipfold's love of language. It often helped him out with tricky crossword clues, although that was as far as his interest went.

Leipfold didn't understand what she was talking about until she told him that she'd be using the Internet to find sensitive information about Tom Townsend, the sort of stuff that the theatre director would probably prefer to keep private.

"These days," Maile said, "you can file a request for search engines to hide results. It's called the right to be forgotten. But that only gets you pulled from the search engines, and the information is still online if you know where to look. Luckily, I do."

"You're wasting your time," Leipfold replied. "You should focus on Eleanor Thompson, the victim's mother. There's something not quite right there."

"One of your hunches?" Maile guessed. But Leipfold said nothing, and Maile ignored his suggestion and carried out the research. It didn't take her long to find something.

Tom Townsend was no angel. At least, not according to the charity chairman who'd accused him of embezzlement.

***

It was later that afternoon, and Maile had finished her report on Tom Townsend and started to look into the ad agency. Leipfold read the report with growing interest.

According to Maile, Townsend's theatre company had agreed to put on a show at a local arts centre. The chairman had handed him a cheque to cover the expenses, but no one turned up on the day of the performance. Townsend had ignored their calls and left no forwarding address, so when they finally managed to track him down, they served up a summons. The results of the hearing had been reported by several local newspapers. He'd won the case and kept the money and then moved on with his life.

Leipfold finished reading the report, stacked it neatly on top of his desk and then walked over to see what Maile was doing.

"Good news, boss," Maile said. "The cameras are still working. Well, most of them. One's offline, probably because something's interfering with the signal, and another is at a funny angle. It's pointing in the wrong direction but it still gives us a view of the street."

"Have you got the house in shot?" Leipfold asked.

"Of course," Maile replied. "That was the whole point of it. Don't worry. If someone enters or leaves the place, we'll know."

"Good. A lot of criminals go back to the scene of the crime. They remember things that they left behind or they double back to see what the cops are doing. Sometimes they take the risk because they have to. Sometimes they do it because they're stupid."

Leipfold didn't care why they did it. He was just glad that it gave

104

people like him a chance to catch people like *them*—the criminal class—in the act.

The day dragged on, and Maile made a surprising amount of progress in the case of the ad agency before switching her attention to Marie Rieirson. Leipfold was about to ask for a coffee when she gestured excitedly for him to come over for a look at her screen. The cameras were grainy at best, but there was no mistaking what was up there.

"That's her," Maile said. "It has to be."

"Who?" Leipfold asked.

"The cleaner," Maile explained. "She found the body. I saw her when I went to set the cameras up. They were loading her into a police car when I was leaving. I wonder why she's back there."

"Are you sure it's her?"

"Positive," Maile insisted. "I'm telling you, it's her. Look, she's just standing outside the house and staring right at it."

Leipfold glanced at the screen and arrived at a decision almost immediately. "Keep an eye on her," he instructed. "I'm going after her. Call me if she looks like she's about to leave."

He grabbed his coat and raced out of the office. With no car or motorbike, he hopped on his bicycle and pedalled as fast as his muscular legs could manage.

***

Maile called him as he was on route, so he answered the phone hands-free and followed her directions as he navigated through the busy London traffic towards Marie Rieirson's house. She started to panic when the cleaner finally stopped staring at the house and started to walk away, but Leipfold told her to stay calm and to concentrate on the job at hand. He was a couple of minutes away at most, so Maile focused on firing off instructions as he pushed himself even harder. The bike was in its highest gear and he was risking life and limb every time he flew past a turning, but he reached the end of Rieirson's road in a minute and a half.

He idled up to the house another ten seconds later, while Maile asked him frantically for updates. The cleaner was nowhere to be seen, but Leipfold knew that time was of the essence and so he took a chance, heading further down the street and slowing at the turn-offs. On the third left, he saw a woman halfway down the road. Without knowing for sure whether it was the person he was looking for, Leipfold chased her down and jumped off the bike beside her. She looked suspiciously over at him, alarmed by his behaviour.

"Can I help you?" she asked.

"I hope so," Leipfold replied, pausing slightly to catch his breath. "This might be a strange question, but do you happen to know Marie Rieirson? Her house is just around the corner."

Without warning, the woman burst into tears. Leipfold found himself offering her a literal shoulder to cry on. He stroked the back of her head half-heartedly until she started to calm down and catch her breath.

"Sorry," she said, dabbing at her eyes with the sleeve of her jacket. "I'm so sorry about that. I've had a rough day. Yes, I know Miss Rieirson. Or rather, I knew her."

"You used to clean for her," Leipfold said.

"How did you know that?"

"It's my business to know things," Leipfold replied. "Don't worry, Miss…uh…"

"Frankowska," the woman said. "But you can call me Jowie. Everyone does."

Leipfold scrutinised her closely. She was a good-looking woman in her twenties with Latin skin and a hint of something else in her blood and face. Leipfold thought she looked exactly like a cleaner *ought* to look, but his only experience of household help came from bad porn movies. She was wearing a short blue dress that ended just above her knees and a pair of plain black heels. She had a silver crucifix around her neck and she wore her hair tied back in a ponytail. She didn't exactly look dressed for the job.

"Well, Jowie," Leipfold continued, "I'm a private detective, and today is your lucky day. You're going to help me to put someone behind bars. Come with me. I'll get you a coffee and you can tell me all about that rough day of yours."

To Leipfold's surprise, Jowie acquiesced, and the two of them were soon sitting side-by-side in a Starbucks with a couple of lattes. Leipfold chatted about the weather and the latest headlines to set her mind at ease, and then he started to press her once she seemed ready to talk. Jowie explained that she'd arrived at her usual time to give the flat a once over, and so she'd let herself in with the spare key and gone through to the kitchen to drop off her supplies. Marie was usually at work when Jowie did the cleaning, so she wasn't surprised that the house was quiet. But the silence was broken when she walked through to the hallway and prepared to climb the stairs.

"She was there," Jowie said, shivering slightly despite the heating, which was cranked up to the max to entice passers-by to come in from the cold. "Right there at the bottom of the stairs. She had blood in one of her ears. She wasn't moving, so I called an ambulance and rushed over. The police said she was probably dead by the time that I got there."

"Did you notice anything suspicious?" Leipfold asked.

Jowie looked at him while she decided how much to trust him. "I'm not sure," she said, eventually. "Maybe. It might be nothing, it's just… well, she just wasn't right."

"What do you mean?"

"It was her expression," Jowie said. "Like a cat that's been backed into a corner. She looked angry, maybe a little scared. I was scared too, but not like that. I think she knew what was coming."

"You mean she knew she was going to die?"

Jowie shrugged and used a napkin to wipe a tear from her eye, being careful not to smudge her eyeliner.

"Is there anything else you can tell me about Marie Rieirson?" Leipfold asked, gently bringing her back to the present.

"Not that I can think of," Jowie replied. "She kept to herself. Only… well, there is one thing."

"Go on."

"It's probably nothing," Jowie explained. "It's just that a couple of weeks ago, when I was cleaning the place, an old lady came by. She knocked on the door and was shouting through the letterbox. Something about money, but that's all I remember. It seemed harmless enough at the time."

"Interesting," Leipfold murmured. "Would you recognise the woman if you saw her again?"

"I only saw her from the top of the stairs, so I couldn't swear to it. But I can have a go if you think it'll help."

Leipfold thanked her and pulled his phone from his pocket. He flicked through the apps until he found the one he was looking for, then booted it up and started flipping through the folders. Jowie didn't recognise the first photo, nor the second or the third. Then she saw the fourth.

"That's her," she said. "I'm sure it's her."

"How sure?" Leipfold asked.

"Pretty sure," Jowie said.

"But not entirely," Leipfold murmured, glancing down at his phone again.

"Who is that woman, anyway?" Jowie asked.

Leipfold shook his head, slowly. "Her name is Eleanor Thompson," he explained. "And before you ask, I have no idea what she was doing there."

***

Leipfold was acting strangely and Maile was worried. He'd seemed okay the night before when he came back from his chat with Jowie Frankowska. But when Maile entered the office on a dreary Wednesday morning, nine days after Donna Thompson's body had been found, Leipfold had the look of a man possessed. He'd spent the night in the office, working feverishly to map out the thoughts that were whizzing back and forth through his head and bringing on the worst migraine that he'd had since his drinking days.

Maile gasped audibly when she entered the room and took in the scene. One wall was covered with scribbled Post-it Notes, blown-up photographs, newspaper clippings and web printouts. Leipfold had assembled them in some sort of order, then moved them so often and jotted so many notes on top of them that it was almost unintelligible. He'd skipped the cliché of setting up a cobweb of strings to connect them all together, but he'd made up for it by ruining the plaster with a thousand tiny pinpricks. If the current state of his debatable masterpiece was anything to go by, he hadn't managed to get anywhere.

He hasn't even looked at the crossword, Maile thought. *That's not like him at all.*

He had the radio on, but he wasn't listening to it. Maile thought that was probably a good thing. It was tuned to Radio 1, and Bieber was singing about it being too late to say sorry. The song set Maile's teeth on edge, and she wondered—not for the first time—why teenage girls were so quick to jump on a bandwagon.

Maile coughed, but the boss didn't turn around.

"Hello?" she asked. "Boss? Are you okay?"

There was no response.

"Jesus," she said. "It must be bad."

Leipfold remained silent, so Maile reached over to the radio and fiddled with the buttons until she'd successfully switched it over to XFM. It wasn't much better, but it would have to do.

Who the hell still listens to the radio anyway? she thought.

Maile wondered whether Leipfold was back on the bottle or whether he'd gone stir-crazy after staying up all night and working too hard. She'd heard stories about people cracking under pressure, but she never thought she'd have to watch as it happened. Not that she could blame him. Business was bad. While the boss never seemed too worried about money when they talked about the Thompson case, she'd caught him looking up payday loans and comparing repayment rates and terms and conditions.

Another thought flashed unbidden across Maile's mind.

Shit, she thought. *I hope he's all right.*

Chapter Eighteen:
A Grip on the Case

LEIPFOLD'S MOOD changed quickly, like the flip of a light switch. He cycled home to grab a shower. Maile assumed he'd take the chance to get some sleep, but he was back within the hour looking fresher than ever. He breezed airily into the office like a new man, ready to go over the case all over again.

Twenty minutes later, his mood changed again, and he snapped at Maile for humming a tune while finalising her latest report on the agency's runaway creative. It was dull, unpleasant work, so she had her headphones half on and half off with one ear free to listen for the phone. She didn't even know she was humming until Leipfold shouted, "Shut the hell up so I can think for a minute!"

Maile acquiesced, and fifteen minutes later he was in a good mood again. He made Maile a cup of coffee by way of an apology and then sat down beside her to take a look at the day's crossword. It took them eight and a half minutes.

"Not bad," Leipfold murmured, cutting it out of the paper and adding it to his collection, which he kept in a folder in his bottom drawer. "Not bad at all, especially with no sleep and not enough coffee. Today's going to be a good day."

Leipfold started whistling a tune. Maile recognised it as the same one she'd been humming earlier, a nu-metal song from the turn of the century that her boss had probably never heard before.

"I'm in a good mood, Maile," Leipfold said. "A very good mood."

"You are? Why's that, then?"

"No reason," Leipfold replied. "None at all. Listen, why don't you take the day off today? It's not like I'm going to need you."

Maile glared at him. Without meaning to, he'd hurt her feelings, just like everyone else always did. That's why she hated getting close to people, but Leipfold was *different*, or so she'd thought. But he wasn't being a dick. He was just tactless, and her gaze softened slightly as she realised he thought he was doing something nice for her. And so she did as he suggested and headed home.

But she wasn't done working. Not by a long shot. She had a couple of lines of enquiry to follow up on, as well as some new marketing ideas that might just save the business. Kat was out, of course. She had a proper job to go to in a shiny office in the city centre where coffee was covered by the company and bosses gave presentations about share prices and returns on investment. But that meant that Maile had the place to herself, and she could lounge around with her feet up while she trawled the net and made notes about whatever she was able to find. And because it was, after all, her day off, she also played a little Warcraft.

***

Jack Cholmondeley was worried.

He was sitting alone in his office, squeezing blue stress putty between his powerful fingers. He liked to play with it while he was thinking, to stretch it out and swing it around or to flatten it into a vague sphere and to bounce it up and down off the surface of the desk. Strictly speaking, it was medicinal. At least, that was what he'd told Gary Mogford. It had been a gift from Mary one Christmas, the latest weapon in the battle against arthritis. Cholmondeley didn't have arthritis, but he did have a hell of a lot of stress to deal with. The blue goo was as decent an aide as anything else, bar cigarettes, but Mary had made him give those up, too.

There was a knock at the door and Constable Groves entered the room with an air of nervousness blowing after her like dust from the street into a shopping centre.

"Constable Groves," Cholmondeley said. He offered her a chair on the other side of his mahogany desk and waited for her to sink into it. "How can I help you?"

Groves shook her head. "It's the other way around today, sir," she replied. "I can help you. We've had the results back on the Thompson girl's mobile phone."

"I thought the tech boys already had a look at it."

"They did," Groves said. "But forensics got their hands on it first. The DNA results were inconclusive, although they're running more tests and they're hopeful. But they did find something."

"What?" Cholmondeley asked. He leaned across his desk towards her, resting his elbows on the elegant woodwork. "What is it?"

"They found a couple of fingerprints," Groves said. "It took a little work to clear them up and they had to enhance them on the computer, but they got a match."

"Will it be admissible in court?"

"Should be," Groves said. "That's what we pay them for. We got three sets of prints."

"Three?" Cholmondeley exclaimed. "Christ, the damn thing changed hands more times than a kilo of coke. Who did they match?"

Groves grinned. She'd already printed out a copy of the report, and she handed it to the old man as she talked him through it.

"The first set of prints belonged to Donna Thompson," Groves explained. "But the phone belonged to her, so that's hardly surprising. Next up, we've got Eddie Burns, the guy who dropped it in."

"That's no surprise, either," Cholmondeley said.

"Agreed." Groves paused for a moment while Cholmondeley flicked through to the next page of the report. "Sir, it's the third print. That's the one you'll be interested in."

"Why?" Cholmondeley asked. His ears had pricked up like the ears of a hound who'd caught the scent, and he leaned still further across the mahogany. "Who did they match?"

"Tony Barlow," Groves said. "The owner of the café where Donna worked. He was good enough to give us his prints when he came in to give a statement. It looks like it paid off."

"So Barlow handled Thompson's phone?" Cholmondeley said. He frowned and stared thoughtfully into space. "So what? He could have done it any number of times. Maybe she left it on the counter and he took it over to her."

"Maybe," Groves admitted, "but wouldn't you rather find out?"

Cholmondeley stared at her for a moment or two. Then he nodded. "Okay," he said. "Bring him in. I want to talk to him."

***

A couple of hours later, when Leipfold had finished trading his grip on sanity for a grip on the case, he decided to head back out into the cold. He pulled on a long coat and locked the door of the office behind him before climbing onto the seat of his bicycle and heading out into the inner-city traffic. The roads were emptier than usual, but they were also damp from a recent rain. Leipfold's tyres weren't flat, but they needed more air and he kept forgetting to fill them. With the winter well on its way, he told himself that it was a tactical move and that flatter tyres gave him more traction in the rain and snow.

Not that it did him much good. As he skidded to a halt outside Eleanor Thompson's house, his tyres caught in a hunk of gravel and sent him spilling from the saddle into the road. He was stunned for a moment when he hit the asphalt, but he had the presence of mind to pull himself up—and not a moment too soon. He was still dragging his bike onto the pavement when a car barrelled past into the night. Leipfold guessed it was running at fifty, and Eleanor Thompson lived on County Drive, a suburban twenty zone with speed bumps in the road and cars parked haphazardly along the side of the street. Leipfold cursed and tried to catch the number plate, but the car was too far away. He could only make out the first couple of letters. But that was all he needed, and more significant than the number plate was the identity of the driver.

There wasn't one.

The black sedan skidded on the road and disappeared into the night, just like Donna Thompson's murderer.

He shrugged his shoulders, leant his battered bicycle against the fence at the end of the drive and then made his way towards the front door. He pressed his ear against it and listened in. Nobody answered when he knocked.

Leipfold frowned and knocked again, but still nothing. He bent down and opened the letterbox, then shouted, "Is anyone in there?"

He was answered by an oppressive, imperfect silence, like the sound of a room full of people who are getting ready to spring a surprise.

That settles it, Leipfold thought. *There's someone in there.*

A terrifying thought occurred to him. Perhaps the old lady was dead as well, lying at the foot of the stairs like Marie Rieirson. Leipfold thought about kicking the door down and decided against it. The movies made it look easier than it actually was. Besides, he caught a glimpse of movement in the window. Even in the darkness there was no mistaking the sharp features of Eleanor Thompson, her feline eyes glinting as she peeked through the curtains.

The two of them made eye contact and there was a flash of recognition in the woman's eyes before she scuttled away and let the curtain fall back into place. Leipfold knocked at the door again and shouted once more through the letterbox, but she still didn't open the door.

Leipfold needed to talk to her, and his questions were too sensitive to be shouted from the street. He took out his notebook and scribbled a short letter while leaning against the wall, before tearing the page out, folding it in half, writing her name on it and posting it through the letterbox.

He whistled as he climbed back into the saddle and cycled away into the night.

***

Maile's research into the Fisher case continued, slowly but surely and with plenty of Xbox breaks. When she paused between headshots, she picked up an email with a new lead and some extra information.

A couple of days earlier, she'd contacted Companies House. After a little to-ing and fro-ing, they'd handed over some information that she'd been unable to find elsewhere. Whatever else it was, Fulwood Scientific was also a real organisation, at least in the eyes of the law.

The company was registered to a man called Will Rickman, and it had a registered address right there in the capital, half a mile away from her flat. And so, with nothing better to do with her day, she decided to pay Mr. Rickman a visit.

Before she left, Maile scribbled a quick note to her housemate, explaining where she was going and what to do if she didn't make it home by the time that darkness fell. Then she grabbed a coat and her handbag, checked her pockets for her keys, purse and phone, and hit the street. She was a fast walker. She always had been, despite her height, especially when she was alone. The cold weather drove her on even though the wind stung her face and dried her lips out.

It took nine minutes from door to door, about the same amount of time it took Leipfold to finish a crossword. Even from a distance, it didn't look like a business address. When she knocked on the door and found herself invited inside, she realised that she was right. It was just a house—no more and no less.

The door was answered by a young man who was lounging around in tracksuit bottoms and a plain blue T-shirt. He introduced himself as Will Rickman and didn't seem to listen when she explained what she was doing there. Inside, Maile was smiling. Sometimes her appearance came in handy, and this was one of those times.

"So," the man said, after leading her into his office-come-living room, "how can I help you?"

Maile smiled politely and explained who she was and who she worked for. Then she said, "I was hoping I could ask you a couple of questions."

"Sure," Rickman said. "Go ahead. I'm supposed to be working, but…"

"You're working?"

"Supposed to be," he said. "I work from home. Mostly freelance stuff: web development, marketing, that sort of stuff. Whatever I can get."

"So you're unemployed," Maile joked.

"Pretty much," he replied.

Maile smiled politely and said, "So, Will, what can you tell me about Fulwood Scientific?"

Will Rickman looked confused at first and then angry. He covered his mouth with a hand and stared at her like she'd brought the wrath of some god down upon him.

"Holy shit," he cursed. "You know about that?"

Maile nodded but said nothing, gesturing for the young man to continue. He looked back at her for a second, saw the determination in her mascaraed eyes and realised how futile it was to try to argue.

"Whatever," he said. "I've got nothing to hide. Fulwood Scientific? It's not a real company. It's just a front."

"A front?"

"A front," Rickman repeated, glancing nervously around the room. "Listen, I don't want any trouble."

"Don't sweat it," Maile said. "Just tell me what you know and I'll hit the road. I'm not a cop, Will. I just want to know the truth."

"The truth," he murmured. "I can do that. Fulwood is just a shell, a fake company for a fake man with a fake name."

"But it's registered to you," Maile reminded him.

"So what?" Rickman replied. "Fulwood is a sham, but it's not my sham. You need to speak to a friend of mine, a man called Mark Baxter."

"How does he come into it?"

"Fulwood belongs to him," Rickman explained. "My name's on the paperwork, but he's the owner and managing director. I have nothing to do with it."

"I see," Maile said, although she didn't. "But in that case, why register it in your name? Why not let Baxter do it?"

Rickman shook his head. "It's not that simple," he said. "Mark's a good friend of mine. I've known him for years. But he's never had much luck with money. He went bankrupt a couple of years ago and never quite got over it."

Maile smiled but said nothing, waiting for Rickman to continue his story. He stared back at her and ran a hand through his chin's fluffy stubble.

"Fulwood is what Baxter uses when his name gets in the way of business," Rickman explained. "That happens a lot, from what I've heard."

"I bet it does," Maile said. "Any chance you've got an address for him? Or a phone number?"

Rickman smiled and said, "I'll give you Mark's number if you give me yours."

"In your dreams," Maile said, crossing her slender arms and looking at him like he was a piece of shit she'd stepped on.

"Worth a shot," he murmured. "Better make yourself comfortable. I'll go grab a pen and paper."

***

Leipfold was about to shut up shop. With Maile away, he'd had plenty of headspace, but he'd also realised that she brightened the place up with her esoteric clothing and her colourful language. Leipfold worked better when he was alone because there were fewer distractions and no obligations to make a fresh pot of coffee. But he had more *fun* when Maile was around.

Leipfold shut his computer down and tidied the papers in his in tray. He wiped down the surfaces, did the washing up and bleached the toilet, and then he had one last pass over the office to make sure everything was in order. Maile often teased him and told him he had OCD, but Leipfold disagreed. He was both obsessive and compulsive, but not at the same time. He just knew that all things had their place, and he worshipped efficiency like other men worshipped money. Wasting time trying to find things had no place in the Leipfold methodology, and Maile had picked that up within a day or two. She'd even found a way to optimise the server so the two of them could dig through his old case files and find anything they needed within a couple of seconds.

Leipfold surveyed the office and smiled like a proud father on sports day. It wasn't much, but it was his and he wanted to keep it. Even if it meant losing his apartment.

The buzzer rang, and Leipfold checked his watch and murmured a soft statement of surprise. Nobody called at this hour—nobody called ever, for that matter—and he knew straight away that it wasn't a client or a social call. His suspicions were confirmed when he opened the door to Eleanor Thompson, who was dressed all in black and holding an umbrella to fend off the winter drizzle.

Leipfold gestured for her to enter the office. "Come on in," he said. "I had a feeling I'd hear from you."

Eleanor Thompson scowled at him and walked into the relative warmth of the office. She shook her umbrella, spattering the walls with rainwater, and then hung it up to dry on the rickety old coat stand beside the door. "I got your letter," she said.

"I thought as much," Leipfold replied. "You could have saved us both a lot of trouble if you'd opened the door when I came over."

"I don't open the door to strangers," Mrs. Thompson said. "Not even strangers that I've met before."

"So why did you come to my office?"

"Why do you think?" she snapped. "It was that damned letter of yours. Can't you just leave me alone?"

Leipfold smiled. "Mrs. Thompson," he began, delicately. "I know you didn't love your daughter."

"Of course not. You wouldn't have loved her, either. And what of it?" she snapped.

"I'm going to ask you again. Do you have any idea how the accident happened? Any idea at all?"

"Why would I?" Mrs. Thompson scowled. "And even if I did, why would I share it with you?"

"To bring her murderer to justice," Leipfold said. "Let's face it, thanks to the message you left and your own admission that you didn't love her, you're currently sitting at the top of the suspect list. Besides," he added, hoping that his hunch was right, "you're her next of kin. Her assets will go to you. And not just that, either. It's funny how the youth of today thinks they're invulnerable. Did you tell her that you had her covered with life insurance?"

Eleanor Thompson scowled again. "She knew about the policy," she said. "The silly girl didn't want to pay her premiums. Would you believe that she wanted me to cancel it?"

"But you didn't cancel it, Mrs. Thompson," he said, staring straight into her eyes and spotting a faint fog, the early signs of cataracts. Leipfold recognised the symptoms from some work he'd once done for an optometrist. For a moment, he felt sorry for the old woman, but the moment passed. "Mrs. Thompson, do you realise that as the sole recipient of your daughter's life insurance policy, you have more reason than anyone to wish her dead?"

"I do," she replied.

"So did you do it?"

She shook her head. "I have no idea what you're talking about," she said.

Chapter Nineteen:
The Thrill of the Chase

THURSDAY ROLLED AROUND SLOWLY, as it often did. Maile was full of unfounded optimism as she entered the office and sat at her desk. Leipfold was already there, sipping on a glass of water while catching up with his emails. Maile dumped the papers on his desk and he started to work through them, putting the crossword on hold until he'd caught up with the world.

"Anything good?" Maile asked.

"Nope," Leipfold said. "Just the usual. Viagra spam. Nigerian princes."

"Any work?"

Leipfold shook his head. "One guy wants us to work for free," he said. "So I told him to get lost."

The detective sank back into a gloomy silence. Maile tried to leave him to it. But she was bored, impatient for him to finish, so she put the kettle on and made them both a drink. Then she pulled her chair across the room and sat down on it. She crossed her legs and stared at Leipfold until he sighed, put a finger down to mark his place on the page and looked up at her.

"What?" he asked. "Can I help you?"

"Nope," Maile said. "But I can help you. Get this. I did a little digging on Tom Townsend. You know, the theatre guy?"

"You mean the asshole who stole money from a charity to put on a show that never happened?"

"The very same," Maile said. "Listen, I managed to hack into his emails. Idiot set his password as 'password041175.' Anyone could have guessed it."

Leipfold frowned. "Why the numbers?" he asked.

"His birthdate," Maile replied. "It's easy to find if you know where to look. You'd be surprised at how many people do that. Of course, I had a little help from my friends."

"Like the Beatles?"

"Whatever," Maile said. "I downloaded his emails into an archive so you can take a look at them. His outbox is in there too, but it's the stuff in his inbox that's most important. He has a folder called 'Abubakar' in his archive. It's password protected, but it's the same password as before. Write it down, so you don't forget it."

"How do you spell it?"

"Like it sounds," Maile said. Leipfold glared across at her and she grinned. "Okay, boss. It's alpha, bravo, uniform, bravo, alpha, kilo, alpha, Romeo."

"The phonetic alphabet," Leipfold observed. "Nice. Why do you know that?"

Maile shrugged. "Gaming," she replied.

Leipfold laughed and turned his attention back to the notes on the pad in front of him. "Abubakar," he murmured. "What does that mean?"

"I googled it," Maile said. "It's the name of a Nigerian guy with ninety-seven wives. I guess Tom Townsend saw him as a kindred spirit. Did you know he was seeing Donna Thompson before she died?"

"I did."

"What about Marie Rieirson?"

"I had an inkling," Leipfold admitted. "What of it?"

"He was seeing Jayne Lipton as well," Maile said. "His archive is full of messages from all three of them."

"Jayne Lipton?" Leipfold asked, looking sharply across at her. "Are you sure?"

"It's all in the emails, boss." Maile grinned. "Jeez," she said. "It's the love triangle from hell—it's a fricking love *rectangle*—and now two of them are dead. What do you make of that?"

"Could just be a coincidence."

"You're right," Maile said. "It could be. But maybe it's not. Who knows? Have you talked to Jayne Lipton? Maybe we should check her side of the story."

"I've talked to her," Leipfold said. "But I didn't know she was screwing around with Tom Townsend."

"What did you find out from her?"

"Not much," Leipfold replied. "But this changes everything. You see, it was Jayne who reported Marie's disappearance. And now we know she had a pretty good reason to make her vanish."

"Could be a coincidence," Maile murmured.

"That it could," Leipfold replied. He paused. "There are a lot of them about at the moment."

***

Maile's report on the case of the rogue creative was well-received by the client. The PO had cleared, the funds had been received and the company had asked to book the duo on a three-month retainer. It wasn't much, but it was enough to cover the rent. Leipfold had amped up the prices to almost double his usual rate. He reasoned that they were getting two for the price of one and that Maile's unusual set of skills gave them a unique perspective on the case, something that the client wouldn't find elsewhere.

Leipfold bought Maile a bottle of wine to celebrate, but she'd insisted that the greatest reward would be to go along with him to talk to Jayne Lipton. The sun drifted lazily across the sky, but the weather was still cold and neither of them felt up to the long walk to Shelden Street, where their suspect lived. So Leipfold booked a taxi and took some cash out, wincing slightly as he checked his balance. He still had enough working capital for a couple of months, thanks to the new client's deposit and the sale of his motorbike, but he'd made a bigger dent than he'd imagined.

The taxi rolled into Shelden Street and pulled up on the kerb. Leipfold paid the driver while Maile checked her phone and climbed out onto the pavement. Then they walked up to the door.

Jayne answered their knock almost immediately. "You're lucky you caught me," she said. "I'm working from home today."

"I thought you might be," Leipfold replied. "I'd be doing the same if I was you."

"What's that supposed to mean?"

"Isn't it obvious?" Maile asked. "You needed to keep a low profile. After all, you reported Marie missing but you were screwing the same guy. I guess you forgot to mention that. And now she's dead."

"She's dead?" Jayne gasped. Her face flushed and she held a hand up to her mouth, but something about it didn't ring true. When they discussed it back at the office, Leipfold said he believed her and Maile said that she didn't, but both of them agreed that they could have been wrong.

"I'm afraid so," Leipfold said. "I'm surprised that the police haven't been to see you."

"I have nothing to hide," Jayne said. "Ask me your questions and then get the hell out of here."

Leipfold shrugged and asked, "Are you in a relationship with Tom Townsend?

"No, I'm not," Jayne replied. "But we used to have sex, if that's what you mean. Tom wanted more and I didn't, so I broke it off. End of story."

"I see," Leipfold replied. "Ever heard of a woman called Jowie Frankowska?"

"That *bitch*," Jayne spat. She had the look of a woman who had just stepped in something unpleasant while wearing her new Jimmy Choos. "Yeah, I know her."

"How?" Maile asked.

"I just do," Jayne replied. "She used to clean the flat when I was living with Marie. A family friend or something. Marie's parents paid her rates because they knew that their daughter couldn't look after herself. I always hated that girl."

"Why?"

"Do I need a reason?" Jayne asked. "There's just something about her. She thinks she's entitled to the world on a plate, but that's not how it works. Oh, don't get me wrong. She did a good job of the place, but she did a little bit more than the cleaning, if you know what I mean."

Leipfold stared at her for a moment, expecting her to continue. When she didn't, he said, "I'm going to need you to be specific."

Jayne laughed, a belly laugh that made her arch her back and flash a glimpse of her pearly whites. "Well, where do I begin?" she asked.

"Money. Movies. Books. Jewellery. If she wanted it, she took it. Slowly at first, then more and more often, until Marie—useless as she was—couldn't miss it. Jowie took her mother's ring, and that was the final straw. Marie was going to tell the police. That was the last time I spoke to her."

***

Later that afternoon, when Maile and Leipfold were back at the office, there was a knock at the door. Maile had her headphones on and didn't notice, but Leipfold did, and he groaned as he got up to answer it.

"I need to fix that intercom," he murmured, casting his mind back to the early days when business was booming and the building still smelled of paint and sawdust. Leipfold had been on Balcombe Street for over a decade, and the intercom had been out of order for half of that. It was probably just a loose wire, but he'd never got round to fixing it.

He opened the door to a familiar face, but it didn't comfort him. He'd been hoping for a new client, but it was just Jack Cholmondeley, suited and booted in uniform, looking solemn. Leipfold invited him in and offered him a cuppa, but Cholmondeley was on duty and so he politely declined, opting instead to remain in front of Maile's desk beside the door, ready to make a getaway.

"Can't stop to chat, old friend," Cholmondeley said, shaking Leipfold's hand and tipping a wink at Maile, who returned it with a glare that could've stripped paint from the walls.

"You always say that," Leipfold replied.

"Doesn't matter. This is serious. We're talking about a murder."

"You're here about Donna Thompson, then," Leipfold guessed.

"Yes and no," Cholmondeley replied. "I'm here about Marie Rieirson as well."

"Am I a suspect again?"

"No," Cholmondeley said. "But someone is. I just got the report back. Let's just say that her death wasn't an accident."

"I could have told you that," Leipfold replied. "The two cases are connected. We just have to figure out how."

"Perhaps," Cholmondeley said. "I've never understood how you do what you do, but in my line of work we need evidence. Assuming that they're connected is pure conjecture. Marie's murder is a fact."

Leipfold frowned and then risked a glance across at Maile. She was still sitting beside her computer, but she read his look like some secret sign language and surreptitiously started taking notes on what Cholmondeley was saying.

"You talk about proof like a priest talks about heaven," Leipfold said. "Prove heaven exists and I'll have faith in your proof. Until then, there's only what happened and what didn't."

"Spoken like a true private investigator," Cholmondeley replied. "You did the right thing when you set up shop on your own. You couldn't cut it as a copper. You don't hate criminals as much as I do."

"You're right," Leipfold replied. "I don't hate criminals. But I do hate crime. If crime didn't exist, you'd be out of a job. You need it and I don't. I can make a living out of jealous wives and paranoid businessmen in the grey areas where no crime has been committed, but you feed on crime like a drug dealer feeds on junkies."

Cholmondeley's face flushed. "Jealous wives, huh? Tell me, if you're so busy then why bother to take on the Thompson case?"

"I figured you'd need the help," Leipfold replied.

Cholmondeley laughed and said, "James, don't ever change." He paused for a moment as the tension seeped out of the room like pus from a popped spot. "Truth is, I was hoping you might be able to help. I'm not saying we're stuck, but we could use an extra pair of hands."

"Yeah," Leipfold said. "I know you could. Listen, I'll be honest. I'm broke, my business is dying and I'm not being paid for the Thompson case. I thought I could solve it and pick up a little business. Now the press has moved on and the cops are stuck. Even if I solve it, I'm not going to make a penny. What's in it for me?"

Cholmondeley smiled. "The thrill of the chase," he said. "Same as always."

Chapter Twenty:
Blood, Perhaps

IT WAS A FRIDAY MORNING, a week and a half after Donna's body was discovered. Gary Mogford was off duty, catching up with *White Dwarf* and waiting for the enamel to dry on his painted figurines. Jenny Groves was on shift but taking a break to call her sister, who was pregnant. And Jack Cholmondeley had just arrived at the station.

He was in a bad mood. Mary was upset because he'd woken up at four in the morning, turned the bedside lamp on and started scribbling away in his notebook. It wasn't the light that woke her. It was the sound of his biro as it scratched across the pages. It haunted her. It always had, although she'd learned the hard way not to look inside it. She'd done it once and been haunted for weeks by the grisly details that she'd glimpsed before Jack had walked in and snatched it away from her. He'd never raised a hand to her in all of the years that they'd been together, but it had been a close call that day and she'd never been foolish enough to take the chance again. Besides, she still had nightmares about what she'd seen, and her husband had lectured her for days on end about how lucky she was for her comfortable life and the disposable income that she didn't need to work for.

"Strictly speaking," he'd told her, "I ought to report you. You could get both of us into a lot of trouble. Damn it, Mary, I could be suspended. I could lose my job."

"I'm sorry," she'd repeated, crying hysterically to begin with before settling down into a slow, seething rage. "It won't happen again."

On that Friday morning, the buried tensions had come to a head again after Mary woke up and asked her husband to either put the pen down or to get out of bed and go to work.

Cholmondeley had chosen the latter, like he always did, and he'd successfully surprised the skeleton crew who worked through the night by cracking the whip as soon as he entered the building. Constable Yates, a pale-faced twenty-something with a promising future ahead of her, noted down his orders in a feverish shorthand. Once she was sure her notes were accurate, she told Cholmondeley about the latest development.

"Frankowska?" he repeated. "Are you sure?"

"Positive, sir," Yates replied. "Shall we bring her in?"

Cholmondeley nodded and then dismissed her with a wave of his hand. He had a mound of paperwork to get through, and his email inbox reminded him of a digital K2—not as tall as Mogford's Everest, perhaps, but a hell of a lot harder to climb. Besides, Mogford had given up on his emails and made it known that if someone wanted him to do something, they had to ask him in person. It had ruffled a few feathers, particularly with the newest recruits who could never seem to find him when they needed him, but it was a system that worked for both of them. Mogford was a younger man, a man of action, but Cholmondeley's days on the streets were long behind him.

There was a knock at the door. After hitting send on a report to his superiors, he answered gruffly and Constable Jenny Groves entered the room with a cup of coffee and a tired smile on her face.

"Morning, sir," she said. "I brought you a coffee. Flat white with a sweetener, right?"

"Right," Cholmondeley said. "Mary won't let me take sugar. She says it's bad for me."

"She's probably right, sir." Groves put the coffee down on Cholmondeley's desk and then stood at attention in front of him. "When you have a moment, sir, could you come through to the interrogation room? Jowie Frankowska is here, but she isn't talking. She says she wants a lawyer."

Cholmondeley sighed and stared absentmindedly at his computer screen. "I guess we'd better find her one," he said, massaging his temples. He thought back to the days when he'd had a little more hair, when a crook was a crook and a villain was a villain. "Do what you've got to do.

I'll be over in a couple of minutes to take a look at her. I want to hear what she has to say for herself."

***

We have her.

Leipfold looked at the message again, then grunted and handed the phone to Maile. She read it, checked the number that had sent it and then read it again. Then she handed the phone back to Leipfold.

"Is that from the cops?" she asked.

"Yeah," Leipfold replied. He scratched his scalp with the end of his pen and stared into the distance. "Jack Cholmondeley," he murmured. "They've taken Jowie Frankowska to the station."

"Have they charged her?"

Leipfold shrugged and slid the biro back into his pocket. "Who knows? Personally, I doubt it. They don't have enough evidence to hold her. Not unless there's something we don't know about. But they'll want to talk to her and hear her side of the story."

"And what *is* her side of the story?" Maile asked.

Leipfold knew the case like the back of his hand, so he didn't need to check his notes to answer her. "Frankowska said she found Marie's body when she went to clean the place," he explained. "She was at the bottom of the stairs, dead already when she got there, looking angry and scared and presumably pissed off, all at the same time. Frankowska called for an ambulance, but Marie was pronounced dead at the scene."

"That's it?" Maile scoffed. "Yeah, definitely not enough to arrest her."

"Perhaps," Leipfold said. "But according to Jayne Lipton, Frankowska was a thief. Maybe she got caught in the act and tried to settle the score. A body at the bottom of the stairs? She could have been pushed."

"And she could have fallen."

"Yeah," Leipfold said. "I don't know. It's a shaky motive, but Frankowska had means and opportunity. And then there's Eleanor Thompson."

"What about her?" Maile asked.

"She links Marie Rieirson and Donna Thompson," Leipfold explained. "And now they're both dead. According to Frankowska, Mrs. Thompson paid Rieirson a visit. She was shouting abuse through the letterbox."

"Hmm," Maile murmured. "And was Frankowska sure it was Eleanor Thompson?"

"Yeah," Leipfold replied. "She recognised her when I showed her a photo."

"Could have been a lucky guess," Maile said, doubtfully. "I mean, what if you're right and she was lining her pockets when she was supposed to be on the job? Let's say she pushed Marie down the stairs. Maybe she didn't even mean to kill her. It's not much more of a stretch to suppose she made the Eleanor Thompson story up to take the focus away from her."

"That's not her style," Leipfold said.

"You only met her a couple of days ago," Maile reminded him. "How well do you really know her?"

"Call it a hunch if you want," Leipfold said. "I just don't think that's how it went down."

Their conversation was interrupted by a short beep and an accompanying vibration that meant that Leipfold had received another message. He unlocked his phone and read it, then whistled softly and set the phone back down on the table.

Maile looked at him impatiently. "Well?" she said when she spotted the vacant look that her boss adopted when he was deep in thought. She knew it best from the daily crossword, although it sometimes appeared when he was trying to decide on his next course of action. "What gives? What is it?"

Leipfold said nothing. Instead, he handed her the phone with his left hand while grabbing a pen with his right. He started scratching his scalp with it while staring into the distance. Maile glanced at the phone, cursed when it asked her for a passcode, then held it over to Leipfold for him to unlock it. He did so without even looking. Maile looked down at the screen again and then gasped as she read the latest message.

Four words from Jack Cholmondeley. *She has no alibi.*

***

It was lunchtime, and Leipfold and Maile were out of the office. They were sitting in the back of a black cab and watching the city roll by on the other side of its windows.

The duo coursed through the roads towards the Thompson crime scene, and then past it and down Wentworth Road towards Tony's Café. Maile figured out where they were going when they were still half a mile away. She recognised the streets from her research and she knew that the café was the only place they had yet to investigate.

The place was almost empty, except for a table in the corner where two builders were eating BLTs and drinking thick, black coffee. A man was serving behind the counter. Leipfold and Maile walked right up to him.

"Table for two, please," Leipfold said.

"You can seat yourself," the man replied. "We're a café, not a restaurant. If you're expecting a waiter, friend, you're shit out of luck."

"Charming," Leipfold said. "Are you the owner?"

"Yes, I am," the man replied. "Tony Barlow. How can I help you?"

"Donna Thompson used to work here," Leipfold said. "She was on duty the night she died."

"That she was," Tony said. "What's it to do with you? What did you say your name was?"

"James Leipfold," he replied. "I'm a private detective. I'm looking into Donna's death. I wondered if there's anything I might be able to learn here."

"I told everything I could to the cops," Tony said. "I'm not saying another word."

"I didn't think you would," Leipfold said. "But don't worry. I'm not here to ask questions. I'm here for a spot of lunch."

Tony's mouth wavered. The corners of his mouth twitched up in a half-smile and he nodded at Leipfold as he handed him a laminated menu. His grubby fingers left a greasy pawprint, and Leipfold stared thoughtfully at it as he led Maile to a table.

"Something on his hands," Leipfold murmured. "Blood, perhaps."

Maile looked across at him. He'd picked a window seat, and they found themselves sitting side by side and looking out through the window at the traffic. A decent enough view, perhaps, but it must have been hell on a Friday night when the drinkers were out and about, causing trouble on Wentworth Road and looking for greasy food to fight their inevitable hangovers. Leipfold, meanwhile, was watching Tony's reflection in the glass. He was staring intently at the back of Leipfold's head, and not because he was waiting for a signal that he was ready to order.

"Why are we here, boss?" Maile asked.

"I wanted to see the place for myself," Leipfold said. "To get a feel for who Donna Thompson was. To find out where she worked and how she lived. What she thought."

"And what do you think so far?" Maile asked.

Leipfold shrugged. "Not much," he admitted. "So far, at least. But I always found it hard to think on an empty stomach."

Maile laughed and Leipfold gestured to the menu. "What are you having?" he asked.

"Depends who's paying," Maile replied.

***

It was later that day and Maile had a problem. She had a good lead on the Fisher case, and she thought she knew who was responsible, but she needed some muscle to go after her suspect. Unfortunately, her muscle came in the form of James Leipfold, a man who'd let himself go since his glory days in the army and who was barely five foot six to begin with. But she couldn't think of anyone she'd rather have beside her.

Will Rickman had sent her an address in Putney. Maile couldn't drive and Leipfold no longer had a motorbike and so, with no money in the kitty, they had to take the tube. Along the way, Leipfold busied himself with the papers while Maile pulled a Palahniuk novel from her handbag. She managed seventy pages before they alighted at Putney Bridge and walked past a couple of hooded youths in the underpass. One of them, Maile noticed, was taking a leak while the other one kept watch. Leipfold and Maile walked straight past them and they found themselves on the high street.

Baxter's address was on Disraeli Road, round the back of Nando's and just down the road from the Putney School of Art and Design. With the daylight slowly fading and the streetlights flickering to life, it looked deserted and unwelcoming. Maile thought she saw a curtain twitch on the other side of the road as they walked up the path towards Baxter's front door.

When Maile knocked at it, there was no reply. Leipfold checked his watch and chuckled softly. If Baxter had a job, which he doubted, then that might explain why he wasn't in. On the other hand, Leipfold supposed it was possible that Baxter was hiding inside the building. But he didn't think it was likely.

Maile knocked at the door again, but there was still no response. She sighed and flashed a glance at Leipfold, disappointed that her lead had amounted to nothing. But Leipfold's eyes were bright and excited. He nodded at her and said, "Just give it some time. Get your book out if you want. We'll wait an hour or so to see if Baxter shows up. If he doesn't, you can set up a couple of cameras and we'll head back to the office."

But as it turned out, they didn't have long to wait. On Leipfold's instructions, Maile hid in the foliage while Leipfold himself leaned nonchalantly against a lamppost, thirty yards away from the door. Neither of them knew what the man looked like, but they both spotted their mark as he approached the door with a key in his hand. He was humming a Metallica tune and paying no attention to the world around him.

Maile stepped out from behind him, blocking off his only exit. He looked at her cautiously and then tried to make a break for it, pushing Maile out of the way and jogging straight towards Leipfold, who launched himself at the man in a flying tackle that sent them both crashing to the ground.

"What the fuck is wrong with you?"

Leipfold groaned, feeling the weight of the years express itself through his aching limbs and angry ligaments. He pulled himself on top of the man and used his weight to pin him down. The man shouted again, this time in an unintelligible mixture of fear and pain.

"Mark Baxter, I presume," Leipfold said.

"What's it to you?" he replied, twisting painfully to try to free himself.

"I think you'd better let us in," Leipfold said. "I'd like a word with you."

Baxter wasn't too happy about it, but Leipfold and Maile gave him little choice. He opened the door of the house with the two of them at his back and glanced longingly over their shoulders at the freedom that he'd just walked away from.

Maile, meanwhile, was talking to Leipfold in a quiet undertone. "How did you know it was him?" she asked.

"I didn't," Leipfold admitted. "But he fit the profile, the address was right, and as soon as he tried to run, I had to stop him. It's an old habit. If someone tries to run, they've done something. If you're innocent, you don't run. You have no reason to."

"Perhaps," Maile murmured.

Baxter, meanwhile, had finally admitted who he was. "Better make this quick," he said. "Mum's working a day shift. She'll be back soon."

"You live with your mum?" Leipfold asked.

"Yeah," Baxter replied. "Don't get me wrong, I hate it here. But I'm skint, so I have no choice. What do you want?"

Leipfold drew himself up to his full height, which still left him three inches shorter than Baxter, who looked at him, confused.

"Information," Leipfold said. "Ever heard of a woman called Doreen Fisher?"

Mark Baxter flinched and his face lost its colour. Maile noticed him glancing at a photograph on the mantelpiece, so she walked across and picked it up, turning the heavy frame over in her hands. She looked a little closer and gasped. It was their client all right, as well as a younger woman that Maile didn't recognise and a scruffy-looking eight-year-old kid. Maile thought it might have been Baxter, but she'd never mastered the unusual art of mentally ageing photographs. To Maile, all kids looked the same.

She held the photograph out so he could see it and said, "Perhaps this will refresh your memory."

Baxter groaned. "Yeah," he said, reluctantly. "Yeah, I know her. She's my grandmother. And that's my mother, Linda."

"Linda Baxter?" Leipfold asked.

Baxter shook his head. "Linda Fisher," he said. "She changed her name after my father left. Can't say I blame her. My dad was a liability. He wasn't around much."

"But you kept his surname," Maile said. "Why?"

"Why not?" Baxter replied.

Leipfold sighed and straightened up again. Baxter hadn't invited them to take a seat, so all three of them were still standing. Leipfold didn't want to show any weakness, even though his knees were on fire from the tackle. He just wanted the interview to be over and done with, quickly.

"Okay," he said, "let's cut the shit. My assistant and I have reason to believe you've been using a false name to contact your grandmother. Sound familiar?"

Baxter just looked at him and said nothing.

"The silent treatment won't work," Leipfold said, scowling at the young man like a boxer trying to psych out his opponent before the bell rang for the opening round. "We can tie Fulwood Scientific, your fake company, back to you, and we can tie the scammer's email address back to Fulwood. If it wasn't you, who was it?"

Baxter shrugged and said, "No comment."

"Listen, Mark," Leipfold said, leaning closer and making no attempt to disguise his contempt. "We can do this the easy way or the hard way. You see, I'm in a unique position. I'm not a cop. I'm a private detective. Your grandmother asked me to look into this case, so that's what I'm doing. But, of course, if you're not going to cooperate, we can always call the police. I'm sure they'd like to hear about the scam you're running."

Leipfold's threat had an instant effect. Baxter slumped like he'd taken a punch to the gut. Maile found herself supporting his weight as he collapsed into an armchair. Once Baxter was down, Maile stepped back and Leipfold stepped forward until he was cornered in, unable to get up or escape.

Baxter sighed and buried his head in his hands. "I don't know how much you know," he said, "but you seem to know enough. I guess I take after my dad and not my mum. *If*—and this is all hypothetical—but *if* I could return the money, would that be the end of it? Would she promise not to prosecute?"

"She's your grandmother," Leipfold reminded him. "She won't prosecute, not if she can avoid it. That's why she approached me and not the police in the first place. She must have had an inkling that she'd been scammed by someone she knew."

Baxter sighed again. He took a moment or two to weigh up the options.

"Okay," he said, eventually. "You got me. But *please* don't tell her it was me. I'll give you the money, you can say it was returned anonymously, and everything's okay, right? Nobody prosecutes, nobody argues, and nobody tells my mum or my grandma what I did and why I did it."

"And why *did* you do it?" Maile asked.

"You have no idea what it's like," Baxter said, his voice shaking because he needed to cry but he couldn't get started. "There's no future for people like me. Oh yeah, I pretend to be an entrepreneur and tell my mum I make a killing, but that's just a lie to keep her off my back. Then I found out about the old lady's savings. She keeps it in a shoebox beneath her bed, for God's sake. If I didn't take it, someone else would have done it. Better to put it to some use instead of leaving it there to rot."

"Why didn't you just ask her?" Maile said. "She is your grandmother, after all. Why go to such elaborate lengths?"

The young man laughed bitterly and hung his head. "She would never have agreed to it, not in a million years."

"Why not?"

"I used to steal from her," Baxter admitted. "I still do, I guess. I mean, it's not like she needs the money. The old crone lives off her pension, and the rest of her cash is just sitting around and waiting for someone to nick it. I figured it was better to take it myself than to leave it behind for some crook to steal."

"You're a crook yourself," Leipfold growled. "You stole from an old woman. You're the lowest of the low, you horrible scumbag. I should call the cops on you."

Maile looked at Baxter like he was a piece of dirt on the bottom of her shoe. She was about to say something when Leipfold cut in to say, "Return the money and we'll call it quits. Your grandmother hired me to get her money back. She didn't say anything about finding out who took it."

Baxter smiled slightly and a little of the colour returned to his face.

Still seated, he offered a hand to Leipfold. "We've got a deal, Mr. Leipfold," he said.

"That we do," Leipfold replied. He shook the man's hand. "As long as you return the money. Where is it, anyway?"

Mark Baxter smiled ruefully and said, "It's in a shoebox. Beneath my bed."

Leipfold laughed a long, deep laugh that built up steam in his stomach and hit his diaphragm like a freight train bursting out from the depot and rolling through the station. The crosswind set Maile and Baxter off, too. Then they all stopped, as suddenly as they'd started. They'd all heard the same noise, and they turned to look at the doorway in unison. It opened a split second afterwards and Baxter's mother, who had barely aged a day since the photo was taken, walked into the living room. She looked at Leipfold and then at Maile, then finally at her wayward son, who was still sitting sullenly in his seat and looking like he wished the sky would fall in.

Ms. Fisher looked sternly around the room and asked, "What's going on here, then?"

***

Later that evening, Leipfold disappeared on a mysterious errand and presented Maile with a set of keys to the office.

"I trust you," he said, "and it takes a lot for me to trust someone. Just don't burn it down while I'm gone."

Maile took it in her stride and ceremoniously added the keys to the chain she wore, which jingled and rubbed against her thigh as she walked. Leipfold had joked about it, until she'd told him that if she ever got in trouble she could wrap it around her fist before she punched someone. After that, the jokes didn't seem as funny.

Maile worked an hour late in the hope that Leipfold might return and save her the job of locking drive bars on the windows and setting the alarm, but he didn't show up and she didn't want to be stuck there forever. She had a date with her Warcraft clan and a bottle of red, and Kat had said something about takeout. So she shut down her computer and stacked the paperwork on her desk into an orderly pile. Then she picked up her stuff, unclipped the chain from her belt and got ready to leave the building.

Although the solstice had passed and the nights were getting shorter, it was dark outside, and it was raining like hell and blowing up a storm.

Like it was the night that Donna Thompson died. Maile's thoughts had been drifting of late, focusing more on Marie Rieirson than Donna Thompson, whose death had started the whole thing off. She thought about the car that had hit her, the invisible driver who'd stepped out of the vehicle long before it was used as a murder weapon, and she shivered slightly as she buttoned up her coat and walked out into the night.

It didn't take her long to realise that someone was following her. She'd seen enough cop shows to know that it was the people who looked casual that she had to worry about, and no one in their right mind would be walking the streets at this time of night, especially not like she was, purposelessly drifting left and right as the mood took her while she thought about the Thompson case.

Maile hit another left and then immediately feinted a U-turn. She caught her pursuer by surprise, although he was hooded and difficult to see in the half-light. For a brief moment, the face was lit up and Maile saw the devil. The man was wearing a mask like a Mexican wrestler or the villain in an old horror movie. Then the shadow passed before the light and reached for her. His fist hooked around her shoulder and pulled her towards him. His fingers felt pneumatic, machine-like. They pinched her so hard that they brought blood to the skin and left long, thin marks on her shoulder. Maile felt the same warm flush of adrenaline that she felt when she was lining up a headshot on her Xbox.

She reacted on instinct, geared up for fight or flight like when some troll left a comment. She'd always preferred to fight, even when she was a little girl, and it was that instinct that dipped her hand into her bag. It came out with her chain wrapped around it, and she punched blindly at her attacker. The impact sent shockwaves up her arm and she dropped the chain while her assailant was falling to the ground. She rifled through her bag again and came back out with her pepper spray. Still on autopilot, her finger pressed the trigger as her attacker pulled himself up and lunged towards her, flinging an arm up at the last second. Maile didn't stick around to see whether she'd hit his eyes or not.

She *knew* him. In that single split second, she knew him by the way he held himself as he shied away from the streetlight. And then she was gone, back along the street towards Leipfold's office. She glanced back again before she rounded the corner, but her attacker was nowhere to be seen. That knowledge didn't comfort her. It meant he was out there somewhere, maybe even trying to head her off. But she prided herself on her willpower, so despite the mounting panic, she was able to keep her head.

She slammed the door shut and locked it from the inside, then hit the lights and leant, panting and shaking, against the wall. She was still catching her breath when she realised with mounting panic that the alarm was off.

I set it before I left, she thought, subconsciously reaching for her pepper spray. *I swear I did. So who's in here?*

Chapter Twenty-One:
Trapped

MAILE POKED HER NOSE cautiously into the office with one hand on the aerosol. She saw nothing and then something, a figure in black beside the coat stand. She raised the aerosol defiantly. She was just about to pull the trigger when—

"Maile," Leipfold said. "Put that down. You're going to hurt someone."

She'd never been happier to see him. Leipfold knew something was wrong when she threw herself at him and wrapped her arms around his neck. He hugged her back half-heartedly and asked, "Is something the matter?"

"Yeah," she replied, disengaging from him and sitting shakily down at her desk. "Someone tried to jump me."

"What?" Leipfold exclaimed. "Are you sure? Should I call the police?"

"No," Maile said. "Not yet. I think it's connected to the case. I want to tell you about it while my memory's fresh. You'll want to try and get hold of the footage as well, if there is any. I think I spotted a camera. I'll get the address for you."

While she was talking, Leipfold walked over to his desk and reached into the bottom drawer. He took out his emergency bottle and poured a small amount into a plastic cup. Then he handed it over to Maile, who drained the harsh spirit and nearly choked on it. When she could talk again, she told Leipfold what had happened, starting with her departure from the office and culminating with her return when she'd peered inside.

"Jesus," Leipfold murmured. "And you're sure you're all right?"

"I'm fine," Maile insisted. "Although I wouldn't mind another hit."

Leipfold grunted and poured another shot before stashing the bottle back in the drawer. *Out of sight, out of mind,* he thought. *We all need our little reminders.*

"Do you think it was connected to the case?" Maile asked.

"Maybe," Leipfold replied. "In fact, I think it's likely. But we can't be certain. This is a dangerous city, Maile, and the world is a dangerous place. It could have been a random attack or some sex pervert trying to have his way with you."

"That's why I carry pepper spray," Maile said. "I made a promise to my mum. She said that knives get you arrested and guns are for fools, but it's better to be safe than sorry."

"Sounds like wise advice."

Leipfold watched impassively as Maile downed the last of her whiskey and took a couple of deep, expansive breaths. He recognised the trick. She was trying to calm herself, to force her heart and her breathing to slow so she wouldn't hyperventilate.

"I can take care of myself when I have to," Maile said. "I might be short, but I can pack a punch. You think we should tell your policeman pal?"

"Are you kidding?" Leipfold asked. "We have to. If it's connected to the case, Cholmondeley needs to know. And if it's not…well, that gives us even more of a reason to tell him. If this is just a random act, there's someone on the streets who might strike again."

"You're right," Maile said. "As usual. So how do we do this?"

Leipfold skimmed through the names and addresses in the back of his Moleskine until he found the number he was looking for.

"Give me a minute," he said. "Let me call the old man and get him over here. This needs to be handled discreetly."

***

Cholmondeley didn't answer the call, so Leipfold left him a message. The cop felt his phone vibrate in his pocket, but it wasn't a good time for him to talk. He'd been checking his suit in the mirror and running a hand through his thinning tufts of hair. He adjusted his tie twice and barked orders indiscriminately before amassing his troops and walking down the stone steps of the police station. It was the part of the job he'd always hated. Jack Cholmondeley had never been short on confidence, but he also hated standing up in front of strangers. He was a cop, for God's sake, not a schoolteacher. But every now and then there were the *special* cases, and this one was threatening to blow up into a shitstorm unless his team released a statement.

Cholmondeley walked over to the podium and tapped the microphone to check it. Satisfied with the muffled echo from the PA, he stared at the couple dozen journalists in front of him and introduced himself with his name and rank.

"Thank you all for coming," Cholmondeley said. "And thank you for helping us to bring this matter before the public. We'd like to assure you that the perpetrator will be caught."

He nodded at Constable Groves and she started to wander from journalist to journalist, handing out press packs and asking them to "take one and pass them on".

"As many of you know," Cholmondeley continued, "we're investigating the death of an IC1 female in suspicious circumstances. I can now confirm that the victim was twenty-five-year-old Marie Rieirson and that she was found dead in her apartment after being reported missing several days ago. You may be familiar with Marie's case due to our earlier appeals for information."

Cholmondeley paused to wipe a bead of sweat from his forehead. He glanced to his right at Gary Mogford, who was watching the proceedings impassively while keeping an eye out for trouble. To his left, Constable Groves was finishing her rounds. She flashed her boss a quick thumbs up before handing out the last five press packs.

"While I'm not at liberty to discuss the full details," Cholmondeley continued, all too aware of the cameras, "I have some limited information to share in the hope that you'll be able to help. We now believe that Marie Rieirson died as the result of a blunt force trauma injury at the base of her skull. While it's possible that this was as a result of the fall she sustained, our current belief is that it occurred before the fall as part of a premeditated attack on the victim with a large, heavy object."

Cholmondeley paused, half for effect and half to get his breath back. Down below him, the cameras were still rolling, and people were taking notes on smartphones or frantically re-establishing their Internet connections.

"As a result of these early findings," Cholmondeley said, "we believe that Marie Rieirson was murdered. We're making this appeal in the hope that a member of the public will come forward with some information that might help us. In particular, we're interested in anyone who saw Miss Rieirson between Sunday the twenty-second and Tuesday the twenty-fourth. We've provided recent photographs of the victim to help with identification. We'd also like to hear from anyone who saw anything suspicious between those dates that may be connected to the case."

Cholmondeley stepped back for a second and allowed Gary Mogford to take the stage. His contribution was short and to the point. He listed the contact number and the webpage that had been set up with further information, and he encouraged the public to get in touch. Then he handed over to Cholmondeley, who stepped up to the podium for the final time.

"This is an ongoing investigation," he said, "and it's prone to rapid developments. While we have no concrete leads to speak of, there are a number of avenues that we plan to investigate. We'd like to reassure the public that if foul play was involved—as we initially suspect—then we'll find the perpetrator and bring them to justice. In the meantime, we ask you all to remain vigilant and to report any suspicions that you might have to the number that my colleague just read out to you. Thank you for your time."

***

Maile managed to find a livestream of the announcement and watched it in silence with Leipfold sitting to the side of her. Cholmondeley finished his statement and then the feed panned back to the journalist, who started to sum up the developments while encouraging viewers to share their comments on social networks. Maile was half tempted to send a message of her own, but Leipfold cautioned against it, saying, "Now's not the time."

"But what do you make of that?" Maile asked.

"We haven't learned much that we didn't already know," Leipfold replied. "But I'm surprised nonetheless. Looks like Jack Cholmondeley has finally seen the light and figured out that he might not solve this crime without a little help from the general public."

"It might work," Maile said. "It's happened before."

Leipfold's phone rang and he scooped it up to answer it. Maile had noticed by now that he had two of them, a Samsung and an HTC, which was how she knew it was Jack Cholmondeley. He was the only person who ever dialled the HTC, and Maile suspected it was no coincidence. She also suspected that if she looked up the numbers, they wouldn't be registered. They'd be cheap disposables, favoured by the criminal class because it made it harder to trace the calls they made.

She watched one side of the conversation as Leipfold brusquely replied to a couple of questions before sitting back to listen to whatever Cholmondeley was telling him. The policeman finished his update and Leipfold hastily told him about the attack on Maile and their suspicions that it was connected to the case. Then he thanked Cholmondeley and put the phone down. Maile wanted to ask him what had happened, but she knew better than to interrupt him when he was scribbling away at his notebook, which is exactly what he started to do once the call was over. But eventually he put the pen down and turned to talk to her.

"They didn't release everything they knew," Leipfold said. "They managed to get some samples from the sedan and the lab came back with a match."

"And"? What did he say?"

"Tom Townsend was all over the thing," Leipfold said. "They had no problem figuring that one out. His prints were on the wheel, for Christ's sake. But they also had prints from an unidentified female, and that's where the surprise comes in. Cholmondeley says they were a match to Jayne Lipton. Remember her?"

"Yeah, I do," Maile said. "Marie Rieirson's friend. The one in the fucked-up foursome with Tom Townsend."

"Exactly," Leipfold said. "And now we can put her in the car that killed her rival, sitting right beside the guy they were competing for."

"There's more," Maile replied. "When Tom Townsend hired the car, he said he used it to take Marie to The Ledbury. But if that was the only time he had it, why was Jayne Lipton inside it? Were they both in there at the same time? If so, when? And if she was in there by herself, could she have tampered with it?"

"It could be a coincidence," Leipfold said.

"No," Maile said, shaking her head. "Coincidences are for the lazy. You taught me that, remember? There has to be a proper explanation."

***

Leipfold promised Maile that Cholmondeley's boys would look into the attack, but she didn't have much faith in their abilities. Ever the cynic, she suspected that an unsuccessful attack on a young woman would take low priority when they had two bodies in their morgue and no one to bring to justice. Besides, she knew the statistics.

That was why, when she returned to work the following morning, she started an investigation of her own. She spent the morning going door to door, canvassing local businesses to see if they had CCTV. Most of them had cameras, but most of them weren't turned on or, if they were, they weren't recording. Luckily, Leipfold's reputation carried weight in the area, and Maile reaped the benefits. She was able to track down a couple of store owners who were both happy and able to give her the footage she was looking for. She took it back to the office on a portable hard drive for analysis. While she was walking, she noticed that she was constantly looking around like a meerkat on sentry duty, expecting to see something—anything—out of the ordinary. Another threat to try to take her down and stop her from working the case.

But it's too late for that shit, she thought.

Leipfold looked up at her but said nothing as she re-entered the office and sat down at her desk. She'd given up on Leipfold's spare machine and started bringing in her MacBook so she could work more efficiently. The boss understood and approved, although she'd lost him when she talked about RAM and CPU.

"It's too slow," she'd explained, "but it'll cost you money for a new one." He understood that, all right.

Maile booted up the MacBook and plugged in the hard drive. Then she made a couple of copies of the footage and started processing the images, identifying the relevant sections by the timestamp and trying to augment the colours and contrast so she could get a better look at what was happening. It was a lengthy, thankless task, but she couldn't call it boring, not by a long shot. Every time she replayed the footage of her attack it started the adrenaline flowing all over again, but she pored over it like a geeky kid on an MMORPG until she turned into a big, sweaty mess.

She took a break from the screen to boil the kettle and to refresh herself in the bathroom. Then she sat back at her desk to review the footage again. There was something there that she hadn't spotted before, some little insight that had been hiding in plain sight since she first took a look at it. She hit the play button again, first scanning the rest of the street and then focusing on the attack. She hit rewind and watched it again. Her attacker had turned his face at the last second, but that wasn't what caught her attention. After all, he was wearing a balaclava, and no amount of enhancement would reveal the face beneath. No, it was the way that he moved, and the way he held himself as he walked along behind her. It wasn't right, none of it was. Nobody walked like that, not normally. It was a distinctive walk, one which hinted at its owner's personality. It was a thespian's walk, the walk of a man who'd practiced for hours in front of the mirror to give himself an edge on the competition, a walk that screamed "look at me!" even as the man in the balaclava tried to hide his face from the light.

Maile knew that walk all right. She'd seen it before when she went to see *Driven* with Leipfold. When she cross-referenced the attacker's height with the height of one of their suspects, she found a match. She had a name.

* * *

Maile was so absorbed by her new-found knowledge that she didn't see Leipfold leave. When she looked up and saw he was gone, her heart skipped a beat and she involuntarily reached for the pepper spray and came up empty. She'd left it in her jacket because she'd figured that she was safe in the office whether she was alone or not. No one would get through the reinforced door unless she let them in. Even if they had a battering ram—or possibly a clan of half-orc warlords—they wouldn't get in before the police could arrive, especially with the station only a mile and a half away.

But then there was a sound from outside. Maile retreated to her desk and pulled her jacket on, just in case. She checked the door and found that Leipfold had locked it, as he usually did when he left. As always, business was slow. Since they averaged three to four walk-ins a week, he wasn't worried about losing out on revenue.

There was a knock at the door. Maile cursed his dire finances and the faceless landlord who'd refused to fix the intercom and then tiptoed up to the spyhole and looked outside.

And then her heart sank because she saw who it was and it scared her.

Tom Townsend knocked on the door again, then shouted, "Leipfold! James Leipfold, are you in there? I need to talk to you." He knocked again. "Leipfold! I know you're in there."

Maile started to panic, and her nimble fingers danced their familiar fandango across the screen of her smartphone. Leipfold answered almost immediately, and Maile talked quickly in a whispered monotone. "Tom Townsend's here, and he wants to come in."

Leipfold tried to cut in to ask what she was talking about, but Townsend was still on the other side of the door and Maile just talked right over him.

"Shut up and listen to me," Maile continued, backing away from the door as though it were a snake that might strike at any moment. "Get back here right now. I mean it. He's outside the door, and I…I'm scared, all right?"

Maile cut the call and looked across the office at the door. It was quiet again, too quiet. Townsend must have worn himself out, or else he'd changed tack and had something else up his sleeve. She keyed in triple nines and held one finger over the dial button, then edged slowly closer to the door. She was struck with the uncomfortable realisation that the entrance was also the only exit. She was *trapped*, for God's sake. And from outside, there was only silence.

Only it wasn't silence, not really. It was an absence of noise, the sound of something that was there but was holding its breath and trying to pretend otherwise.

And then the voice came.

"I know you're in there," Tom Townsend said, his voice lifting softly like a child singing a nursery rhyme. "I can hear you."

Chapter Twenty-Two:
A Confession

MAILE SHOOK HERSELF and made a beeline for the window. She was starting to panic, and she couldn't think properly when she started to panic. She opened up the window and gulped in the fresh air, then scanned the side of the building for an emergency exit or a balcony.

What the hell, she thought. *I'd take a drainpipe if we had one.* But there was nothing, no way down that wouldn't hurt when she hit the ground, and Tom Townsend was hammering away at the door.

She went to hit the dial button, knowing that Leipfold would be pissed if she called the cops to his office, and then she paused as she saw him from the corner of her eye, skulking along the street with his coat pulled up close and his head down like he was looking for money in the gutter. He was typing away on his phone, and she saw the result of it when his message flashed up on her screen a second later: *Stay put. Don't take any risks. I'm coming.*

Maile toyed with the idea of calling down to him, but she didn't want to give Townsend the chance to overhear her or the satisfaction of knowing that his attack last night—if she was right and it *was* him—had thrown her off balance. So she messaged Leipfold back.

He's right outside. Be careful. I think he's dangerous.

She watched as Leipfold read the reply and then quickened his step along the gum-spoiled pavement. Townsend was still at the door, still shouting for Leipfold to come out and face him. Then the knocking stopped and was replaced by the susurrus of a quiet conversation. Maile could hear Leipfold murmuring platitudes, and she could picture him trying to calm Townsend down while keeping a reasonable distance, but she couldn't hear the other man's responses. Then silence reigned again.

And then a key turned in the lock and the door opened, and Tom Townsend marched sheepishly into the office.

"Don't worry," Leipfold said, following their guest inside and closing the door behind him. He slid the lock into place. "This is all a big misunderstanding. Mr. Townsend here means you no harm."

"That's right, miss," Townsend confirmed. He had a faint redness in his eyes and a small rash on his cheek. She almost felt a little sorry for him.

"Do you want to explain yourself, Mr. Townsend?" Leipfold asked. "Or should I?"

"I didn't mean anything by it," he said, holding his hands up. "And I'm sorry if I scared you back there. I mean, just now, I wanted to speak to Mr. Leipfold. And I'm sorry for last night as well. I thought…well, I thought you might be able to help me."

"No way," Maile growled, still regarding him with some suspicion. "So it *was* you. Why were you following me?"

Townsend opened his mouth to reply, but Leipfold raised a hand and he closed it again.

"Allow me," Leipfold said. "Mr. Townsend here has some valuable information. Information that's relevant to the Rieirson case and maybe even to Donna Thompson. But it's not the kind of thing you can say in the middle of a busy street. That's why I invited him in here. Be nice to him. He's a guest."

"I was nervous," Townsend said. "Honestly, I was. I thought if I waited until no one was around, I could talk to you. Maybe even get you to take a message to Mr. Leipfold. See, I was worried that if I told him the truth, he might not let me out of here. But I thought that you, miss, would understand."

"Call me 'miss' again and I'll kick you in the crotch, asshole."

"Let's all take a moment to *calm down*," Leipfold shouted. Maile's face was flushed and her knuckles were white, while Tom Townsend looked ready to vomit. He had to lower himself into one of the plastic chairs in their makeshift reception area. He held his head in his hands and looked down at the floor.

"I'm sorry, okay?" Townsend said. "I swear. I didn't mean anything by it. I just needed someone to talk to. When I saw you leave Leipfold's place, I thought you might be the one. Close enough to listen to what I have to say without trying to arrest me."

"I don't believe you," Maile said.

"Please!" Townsend cried. "Look, no harm done, okay? Let's just forget about it. I won't press charges or come near you again if you promise not to spray me in the face. Deal?"

"Deal," Maile said. She frowned at him and leaned back against the wall with her arms crossed. Leipfold stood between them, looking from one to the other like a panic-stricken kid in the middle of a family argument. Townsend sagged visibly and then stiffened up again when Leipfold asked what he wanted to tell them.

"Oh, *that*," he replied. "Yes, well…it's not easy. I wanted to make a confession."

"I'm not a priest," Leipfold reminded him.

"No, you're not," Townsend said. "But you are a detective, and maybe you can help me. You see, I didn't attack your assistant. I was just trying to deliver a message. But I think I killed Marie Rieirson."

Leipfold sighed while Maile stared, wide-eyed, at Tom Townsend. Without looking away from him, she pulled a stick of gum from her pocket and dropped it into her mouth. Townsend, meanwhile, was still sitting on the plastic chair with his head in his hands. He didn't look like a murderer. He looked like a dog who'd crapped on the carpet and been confronted by an angry owner at two o'clock in the morning.

"Now," Leipfold said, "before you tell me anything, I need to remind you of something."

"What's that?" Townsend asked.

"I might not be a policeman," Leipfold said, "but if I feel I'm morally or legally bound to do so, I may share information with the police force. If you've come here to get me involved in something criminal, you might want to remember that."

Townsend shrugged. "What's the use?" he asked. "I'm done for either way, Mr. Leipfold."

Leipfold turned to Maile and said, "Get him a dash of whiskey. From the bottle in my bottom drawer." She hurried off to obey him as

Leipfold turned back round to look at the man. "What is it?" he asked.

"Marie Rieirson," Townsend said. "I think I killed her. Marie and I, we used to argue. Not often, but when we did, it was like a firework. A big scream and then an explosion, if you know what I mean. That's how it happened."

"How what happened?" Leipfold asked.

"She found out about the others," Townsend explained. "We argued. Then we fought, and she pushed me. I pushed her back. Harder than I should have, perhaps, but it's not like I raised my fists to her."

Leipfold shrugged. "And then what happened?"

"Then she fell down the stairs and hit her head," Townsend said. "And you know the rest. I panicked and left her there. I thought if I kept my head down, no one would know I'd been over there. But I just couldn't live with it. I had to tell someone, but not the police. Mr. Leipfold, I don't want to go to jail. I didn't mean to kill her."

Leipfold looked Townsend up and down, then nodded slowly and walked over to his desk.

"I believe you, Mr. Townsend," he said. "But some things are out of my hands."

"What do you mean?" Townsend asked.

But Leipfold held a hand up to cut him short. He opened the top drawer of his desk and took out his spare mobile phone, then dialled the only number in its memory. Cholmondeley picked it up on the second ring and then listened, in silence, as Leipfold told him what had happened.

Townsend watched mutely, too numb to try to stop him. Leipfold ended the call with a final "goodbye" and put the phone back in the drawer. Then he walked back over to Townsend and pulled up a chair beside him.

"Listen," he said. "I've put a call in to a friend of mine."

"Is he a policeman?"

"Yes," Leipfold said. "But he's a good man. I trust him. If what you say is true, he'll help you. I'm sorry, Mr. Townsend. I'm just a private detective. It's out of my hands."

Townsend stared at him for a second, his eyes wide and uncomprehending. They darted to the door, and for a split second Maile saw the man as he'd appeared the night before, like a feral cat backed into a corner and ready to scratch someone's eyes out. Then it faded and he was harmless Tom Townsend, the actor and director, all over again.

He ran for the door and let himself out, then fled on foot along the street. Four minutes later, the police arrived, and Leipfold and Maile led Jack Cholmondeley upstairs into the office.

***

Cholmondeley didn't stay for long, and he refused the cup of tea that Maile offered him. Secretly, she was pleased. Her hands were shaking, her nerves were shot, and she wanted him to hurry the hell up and chase down Tom Townsend.

Leipfold filled him in on Townsend's confession and handed over a copy of his file on the man. Cholmondeley thanked him for the information, tipped his hat and took leave of the office. Maile was about to chase after him to ask him to promise to catch Tom Townsend when Leipfold grabbed her arm to stop her. She glared at him.

"Let it be," he said. "He'll find him. And besides, something isn't right."

"Yeah," Maile growled. "Tom Townsend isn't right."

"Maybe not," Leipfold said. "His story definitely wasn't. That man is innocent."

"How can you say that?" Maile asked. "He stalked me and tried to attack me. If he says he killed Marie Rieirson, he killed Marie Rieirson. Why would he lie?"

"Why would he lie, indeed?" Leipfold murmured. He sat in a troubled silence for a moment or two, then added, "He was protecting someone. He must've been."

"But who?"

"I don't know, Maile," Leipfold said, shrugging in his seat and massaging his temples to reduce the pressure that was building up and threatening to spill out like steam from a kettle on the boil. "I just don't know."

Maile stared at him for a couple of seconds as he slumped forwards on his desk with his head in his hands. She was worried, but then she *always* worried about him, and she had done ever since she first agreed to join him. She was about to offer him a glass of water when he stood up abruptly, pulled his leather jacket on and got ready to leave the office. She glared at him.

"You're leaving me alone again?" she asked. "What if Tom Townsend comes back?"

"He won't," Leipfold replied. "And besides, you can look after yourself."

Maile smiled. He trusted her, and that was good. But she needed to prove she was worth it, even if that meant getting into another altercation. But she wouldn't go out *asking* for trouble. Her place was behind a computer screen.

"Where are you going?" she asked. Leipfold was patting his pockets and checking he had the only four things he needed: his keys, his wallet, his pen and his notebook.

"I'm going to pay a visit to Greg Bateman," he said. "You know, the self-driving car guy. I want to ask him a couple more questions. Don't wait up."

***

Bateman's Motors was too far away to cycle to, so Leipfold hopped on the bus instead. It was delayed, but he didn't mind. He liked the hum of life that personified public transport, the interlinked web of relationships almost visible in the air, there for the taking for anyone with the patience and the desire to look for it.

It was dark outside by the time he made it to Bateman's place, but the lights were still on and the car park, while not exactly overflowing, was home to a half-dozen vehicles of various makes and models. Leipfold laughed to himself. He could guess which cars belonged to which employees based upon the staff that Bateman employed. The boss owned the Merc, and the little blue Ford Focus was his receptionist's. The nondescript white van and the VW Golf with the lowered suspension belonged to Bateman's mechanics, probably bought from the lot at a discount.

Greg Bateman himself was behind the front desk when Leipfold walked through the automatic doors. He groaned audibly as he spotted him.

"Oh no," Bateman said. "Not you again."

"Nice to see you, too," Leipfold replied. "Have you heard the news?"

"What news?"

"Tom Townsend confessed to murder," Leipfold said.

"No way," Bateman replied, raising his eyebrows. "You mean he killed that girl with my car?"

"That wasn't the murder he confessed to," Leipfold said. "But *someone* killed Donna with your car, all right. And that's why I'm here to talk to you. I need you to do me a favour."

"Whatever it is, forget it," Bateman said, shaking his enormous head and bunching his hairy knuckles together. "You're more trouble than you're worth."

"Please," Leipfold said. "It's a quick one. I just need you to look at someone and tell me whether you recognise them."

"Whatever," Bateman said, but despite his reluctance he couldn't stop himself from glancing at the printout that Leipfold was holding. He stared at it for a couple of seconds and then shook his head again. "Nope, never seen her. Sorry."

"Fair enough," Leipfold said. "Thanks for your time."

He took a couple of steps away from the front desk and pretended to look out through the windows. It was dark outside and so he couldn't make out the car park, but he could see Greg Bateman's worried reflection. Leipfold shrugged and reached into his pocket. He pulled out his phone and dialled a number.

"Hello?" he said, his back still turned to the po-faced salesman. "Detective Inspector? It's Leipfold. I've got a guy here obstructing the course of justice. You might want to get over here and have a word with him."

There was a pause. Then Leipfold said, "Yeah, Greg Bateman, the car guy. You know, the one who owned the murder weapon? He says he didn't see anything so I thought you'd like to take him for an eye test."

Leipfold winked at Bateman and mouthed, "He's on his way."

Chapter Twenty-Three:
It Could Be Worse

"OKAY, OKAY," Bateman said, grinding his teeth and glaring at Leipfold, who still had his back to him. "I recognise her. Just put the phone down. I'll talk."

Leipfold touched the screen of his phone and put it back into his pocket. The device wasn't even on. The battery had died a couple of hours earlier, and Leipfold was the kind of man who always forgot to charge it. But Bateman didn't need to know that. Leipfold glared across at the man as he returned the phone to his jacket pocket.

Bateman called the receptionist and asked her to take over the front desk while he showed Leipfold to a room around the back. Bateman usually used it to schmooze potential customers by offering them high-end coffee and a short spell in his leather seats, but he liked it for its privacy and it was perfect for an off-the-record chat with a private detective.

"Okay," Leipfold said, as they sat down on opposite ends of Bateman's mahogany table. "So what can you tell me?"

"What do you need to know?" Bateman asked.

"Start from the beginning," Leipfold said, showing him the photograph again. "How do you know this woman?"

"She came in to hire a car," Bateman said. "I've got her records somewhere. I can dig them out for you if you'd like."

"You do that," Leipfold said. "I'll get a copy of them before I leave. Go on."

"Her name is Thompson," Bateman said. "Eleanor Thompson. I only met her a couple of times. Didn't talk to her much. That's not my job. I just need to smile and hand over the keys once they sign the paperwork."

"So how did you meet her?"

"She hired a couple of cars from me," Bateman explained. "So what? A lot of people hire cars from me."

Leipfold sat suddenly upright, a sense of urgency in his eyes. "Yes, Mr. Bateman," he said. "But there aren't a lot of people connected to my enquiry. I want you to tell me something, something important. I can't overstate how important this is. I need you to tell me which vehicles she hired."

"Oh," Bateman said, "that's easy. She only ever hired one of them."

"Let me guess," Leipfold replied. "Was it a black sedan? A self-driving model?"

Bateman glanced over at the detective and sighed. "How did you guess?" he said.

***

"James? Are you there?"

It was Detective Inspector Jack Cholmondeley calling the HTC, and he knew damn well that Leipfold was there because he'd picked up the call. He'd just been expecting his friend to say something by way of a greeting.

"I'm here," Leipfold said. He was on the move and had reluctantly picked up the call while walking through the city. He hated talking on the phone in public because he hated the kind of people who talked on their phone in public, but he couldn't turn down a call from Jack Cholmondeley. "What's up?"

"Where are you?" Cholmondeley asked.

"Never you mind. What's up?"

"I wanted to give you an update," Cholmondeley said. "But if anyone asks, you didn't hear this from me. Tom Townsend is on the run."

Leipfold sighed. "I feared as much," he admitted. "He seems like the type. Any idea where he's gone?"

"No," Cholmondeley replied. "That's why I called you. I thought you might have some insight."

Leipfold paused and thought for a moment. He considered everything he knew about the man and drew a tenuous conclusion.

"He's a thespian," Leipfold said. "The kind of man who believes in the power of narrative. He's not the kind to go gently into that good night. He'll want to go out with a bang and make some kind of a statement."

"A statement?"

"Yeah," Leipfold said. "A stand-off with the police, perhaps. Or maybe he'll fake his death and flee the country. Your guess is as good as mine. The point is that he was never going to just hand himself in. He's not that type."

"But what do we do?"

"He'll show up," Leipfold replied. "He might be familiar with a few plays and have read a few books, but he's no criminal mastermind. Keep an eye out at the airports and the ferry terminals. Put some surveillance on his friends and family. Monitor his home and his studio. If you want to catch him, you'll catch him."

"Will you help me to look for him?" Cholmondeley asked.

Leipfold paused for a moment and the sound of the traffic filtered down the phone line.

"Well?" Cholmondeley said. He sounded tense and stressed. Leipfold didn't blame him. Not with a job like that.

"I'll think about it," he replied.

***

Leipfold slept late on the morning of January twenty-ninth, nearly two weeks after Donna Thompson's body was found. The light filtered in through the gaps in the blinds and cast bleak shadows around the single-room apartment that Leipfold called home because he hung his hat there.

He *hated* living there. He always had. But he didn't have much choice—not with his income. Despite intending to stay for just a couple of months until he found somewhere better, he'd ended up living in the tiny bedsit for the best part of a decade.

Still, he reflected. *It could be worse.*

Leipfold sat up in bed with his back against the wall, then reached over to his dressing table and picked up his two mobile phones. His direct line to Cholmondeley had stayed silent. Leipfold suspected the old man was enjoying a well-deserved day off, probably taking Mary shopping or giving her a lift to the salon. But he had a message from Maile. Just two simple words that cut straight to the chase: *Call me.*

He sighed and crawled out of bed, took a quick shower to clear his head and then pulled on the first clothes he could find when he rooted through his wardrobe. Leipfold owned a dozen copies of the same three outfits: smart casual, smart and super smart. He even owned thirty-six pairs of the same socks so he didn't have to worry about matching pairs after he picked up his clothes from the launderette. There was no chance of him owning a washing machine, not in a flat that was smaller than most caravans.

When he was clean, dressed and ready to roll, he picked up his phone and gave Maile a call. When she answered, he could hear explosions and gunfire in the background and he guessed—correctly—that she was spending her Sunday scoping headshots on her Xbox.

"What's up, boss?" she asked.

"Not much," Leipfold replied, smiling to himself and wondering whether her place was nicer than his. "I just woke up and got your message."

"Yeah," Maile said. "I wanted to know how it went at Bateman's Motors. You never gave me an update."

"It went well. I showed him a photo of Eleanor Thompson and he recognised her, all right. It just took a little discussion."

"Discussion?" Maile laughed. "That doesn't sound like you. What did you threaten him with?"

"Never mind that," Leipfold said, stifling a yawn. He cradled the phone against his ear while he filled the kettle and started to boil it. "The point is that Eleanor Thompson hired the car a couple of times. What's an old biddy like her doing with something out of *Silicon Valley?*"

"Maybe she has a techie side," Maile suggested.

"Bollocks to that," Leipfold scoffed. "No, she's involved in her daughter's death. I just need to find out how."

"So what put you on to her? I mean, how did you know to show her photo to Greg Bateman?"

"I followed her," Leipfold said. "When I left you alone and Tom Townsend showed up. Eleanor Thompson is a creature of habit, just like I am. I made a few enquiries in the neighbourhood, found out when she leaves the house and then I followed her. She stopped by Bateman's Motors on her way back from Waitrose, and I thought, 'What's she doing there?' So, I decided to find out. Besides…"

"Besides what?" Maile prompted as Leipfold trailed off into silence.

"Something about her doesn't sit right with me," Leipfold said. "The first time I visited her place—when Jack Cholmondeley was there—it reeked of bleach. But it wasn't just the house that smelled. It was all over her clothes. But why? She has a cleaner, you know. A young lady called Jowie Frankowska. Remember her."

"Of course," Maile said. "Marie's cleaner. The one the cops pegged for the same murder that Townsend confessed to."

"The very same," Leipfold said. "The plot thickens. Now is it just coincidence that links the cleaner to the two murders? And for that matter, why was Eleanor Thompson, an elderly woman who's used to the finer things in life, on her hands and knees to scrub the floors when she has a cleaner to do it?"

"Perhaps she was trying to hide something," Maile suggested.

"Perhaps," Leipfold admitted, begrudgingly. "Or perhaps she had a guilty conscience. Either way, we'll never know. The police never saw her as a suspect. Even if there *was* something for forensics to find, I doubt anyone ever looked for it."

****

When she got off the phone with Leipfold, Maile drifted into thought for a couple of minutes. Then she turned off her console and booted up her laptop. She was lying back on her bed with her head propped on her pillows, still wearing her Pokémon pyjamas. If Sunday was supposed to be a day of rest, she was determined to do it properly.

But there was no rest for the wicked, and she wasn't the type to stay idle when there was work to be done. So she booted up her secure browser and logged on to IRC so she could communicate privately with a couple of her contacts. She checked the chat, but Krypt0 was away from his keyboard and Mayhem and Brn0ut were offline, which left only KAOS and ProfSyntax. But both of them responded to her messages, and KAOS knew a guy who knew a guy who could help her.

Maile looped her hair absentmindedly behind her ear and then flashed her hands across the keyboard. She was calling in a favour and she knew it, but most of her friends were either anarchists or activists and they worked on a sharing economy. If they scratched her back with this favour, she'd scratch theirs in the future. Besides, she was a girl, and they liked that.

It took their impromptu team a little over three hours to achieve its mission and they broke a half-dozen laws in the process. But it was a success, and Maile was able to get her hands on a couple of important pieces of information. Excitement built in her chest as her eyes rolled over the documents. She was absorbed by the joy of discovery, like a little kid at Christmas.

First off, ProfSyntax had reverse engineered the login to Eleanor Thompson's email account. He'd used a piece of software to crack the password in a brute force attack, guessing every combination of letters and numbers until it found the solution. They'd hedged their bets on the elderly woman using a simple password, and it paid off. They were inside her account and reading her mail in less than an hour.

That was the easy part. The hard part was using her email address to access her banking records, but that's where KAOS and his contact came in. The two of them had worked in relay, communicating sparsely with the rest of the group as they searched for weaknesses, eventually duping her mobile phone number and resetting her password via SMS. Once they were in, they pulled off as many reports as they could get their hands on and then emailed them all over to Maile.

She thanked the guys for their help and promised to get back to them with any news, then started to pore through the documents. For the most part, there was nothing unusual. Just the usual bills that she expected from a one-woman, middle-class household. Direct debits for her mortgage and insurance, her gas, water and electric, her council tax and her monthly membership to the local spa, plus dozens of assorted payments for smaller amounts, mostly at Waitrose and Marks and Spencer. But there were a couple of anomalies, too. Three payments to

Bateman's Motors, for example, which seemed to confirm Leipfold's assertion that Thompson and Bateman were somehow connected.

Plus, there was a twenty-thousand-pound deposit with no name attached to it. Maile asked KAOS to keep digging.

That was about it for the finances, but there were still several thousand emails to work through. Maile copied the archive to her portable hard drive and then started the long, repetitive process of filtering through them all and looking for something of interest.

When she found something, she cried a little yelp of excitement and stopped typing for long enough to punch the air. She heard Kat bustling past outside and wondered whether to invite her in to tell her all about it, then realised that she'd neither care nor understand. So she called James Leipfold instead.

***

"I found something," Maile said, once Leipfold picked up the phone. "I know you said it could wait until Monday, but I don't work like that. Once I have an idea, I need to follow it up."

"Slow down," Leipfold replied. "Start from the beginning."

"Looks like Eleanor Thompson took a big payment from someone," Maile said. "A couple of days before her daughter died."

"How much are we talking?" Leipfold asked.

"Twenty thousand pounds," Maile replied. "That's a hell of a lot of money, boss. And there's more. I went digging through her emails and found a few documents. Get this. One of them was from Marie Rieirson. Looks like she didn't cover her tracks as well as she should have."

"What are the documents about?" Leipfold asked.

"Well, that's just it, boss. They're schematics."

"Schematics?"

"Yeah," Maile said. "You know, diagrams and specifications, that sort of thing. Parts of them were highlighted, and boy oh boy, you should read the comments on that thing. Looks like Marie went to town on it."

"Maile," Leipfold said, "what were the schematics for?"

He could almost hear her grinning on the other end of the line as she said, "An autonomous sedan, of course. The same make and model that was used to kill Donna Thompson."

Leipfold gasped, and there was silence on the line as he tried to figure out the odds of the evidence being accepted in a court of law. They were pretty slim. He was more likely to land the two of them in a cell if he put the evidence forward. But no matter how illegally it was obtained, it was as damning as a smoking gun.

"Boss?" Maile said. "Are you there?"

"Yeah," Leipfold said. "Yeah, I'm here. Listen, I'll call you back, okay? I need a second to think this over."

Maile agreed. Leipfold killed the call and took a moment to brush his hands through his hair as he looked vacantly around the bedsit. He wondered where he'd left his notebook, dismissed it as unimportant and started to think about the case, feeling the clues fall into place like checkpoints along a racecourse. The solution was right there, he could see it all right, and then—

Leipfold's phone rang, breaking his concentration and wiping his mind of the answer that had been floating there in front of him, ready for the taking. He checked the caller ID, didn't recognise the number, and grumpily answered the call.

"Maile," he said, "I still need—"

"It's not Maile," the caller said. "It's Tom Townsend." There was a pause. "Listen, I'm sorry if we got off on the wrong foot. Just…just don't try to track the call, okay? I've seen the movies. I'm on a disposable phone, and I'm not going to tell you where I am. I'm trying to keep a low profile."

"I'm sure you are," Leipfold replied. "Tom, I can't help you. We've been through this."

"I know. I just wanted to set the record straight."

"I'm listening," Leipfold said.

"Okay," Townsend began. "Well, first things first. I was seeing all three of them, okay? Donna, Marie and Jayne. All of them and all at the same time."

"I know," Leipfold replied. "Sounds complicated."

"It was," Townsend said. "Honestly, you have no idea. All of the lies, all of the time. No one should spend their life playing a character, know what I mean?"

"Sure," Leipfold said. "Is that it? I mean, you're breaking cover here. Why risk it to talk to me?"

"I just wanted to say that I had nothing to do with Donna's death, Mr. Leipfold. I swear it. I told you about Marie Rieirson, so why would I lie about Donna? You've got to believe me, Mr. Leipfold. It wasn't me."

"I believe you," Leipfold said. "Now get off the damn phone, and go and do whatever it is you have to do. You're supposed to be on the run, for God's sake. Maybe you should act the part."

"But I—"

"It was nice speaking to you, Mr. Townsend," Leipfold said. "I'm going to put the phone down now, okay? I have a headache."

Chapter Twenty-Four:
A Favour

IT WAS MONDAY MORNING and Leipfold's headache hadn't shifted. He grunted moodily at Maile as she entered the office, and then he gestured for her to keep her voice down. She flashed a smile at him and wrote something down on a scrap of paper, then held it in front of his face. It consisted of a single word: *Coffee?*

Leipfold nodded and popped a couple of ibuprofen while Maile boiled the kettle and hunted for mugs. Then he began to massage his temples again, realising that he'd been doing it a lot and that he owed himself a break from it all. He had no idea when he'd last taken a holiday, but he reflected grimly that it had been before his time on the inside, before he'd quit the bottle and dedicated his life to trying to make some sort of difference. But he couldn't go away, not with his business and his finances in the state that they were in, and so he settled for the next best thing.

He picked up the paper and turned to the crossword. It took him twenty-seven minutes, sixteen seconds—a record low. Leipfold sighed and turned the timer off, then barked for Maile to bring him another coffee. She did as he asked and set it down in front of him. Leipfold sighed again.

"What's up, boss?" Maile asked. "You don't seem like yourself today."

"It's nothing," Leipfold said. He frowned. "I had it, you know. Everything came together and I had it. And then I lost it again."

"Are you okay?" she asked. "You don't look so good, maybe you should—"

"Tom Townsend called," he said, interrupting her. "He said he didn't kill Donna Thompson."

"Yeah, but he would say that." Maile frowned. "Where is he, anyhow?"

"He's on the run," Leipfold said. "But don't worry. Cholmondeley will find him in the end. In fact, I have a feeling that we'll hear from him again. Sooner rather than later."

"Whatever," Maile replied. "I bet he *did* kill Donna Thompson. He seems the type."

"What type is that, then?" Leipfold stared at Maile, who shrugged but remained silent. "No, I don't think he killed her. But enough about that. I need you to do me a favour."

"You do? Sure, anything to help." Maile rushed over to her desk, ready to get back to work at her keyboard. "What do you need?"

"I need you to make a phone call," Leipfold said.

"A phone call?" Maile inhaled sharply and whistled through her teeth. "I'm bad at those."

"So am I," he reminded her. "Remember when I took that sales call and told the guy to shove a carrot up his—"

"Yeah," Maile said. "I remember. Okay, point taken. Maybe I should do it. Who am I gonna call?"

"There's something strange in the neighbourhood, Maile," Leipfold said, deadpan as always. "You're going to call Jack Cholmondeley."

***

It felt weird to talk to Leipfold's cop friend on the phone, but at least he remembered who she was. Leipfold, meanwhile, was humming a Mötley Crüe song and scribbling absentmindedly away at a grubby whiteboard. It was leaning against the wall, already half full of his spidery handwriting.

Cholmondeley agreed to carve out some time to speak to them, but he insisted on doing it at the station.

"Not as suspects, you understand," he said. "I just can't get away from my desk for too long. Things are getting hectic over here."

Maile said that was fine and arranged a time for an appointment. The two of them made their way to the station a couple of hours later. That gave Leipfold enough time to expand upon his notes and to inch

164

ever closer to an answer. Then they made their way downstairs and into the back of a waiting taxi.

There was a short holdup at the station's reception when Leipfold lost his temper with Constable Cohen on the desk, but then they were led to a private room by a frazzled Constable Groves, who offered them a drink of water. Leipfold refused, but Maile took her up on it. Constable Groves disappeared for a couple of minutes before re-entering the room with a plastic cup in her hands and Detective Inspector Jack Cholmondeley stalking silently behind her.

"Jesus, Jack," Leipfold said. "You look terrible."

"Thanks," Cholmondeley replied, smiling ruefully. "You're not looking so good yourself."

"I don't get paid to look good." Ever the pragmatist, Leipfold knew exactly how he looked, like a man who'd gone on a bender and ended up coming down from amphetamines after forty-eight hours on his feet. But he didn't care about that, and neither did Jack Cholmondeley.

Cholmondeley told Constable Groves to leave them, an order she obeyed on the double. Then he turned to Leipfold and said, "So, James. How can I help you?"

"I need a favour," Leipfold replied. "You still owe me, remember. And I have a feeling that if you help me out, I'll be able to give you the answer to a question that's been bugging us both for the last two weeks."

"Who killed Donna Thompson?" Cholmondeley murmured.

"Precisely. Now listen, and listen closely. I think I have the solution. But I'm still going to need your help."

"Have you got any proof?" Cholmondeley asked.

"No," Leipfold admitted. "And that's what I need you for. I've got it. I'm sure of it, but there isn't a court in the land that would lock someone up because James Leipfold says he has the answers. No, that just won't do. We need to work together on this one. I've figured out the answer and now I need you to help me prove it. This isn't some scumbag robbing a purse from an old lady. This is something else, a promising young life ended early. *Two* promising young lives ended early."

"You're talking about Marie Rieirson, too."

"Yeah," Leipfold said. "I am. Will you help me?"

Cholmondeley sighed. He walked over to the door, opened it, stuck his head around the frame and shouted, "Constable Groves!"

Then he sat back down again, spread his hands on the table and looked Leipfold directly in the eye. "You need a favour, huh?" he said. "Better make it fast."

***

When Leipfold and Maile got back to the office, Maile's mood rapidly deteriorated thanks to a review of Leipfold Investigations that she found online.

Leipfold had told her not to worry about it, saying, "No one ever reads those things."

"That's not the point," Maile argued. "It's the principle. Look at what he said."

"I saw it, Maile. Don't worry about it."

"But it's lies!" Maile shouted. "All of it."

"Just let it go."

"But none of this stuff is even true," she protested. "It's all made up to slander the business. This could cost us clients. Don't you want to find out who posted it?"

"I'll take care of it," Leipfold said. "I promise. If it makes you feel better, find out who posted it. Do a little research."

Maile laughed and proffered a mock salute. "Whatever you say, boss," she said.

***

Maile gave Leipfold the reviewer's details before knocking off work and heading home to split a bottle of wine with Kat while watching reality TV shows. They ordered a couple of pizzas with jalapeño poppers and potato wedges and then Maile played an MMORPG while Kat doubled down on the wine and started swearing at the television. She wore herself out at around midnight and went to bed. Maile caught some sleep shortly afterwards.

Maile woke up late on Tuesday morning, and she barely had time to brush her teeth and wash her face before wrapping the leftover pizza in aluminium foil, stashing it in her handbag and making her way to Leipfold's office.

When Maile arrived, Leipfold was struggling to unlock the front door. She bustled along the street towards him and then saw what the problem was. Leipfold's right hand was battered and bruised, welded into the shape of a claw and too clumsy to manipulate the key. As Maile approached, he dropped it, so she bent down to pick it up and then unlocked the door for him before making her way up the stairs to the first-floor office. She held the door open for Leipfold and then tossed his keys on to his desk.

"What happened?" she asked.

"What do you think?" Leipfold replied. "I tracked our reviewer down. They're not going to bother us again."

Maile looked distastefully at Leipfold's hands. "You hit them?"

Leipfold shrugged. "I don't want to talk about it," he said. "Just forget it."

Maile flinched a little as Leipfold walked around her, but he didn't notice. He sat down at his desk and glanced at the latest set of case notes, then looked up again as he sensed her staring at him. She hadn't moved.

"What?" Leipfold asked.

"Violence isn't the answer," Maile said. She had her arms on her hips and was glaring at Leipfold like he'd just kicked a puppy.

"You pepper sprayed Tom Townsend in the face," Leipfold reminded her. "And besides, sometimes there isn't much of a choice. Don't worry about it."

"You broke the law."

"Perhaps," Leipfold admitted. "But I'm not a policeman. I can get away with it. But I don't want to talk about it. Let's change the subject."

"Okay," Maile said. She looked around the office, trying to find some inspiration. It wasn't like she could ask what he thought of the latest Babymetal album. Besides, he was difficult to talk to at the best of times. She settled on the only major thing that the two of them had in common. "The Donna Thompson case."

Leipfold shrugged. "What of it?"

"Aren't you going to tell me what's happening?" Maile asked. "Why did you call in that favour with Jack Cholmondeley? What happens next? And who killed Donna Thompson and Marie Rieirson? Do you even know?"

"You'll find out soon enough."

"Was it Eleanor Thompson?" Maile asked. "Looks like that's where the money is."

"It might have been," Leipfold said. "And it might not. We're going to give her a chance to explain herself. But there's something that I don't understand here."

"What's that, then?"

Leipfold shrugged again. "Last time I talked to Eleanor Thompson, I asked her for her alibi for the night Marie died. She didn't have one."

"So she had opportunity," Maile said.

"Yeah," Leipfold said. "But that's not what I meant. See, it's just not Eleanor Thompson's style. Remember the night her daughter died? She was nowhere near the scene of the crime, nobody was. It's a different MO. When Donna Thompson died, the killer did it from a distance. When Marie Rieirson was killed, someone got up close and personal."

"She still could've been involved."

"Perhaps," Leipfold said. "But if she was, she would've been smart enough to organise an alibi. Maybe the lack of an alibi should make me more suspicious, but in this case, knowing what we know about her, I think we can rule her out. She's more cunning than that."

"So who killed Marie Rieirson?" Maile asked.

Leipfold shrugged. "I have no idea," he said.

Chapter Twenty-Five:
The Suspects Gather

ON WEDNESDAY MORNING, the sun dawned on the first day of February and life seemed almost back to normal. Maile and Leipfold completed the crossword in just under nine minutes. Shortly afterwards, the postman arrived with no new bills, one mail-order catalogue and two pizza menus. Three new emails came in to arrange a call for a preliminary quote. Maile was delighted, but if Leipfold was happy then it didn't show.

"Cheer up, boss," Maile said. "You look worried. Whatever it is, it might never happen. And besides, at this rate, you'll earn enough cash to buy your bike back."

"Maybe," Leipfold said. But it was just a murmur, and Maile guessed that he was barely listening. He seemed listless and lethargic, but that all went out the window when Detective Inspector Jack Cholmondeley paid a visit. It started with a knock at the door. Maile spied him through the peephole, then admitted him with polite astonishment and directed him to take a seat at her desk so he could sit on the comfortable computer chair instead of on the plastic seats in reception.

Cholmondeley took her up on her offer and Maile went to make a round of coffee. When she set the mug down in front of him, Cholmondeley was saying, "…a few strings, but I was able to do what you asked of me. I hope you're right, old friend."

"When have I ever let you down?" Leipfold asked. He nodded a silent acknowledgement to Maile as she handed him a coffee and dragged a chair over to sit down beside him.

"Nineteen ninety-eight," Cholmondeley said. "The Case of the Missing Gnome. I remember it well. But I take your point."

"That was a one-off," Leipfold snapped. "And you know it. It's different this time. I can help you."

Cholmondeley sighed and checked his watch, then drained his coffee in one. Maile stared at him and then looked down at her own cup, which was still steaming.

The guy's throat must be made from asbestos, she thought.

"You'd better be right," Cholmondeley said. "Face it. You're only putting your reputation on the line. You're asking me to risk my career."

"You've done it before," Leipfold reminded him.

Cholmondeley paused. "Okay," he said. "Here's the deal. We'll meet tomorrow night. Seven p.m. at your office. I'll have a few of my men on standby in case your hunch plays out, but this one's on you. I'm committing resources in the middle of a busy case, old friend. You'd better make it worth my while."

"Yeah, yeah," Leipfold said. "I get it. Seven p.m. at my office. I want you to come along as well. Wear a wire."

"A wire?"

"Yeah." Leipfold drained his coffee and then gestured for Maile to fetch him a refill. She walked over and took his cup, but when she walked into the open-plan kitchen, she didn't put the kettle on. She wanted to hear what they were saying, and she couldn't do that if it was thundering away beside her.

"Why do I need a wire?" Cholmondeley asked.

Leipfold smiled. "Because you might want a record of what happens," he said. "And because if I take a recording, there's no chain of command, no nothing. You won't be able to prove it hasn't been doctored. But if you wear a wire, you can use it in a court of law."

"What are you expecting to happen?"

"You'll see," Leipfold said. "Just wear the wire, get here on time and enjoy the show."

Maile watched as the two men shook hands, then turned back to the kettle as Leipfold showed Cholmondeley to the door. She made a couple more cups of black coffee and was back at her desk by the time that they stopped talking. Maile watched Leipfold as he walked over to his desk and checked his emails.

Maile coughed and Leipfold looked up at her. She smiled, sheepishly. "So what was all that about?" she asked.

***

Leipfold kept his cards close to his chest, and Maile learned nothing that she didn't know already. She didn't know how to feel about it. Leipfold thought he knew what had happened, but he wouldn't share it with her. She couldn't decide whether he didn't trust her or whether he didn't trust himself.

"What if you get hit by a bus?" she asked. *Or a driverless car*, she mentally added. "If something happens to you, the answer dies with you."

But Leipfold just shrugged. "Nothing's going to happen to me, Maile," he said. "You worry too much."

"You'd worry too if Tom Townsend had jumped you outside the office."

"Maybe he didn't mean to jump you," Leipfold said. "But I see your point, I guess. Trust me on this one, Maile. You don't have long to wait."

Maile grumbled about it, but she didn't have much of a choice. Meanwhile, Leipfold's train of thought had rolled on out of the station.

"I need you do me a favour," he said. "Another one. But don't worry. You're going to like it."

Maile frowned at him. "You want to bet?" she asked.

"I need you to type up my case notes," Leipfold said, pretending not to hear her. He rose from his seat, walked across the room and dropped his notebook on her desk. "Maybe you'll find your answers. I've never been one for formal reports, but sometimes a client asks for them. In this case, our client is Jack Cholmondeley, and he likes things to be more thorough than most. I need you to type up my notes and start work on a final report. Just the bare bones. I'll finish it off tomorrow."

"After whatever it is that you're planning?" Maile asked.

"Exactly," Leipfold said. "You learn fast. In the meantime, we've got a couple of new cases to look at. Or rather, *I* have new cases to look at. You'll need to stay at the office and hold the fort."

"What about the Thompson case?"

"What about it?" Leipfold asked. "I'm done with it. We need to look ahead to the next one. It's about time this place made some money."

***

It was the following day, and Leipfold was in a good mood as he made his way back to the office. His initial meetings had gone well, and neither of the new prospects seemed overwhelmed when he explained his rates and gave them a quote for a month's retainer. Leipfold was pretty sure he'd get the first job. The other one could go either way, but it had potential.

The door to the office was unlocked, but Leipfold didn't notice. Nor did he notice that Maile was missing—at least, not until the early afternoon. His confusion turned to concern when she didn't answer her phone. Stranger still, she wasn't responding to instant messages, and she didn't answer the door when he cycled over to her house.

Leipfold was worried, all right. But when he got back to the office, it took on a more sinister turn. The postman had arrived. Along with the usual stack of unpaid bill reminders and charity appeals, he'd also brought a handwritten postcard with a not-so-cheerful message: *Stay off the Thompson case or you'll never see the girl again.* There was no signature.

Leipfold cursed softly and delicately set the card on his desk, then fetched the lid of a cardboard box to place over it to protect it from further contamination. He knew that the police liked their evidence to be clean, and he suspected that they'd want to take a look at it. He was worried, of course, but he was also James Leipfold, and James Leipfold didn't panic when it came to facing danger.

Instead, he grabbed his second phone, which he'd used more often than his main line since taking on the Thompson case, and he put in a call to Jack Cholmondeley.

"It's me," Leipfold said, as the policeman picked up the phone with a grunt that reminded him of a horse on its way to the knackers. "Maile's gone missing. There's no sign of a struggle, but she's not answering her phone and there's a note. You know, one of *those* notes. She's in trouble."

"Slow down. We've got to stop talking like this," he said. "What do you want?"

"Maile's gone," Leipfold repeated. "I need you to put out an APB for her. You know what she looks like. I'm worried, Jack. Her coat's still here at the office. She wouldn't have gone far without it. It's cold enough to freeze the balls off a brass monkey."

"I'll get my best men on it," Cholmondeley promised. "Just calm down."

"I'll calm down when you find her," Leipfold replied. "We need to cancel the meeting."

"What meeting?"

"Tonight," Leipfold said, checking his watch. "In a couple of hours at my office."

"Oh," Cholmondeley replied. "That meeting. Afraid not, old friend. The meeting goes ahead. You need to tell me what you know so we can catch the bastard. And besides, it wasn't easy to arrange it."

"Maile's missing, Jack," Leipfold said.

"I know," Cholmondeley replied. "And like I said, I'll get my best men to look into it. In the meantime, we both have a job to do. Don't screw this up for me, okay?"

Leipfold sighed deeply and glanced at his watch. It was 5:14 p.m. He pinched the bridge of his nose and sat back down in his chair.

"Okay," he said. "I'll do it. But you have to find her for me, you hear?"

***

Leipfold was still worrying about Maile and applying his not inconsiderable powers of deduction to the riddle of where to find her— because he already had a good idea of who'd taken her—when there was a knock at the door. He looked through the spyhole and saw his first visitors of the evening.

Detective Inspector Jack Cholmondeley was in uniform and cut an imposing figure despite the lighting, which made him look even older than usual. He was wearing a wire, as promised, and he'd brought backup in the form of a fresh-faced Constable Groves. Leipfold let them in and offered them a cup of tea, keen to stay busy to fight his mounting anxiety, but there was another knock at the door before they were able to answer him.

Leipfold scurried over to open it and returned with Jowie Frankowska. She'd been released on bail pending further enquiries, but Cholmondeley had found it easy enough to talk her into coming. Jowie had treated herself to a manicure. If she was disturbed by her brief spell in custody, she didn't show it. To Leipfold's eye, she looked even healthier than she did when last he saw her.

An awkward tension descended, like a bad smell that refused to go away. Frankowska sat as far away from Groves and Cholmondeley as possible, then stared at them both in silence. Leipfold watched it all with a wry smile, and he was almost annoyed when there was another knock at the door and Greg Bateman came in.

"Hi," he said, shaking Leipfold's hand and glancing apprehensively around the room. "Got the money?"

Leipfold looked at him, confused, until Cholmondeley leaned over and explained, "I may have said something about a reward."

"Did you now?" Leipfold murmured, but he was saved from confronting the reality of his empty bank account by another knock and the appearance of two more guests, Jayne Lipton and Eleanor Thompson, who both made it clear that they'd travelled separately and met each other on the stairs. Leipfold greeted them there and took their coats before directing them to the seats in reception. Jayne looked pale and was dressed casually, and Eleanor Thompson was the polar opposite, healthy-looking, alive and in a modest black blouse with matching trousers and a pin holding her hair up in a bun. She reminded Leipfold of a dying spider.

Next up were three people from Cholmondeley's list. The first to arrive was Tony Barlow, the café owner. He was still in his uniform—food-stained jeans and a baggy T-shirt, though he'd left his greasy apron at home. He looked angry. He clearly didn't want to be there, and Leipfold wondered how Cholmondeley had talked him into showing his face.

Then Eddie Burns arrived, dressed in blue overalls and fresh off the job. He was in a better mood than Barlow, but he seemed confused about why Cholmondeley had summoned him. The policeman took him aside to have a couple of words with him while Leipfold answered the door again. This time it was Adrian Ford, the cab driver who'd passed Donna on the road on that fateful night. He looked sombre and perturbed, and he slouched into a seat without a word. He refused a drink when Leipfold offered him one.

The air was thick with sound for a few minutes as the guests got their bearings. Leipfold handed drinks out, but he didn't talk while he was doing it. He was preoccupied with the knowledge that someone in the room was a murderer—and the fact that Maile was still missing.

Once the drinks had been handed out, Cholmondeley glanced meaningfully at his watch and cleared his throat. The hubbub died down, and Leipfold and Cholmondeley moved over to stand at the head of the circle.

"Ladies and gentlemen," Leipfold said. "Thank you all for coming."

And then he was interrupted by another knock at the door.

Chapter Twenty-Six:
Trial By Media

NOBODY MOVED. Every face in the room turned to look at James Leipfold, who was in his element. His concern for Maile wasn't quite forgotten, but it had been filed away so he could focus on the investigation.

"Ah," he said. "That'll be our final guest for the evening."

Cholmondeley stared at Leipfold as he walked over to the door and opened it up. The rest of the guests were looking from one face to another, trying to figure out who else they might be expecting, and for a single, split second, Cholmondeley wondered whether Leipfold had tracked down Tom Townsend and talked him into surrendering. He nodded at Constable Groves, who edged her hand towards the cuffs on her belt, but then the visitor entered the room and Cholmondeley frowned as he realised he'd never seen him before.

Leipfold led the man into the room and gestured for him to sit away from the circle, on Leipfold's own computer chair. Then he walked back to the centre of the circle and stood beside Cholmondeley. He beamed and clapped his hands together.

"Sorry about that," he said. "This is Alan Phelps, a good friend of mine. Mr. Phelps works at *The Tribune*. Isn't that right, Alan?"

Phelps grunted noncommittally and pulled a notebook from his pocket. He reached in again and took out a pen, and then he followed that with his mobile phone. He started a voice recording and set it down on Leipfold's desk.

"Mr. Phelps is here on my behalf," Leipfold continued. "See, business isn't exactly booming, and so Alan and I made a deal. I'll give him the biggest story of his career, and he'll give me enough coverage to keep me busy for the next six months. Isn't that right, Alan?"

"Sure," Phelps said, shrugging slightly and sitting back in the chair, poised with his pen and ready to absorb all of the action. "Whatever you say, Mr. Leipfold. Just remember that I've got to be out of here within the hour, okay?"

"Sure thing," Leipfold replied. "Let's move on. We've got a lot of ground to cover."

Cholmondeley cleared his throat and stepped forward, holding up a hand to signal to the room that he was the one in charge, at least officially. Leipfold nodded and stepped back to give him the floor.

"My name's Detective Inspector Jack Cholmondeley," he said. "Some of you know me and some of you don't. If you don't know me, count yourself lucky. Mr. Leipfold here is a private detective. That means he's good at sniffing out the truth by whatever means necessary. I think he'll be the first to agree that he doesn't always play by the rules."

Leipfold laughed but said nothing as Cholmondeley continued. "Me, though, I play by the rules. I'm a copper through and through. That's why I'm here. No one is under arrest right now, but I think I should make myself clear. Every person in this room barring myself, Constable Groves, Mr. Leipfold and Mr. Phelps is a suspect."

"That's right," Leipfold interjected, patting Cholmondeley on the back. "And we're not just here for Donna Thompson. We're here for Marie Rieirson as well. The two cases are connected, and I'm about to tell you how. Of course, if there's anyone with a guilty conscience here, now would be a good time to step forward."

There was an uneasy silence, broken only by the sound of Alan Phelps scrawling notes inside his Moleskine using a tired blue biro.

Leipfold shrugged and said, "As you wish."

He turned to look around the room, meeting the eyes of each of his suspects and observing their reactions before moving along to the next one. When he was satisfied that he held their full attention, he dropped his bombshell.

"Ladies and gentlemen," Leipfold said. "Someone in this room is a murderer."

***

Nobody moved and nobody spoke. If Leipfold was hoping for someone to give something away, he was shit out of luck. Unfazed, he flashed a cynical smile at Jack Cholmondeley.

"Let's start with Donna Thompson," Leipfold said. "After all, her murder was what started the investigation."

"And it *was* murder," Cholmondeley interrupted. "A clever murder, but murder nonetheless."

"That's right," Leipfold said, "and so—"

"I'm sorry," Frankowska interrupted, her voice calm and steady and her accent hardly noticeable. "But who's Donna Thompson?"

"Please," Leipfold said, holding a hand up, "no interruptions. I'll get to it."

Frankowska scowled at him but stayed silent. Leipfold took a moment to cast his eyes around the room before continuing. "As I was saying, Donna Thompson was murdered with a self-driving car. That's why Mr. Bateman is here. Mr. Bateman, you're already aware that one of your vehicles was used as a murder weapon. Care to tell us how that happened?"

"I have no idea," Bateman replied. "I've already told you, Mr. Leipfold. I have nothing to do with this. I'm just here to clear my name, to get paid and to go home. Please don't insult me by pretending I have something to do with this."

"Pipe down, Bateman," Cholmondeley warned. "The crime couldn't have occurred without that car of yours."

Bateman's eyes flashed with anger, but he settled back down. Leipfold turned his attention to Eleanor Thompson.

"Now, Mrs. Thompson," he said, "We all know that you didn't get on with your daughter. Let's face it, you're better off with her out of the way. And, as Donna's next of kin, you're first in line to collect on her life insurance."

"That doesn't make me a murderer, young man," she snapped.

"Perhaps not," Leipfold conceded. "And yet you've been acting unusually for a woman who claims she did nothing wrong. The bleach, when Cholmondeley and I paid you a visit at the start of the case. The fact that you'd hired the car before, as Mr. Bateman here can attest to. And, if I may be blunt, the total lack of emotion you've shown since your daughter died."

"That's not true," Mrs. Thompson protested. "That's not true at all. I loved my daughter. I just don't know how to show it. If you ask me, the silly cow brought this upon herself somehow."

"It was nice of you to leave some flowers at the crash site," Leipfold continued.

"You know about that?"

Jowie Frankowska stifled a yawn, and Detective Inspector Jack Cholmondeley flashed an annoyed glance in her direction. Leipfold nodded at Eleanor Thompson and said, "Of course. It's my job to know things."

"Still doesn't mean I'm guilty," Mrs. Thompson replied. "I *felt* guilty, that's all. I pushed her away, I always have. Perhaps she'd still be alive if I'd been a better mother."

"Makes sense," Cholmondeley murmured, but Leipfold didn't share the sentiment.

"I don't think that's it at all, Mrs. Thompson," Leipfold said. "I think you felt bad because you played a part in your daughter's death. You wanted to make amends."

"What?" she screeched. She stood up slowly with the aid of a collapsible walking stick. "I will not be insulted like this, Mr. Leipfold. I'm leaving."

"Sit!" Cholmondeley shouted, his voice booming out like a firework on a quiet night. "Mr. Leipfold is talking. You can either listen to him now or listen to him back at the station."

"The station?" Mrs. Thompson asked. "Am I under arrest?"

"Not at the moment," Cholmondeley said.

"Good," she replied. "I didn't kill Donna."

"No," Leipfold agreed. "You didn't. But you know who did."

***

Leipfold's latest revelation was greeted with a mixture of shock and apprehension. Eleanor Thompson was speechless for once, and the whole room held its breath.

Then Tony Barlow piped up. His face was flushed and his eyebrows were raised, and he looked like an angry cat. Leipfold hoped he wasn't getting ready to pounce.

"Excuse me, Mr. Leipfold," Barlow said. "I don't want to interrupt you or anything but…well, I hope you'll pardon me for asking, but what the hell are you talking about?"

Leipfold sighed and crossed his arms, simultaneously shooting an I-told-you-so look across at Jack Cholmondeley. The cop winked at him and gestured for him to continue.

"You shouldn't even be here, Mr. Barlow," Leipfold said. "I don't believe you have anything to do with the crime."

"That's what I've been saying all along," Barlow insisted. "But nobody seems to be listening. Why did you even bring me here?"

"You'd better ask Jack Cholmondeley," Leipfold replied.

The cop simply shrugged and said, "He was on our list of suspects. You said to bring everyone who played a part in the case. Mr. Barlow here more than qualifies. He was at the scene of the accident, a fact that he first denied and later admitted, and his fingerprints were found on the victim's phone."

"I worked with her," Tony said. "I must have touched her phone a hundred times. That doesn't mean I had anything to do with her death. I already told you, I found her after the accident."

"Yes," Cholmondeley said. "You found her and you took her wages back and then just left her there like a piece of roadkill. And let me tell you right now, I know how your prints got on the phone. The forensic boys carried out some tests and there's not a snowball's chance in hell that the print was more than half a day old, especially not with the weather on the night in question. No, you touched her phone that night."

"So what if I did?"

"You picked it up," Cholmondeley said. "That night, when you took her wages. You took her phone as well. My guess is you were planning on selling it. After all, it was still in working condition when it finally made its way to us. But something spooked you and you decided to toss it."

Tony Barlow was taken aback. His flushed face had blanched and the colour had drained away from it. The change was remarkable, as though he'd had the blood sucked right out of him in the space of a heartbeat.

"If this was true," he spluttered, "and I'm not saying that it is…"

"Don't worry," Cholmondeley said. "We're not going to press charges. We could, but we don't want to. We have better things to be doing with our time."

"Speaking of which…" This came from Eddie Burns, who was sitting off to one side of the group and watching the conversation with a half-smile. He'd risen from his seat and was looking towards the door.

"Sit down," Cholmondeley said. Burns did as he was told. "Your prints were all over the phone, too. This affects you just as much as it affects Mr. Barlow over there."

"But it doesn't affect me," Barlow protested.

"It does," Cholmondeley said. "At present, I'm not going to charge you, but make no mistake. I'll want to see both of you in court to testify. We need to establish the chain of events that led to Donna's phone being returned to the station."

Barlow and Burns exchanged glances, but they both piped down again and waited for Leipfold and Cholmondeley to continue. The tension in the air was palpable. It felt electric and smelled like metal, and people shifted uncomfortably in their seats while they waited for whatever would happen next.

Then Adrian Ford, the taxi driver, cleared his throat and asked, "What about me?"

"I don't believe you had anything to do with Donna's death, either," Leipfold said.

Cholmondeley nodded absentmindedly and added, "I had my suspicions at first, Mr. Ford, but I can't find a motive and I've got nothing on you except your failure to stop and report the accident."

"I already told you—"

"I don't want to hear your excuses, Mr. Ford," Cholmondeley said. "You'll have plenty of time to air them in court. I don't believe that you're responsible for Donna's death, but I certainly don't think you did anything to help us to progress the case. You're lucky you're not nicked for obstructing the course of justice and failing to report an accident. But if you come along to testify, we'll cut you a deal. You won't face charges."

"I, uh…"

"It's okay, sir," Groves said, blushing slightly as a roomful of eyes turned to look at her. "You don't have to decide right now. We'll give you some time to think about it."

Leipfold coughed and brought the attention back over in his direction. Then he turned to look at Greg Bateman, the bald and bulky car salesman who looked far too big to be sitting on one of the agency's uncomfortable reception chairs. Leipfold smiled at him.

"Mr. Bateman," Leipfold said. "You said that you lent your car to Mrs. Thompson and Tom Townsend."

"That's correct," Bateman replied.

"Call me crazy," Leipfold said, "but I don't think either of them was responsible for Donna's death. Who else hired the car?"

Bateman looked at Leipfold, searching his impassive face for some sort of clue about what he was hinting at. He came up short and spluttered something vague and unintelligible.

"Jayne," Leipfold said, gesturing to the young woman who was sitting beside him. "Do me a favour, please. Show Mr. Bateman a photo of Marie Rieirson."

"What makes you think I have one?" she asked.

"Your generation always does," Leipfold replied. "You must have her on a social network or something. You millennials take selfies, right? Or did Radio 4 lie to me?"

Jayne Lipton murmured something beneath her breath, but she was also able to pull up a picture of her friend with a few quick clicks and a Google search. Then she held out her phone to Greg Bateman.

Leipfold and Cholmondeley watched Bateman's face as he looked at the screen. There was a flash of recognition in his eyes, and he looked up from the screen and back across at them.

"That her?" Bateman asked. "Yeah, she took the car out a couple of times. So what?"

"Well, that settles it," Leipfold said. "The coincidences are starting to pile up. Did Tom Townsend tell her to come to you?"

"No," Bateman replied. "She's been a customer for years, ever since she first got a license. In fact, I'm pretty sure she referred Tom Townsend. That's why he wanted to hire the damn thing. Told me he wanted to impress her with it to show her he was listening."

"I see," Leipfold said. There was an awkward pause as he stroked his chin and mulled things over. "Strange, that. See, I happen to know that Mrs. Thompson transferred a large sum of money into Marie Rieirson's bank account, shortly before her daughter's death."

"What are you trying to—?" Eleanor Thompson began, but she was cut short by Leipfold and Cholmondeley, who both turned on her and told her to shut up at the same time.

"What's that got to do with me?" Bateman asked.

"Nothing at all," Leipfold replied. "In fact, for what it's worth, I don't think you knew what your customers were up to. Ever notice anything unusual when the vehicle was returned to you?"

"You mean other than the damage from the crash?"

"Yeah," Leipfold said.

"Well," Bateman replied, "now that you mention it, there was *one* thing. Last time Marie took it out, it came back with some sort of problem. Nothing serious, not as such, but..." He waved his hands expressively, but Leipfold couldn't grasp what he was talking about. He wished that Maile was there to talk tech with him, then realised that she wasn't and that she was almost certainly in danger. And then he remembered that Jack Cholmondeley had his men out there searching for her and that the best thing he could do was to keep his head in the here and now.

"What was the problem?" Leipfold asked.

"Something to do with the guidance system," Bateman explained. "It kept veering from side to side like it was avoiding an obstacle that wasn't really there. I gave it a factory reset and that did the trick." He paused. "Why do you ask, Mr. Leipfold? Does it have something to do with the case?"

Leipfold closed his eyes and paused for a moment. Then he opened them up again and looked Bateman dead in the eye. "It has everything to do with the case, Mr. Bateman," he replied. "Believe it or not, Marie Rieirson knew her way around a computer. I got my assistant to do a little digging. Turns out that she's just as interested in autonomous cars as you are, Mr. Bateman. Perhaps more so. She certainly knew enough to bypass the inbuilt software and to run her own routines. You can get guides for that from the Internet, you know. It's easier than you might think."

"Is that true?" Cholmondeley asked. Leipfold jumped, and so did Greg Bateman. They'd both forgotten he was in the room.

"It's true enough," Bateman agreed, reluctantly. "I've tested a few mods myself, but I wouldn't recommend it. Too much hassle. Besides, it invalidates the warranty."

"Well," Leipfold said, "you're not the only one who messed with the software. Maile, my assistant, was able to bypass it in an hour or so. And Marie Rieirson managed it, too."

"What do you mean?" Cholmondeley asked.

"It was Marie," Leipfold said. "She killed Donna Thompson. Granted, she probably didn't mean to. I think she just wanted to scare her."

"Scare her?" Frankowska asked.

Leipfold whirled around to face her. "Yes!" he cried, tucking his arms behind his back and leaning towards her. "You see, Mrs. Thompson paid her to do it."

"Lies!" Eleanor Thompson screeched, shooting back up to her feet with a surprising lick of speed. "All lies! I'm leaving now. Get out of my way please, Mr. Leipfold."

"You're not going anywhere," Cholmondeley boomed. "Constable Groves, restrain that woman. Mrs. Thompson, if I want you to leave, I'll give you permission to leave. Until then, sit down and shut up."

Leipfold was in his element again. He winked at Mr. Phelps from *The Tribune*, who had given up on taking notes and was watching the proceedings with a morbid fascination.

When the hubbub had died down again and Eleanor Thompson was back in her seat, Leipfold said, "The paper trail betrays you, Mrs. Thompson. You paid Marie Rieirson to scare your daughter. I'm guessing you wanted her to leave the theatre. What was the plan? Were you going to follow it up with a threat? Were you going to bully your daughter until she gave up her dreams to follow yours?"

"This is preposterous."

"Preposterous and true," Leipfold said. "Only something went wrong."

Eleanor Thompson said nothing. She just sat there in her plastic chair, shaking with rage, steely eyed.

"Can you prove all of this?" Cholmondeley asked.

"Yeah," Leipfold replied. "To my satisfaction, at least. Proving it in a court of law is up to you boys. In the meantime, I guess we'll let *The Tribune* and its readers decide."

"Trial by media," Cholmondeley murmured. "I like it. But what about Tom Townsend?"

"And what about me?" Frankowska added. "Mr. Leipfold, why did you bring me here?"

"I'm getting to it," Leipfold replied. "But first, let's talk about Tom Townsend."

***

"Now," Leipfold began, "you might have seen the story in today's *Tribune.*"

"It was one of mine," Phelps added.

"Indeed," Leipfold said, nodding at the journalist before pacing backwards and forwards across the creaking floorboards. "As much as I don't want to offend you, Mr. Phelps, I'm going to assume that not everyone in this room is a regular reader of your newspaper."

"None taken."

"Excellent," Leipfold said. "Well, as I'm sure Mr. Phelps here remembers, he wrote an article about the mysterious disappearance of Tom Townsend. As Phelps correctly stated in the article, Townsend has prior experience when it comes to disappearing in the middle of a show and leaving people in the lurch because of it."

"That's right," Phelps confirmed. "He scammed an arts centre out of some money. Agreed to put on a show, took the cash they gave him for expenses and then disappeared into the night. I thought it possible— and indeed likely—that the same thing had happened again."

"That's where you were wrong," Leipfold said. "The great crossword compiler, finally beaten. Tom Townsend is on the run all right, but not because of the money." He paused to take a swig of water from a plastic bottle. He drained it, threw the bottle at the bin, missed it, scowled and wandered over to the fridge. He continued to talk as he rooted around for another bottle. "This crime wasn't about the money, and Tom Townsend was an innocent man, at least in the eyes of the law. Until today."

"But he confessed to killing Rieirson," Cholmondeley said. There was a hushed silence in the room. Everyone was fixated on the back and forth between the two men as they puzzled over the case and tried to make some sense of it.

"That he did," Leipfold replied. "But that doesn't mean he did it. He's a clever guy. That's why he told me instead of you, old friend. I'm not a copper, so he can't be done for wasting police time."

"But why lie?"

"Easy," Leipfold said. "The fool is in love. Oh sure, he's linked to both of the murders. It's easy to think that he did it, but that's not the case. He's not the murderer. He's the motive."

"He's a horrible young man," Mrs. Thompson said. She looked defeated, tired and spent and ten years older than when she entered the room. "He took my daughter away from me."

"I'm guessing you met Marie when you went to visit him," Leipfold said. "You wanted him to drop your daughter from the play he was directing."

"*Driven*," Mrs. Thompson said. "What a farce. You're right, Mr. Leipfold. I did go to see Tom Townsend. I thought if he dropped Donna, she'd quit that awful job she had and try to do something with her life."

"But Townsend didn't drop her, did he?" Leipfold said. "And so you and Marie hatched a plan to get her out of the way."

Mrs. Thompson glared first at James Leipfold and then at Detective Inspector Jack Cholmondeley, who stared straight back at her until she blinked. "I'm not saying anything else," she said. "Not until I've talked to my lawyer."

"Fair enough," Leipfold replied. "I'm done with you, anyway. In the meantime, back to Tom Townsend. See, the man is a player, a real womaniser."

"Who was he sleeping with?" Cholmondeley asked.

"Donna Thompson," Leipfold replied. "Marie Rieirson, too."

"And me," Jayne Lipton said, shaking her head sadly.

"I thought so," Leipfold murmured. He turned to face her. "And did you know about the others?"

"I knew about Marie," Jayne said. "She was my best friend, after all. We told each other everything. In fact, it was Marie who introduced me to Tom, back when she first started working with him."

"Excellent," Leipfold replied. "Although not so much for you, perhaps. Either way, Tom was sleeping with Donna and he wanted to keep her around. I'm sure of it. Mrs. Thompson is no fool," he continued, pointing at the woman on the other side of the room. She glared back at him but wisely stayed silent. "She tried to pay Townsend off but it didn't work."

"Why not?" Lipton asked.

"Because he was sleeping with her daughter," Leipfold explained. "And he didn't want it to stop."

"I see," Cholmondeley said. "And why did he lie about killing Marie Rieirson?"

"He was protecting the women in his life. With Donna dead, he suspected that Marie or Jayne was responsible. Jealousy is a powerful motive, after all. Then, with Marie dead, I think he wanted to divert attention away from Jayne, the only woman he had left."

"What a gentleman," Jayne said. "But I didn't kill Donna."

"I know you didn't," Leipfold said. "Marie Rieirson did. But Tom didn't know that."

"So where is he now?" Jayne asked.

"About to receive a visit from my men," Cholmondeley replied, jumping in to answer the question on Leipfold's behalf.

"Why?" Jayne asked, staring stupidly up at Leipfold who glared back at her, a glint of steel in his eye and a heavy weight in his heart. Eleanor Thompson murmured something that sounded suspiciously like "what's the silly fool done now?" Leipfold barely heard it. His head was full of the high-pitched whine that precedes a migraine and he was in a bad, bad mood.

"Tom Townsend didn't break the law until today," Leipfold said, "when the bastard kidnapped my assistant."

Chapter Twenty-Seven:
Cautioned and Cuffed

LEIPFOLD'S INSIDES felt like molten lead, but he wasn't the type of guy who was ruled by his emotions. He kept his face steady as he surveyed the room again, taking in the corkboard on the wall with his case notes, the hat stand by the door, the plastic kettle on the kitchen worktop and the circle of strangers all brought together by a common cause. Leipfold looked around the circle again. The tension in the room and the tension in his head built into a crescendo and then passed away like a wave.

"Now," Leipfold said. "Where were we?"

Jowie Frankowska flicked her long hair back and asked, "Where do I come into this?"

"Ah," Leipfold replied. "Good question. You, young lady, are innocent. Yes," he continued, waving aside Cholmondeley, who'd exchanged a frustrated glance with Constable Groves and opened his mouth to say something. "I know how it looked. But poor Miss Frankowska here is guilty of nothing. She simply had the bad luck to discover the murdered body of a murderess."

It took a moment for this to sink in. Cholmondeley, content to take a back seat, still had his mouth open, watching events proceed with the same rapt attention that his wife offered up to daytime reality TV shows.

"In fact," Leipfold continued, "I'd like to thank you. It was you who told me that Mrs. Thompson paid a visit to your former employer. That was what set me on the trail of their partnership. Care to explain why you were shouting through Marie Rieirson's letterbox, Mrs. Thompson?"

"Not without my lawyer," she reminded him, ashen-faced but still strong and unafraid.

"Fair enough," Leipfold replied. "Can't say I blame you. I'd be asking for a lawyer too if I was in your shoes. Things are looking pretty bleak for you."

"But I don't understand," Jowie said. "I thought you said Marie killed Donna Thompson."

"I did."

"So who killed Marie?"

Leipfold frowned. "Good question," he said. "That one had me puzzled for a while."

"Mrs. Thompson?" Cholmondeley suggested.

"No," Leipfold said, holding a hand up to silence the woman before she could say something. "She didn't kill anyone. She just condemned her daughter with her own stupidity."

"Then who?" Frankowska asked. "I have a right to know. After all, the police thought that I did it. I should sue!"

"Sue all you like," Cholmondeley growled. "You won't win."

"Relax," Leipfold said. "Everyone calm down."

"Calm down?" Frankowska repeated, her voice sounding shriller by the minute and her accent kicking in as anger overtook her. "How can we? You said that one of us is a murderer. If Marie killed Donna Thompson, who murdered Marie? I know it's not me and I doubt it was you, so who was it?"

"Well now," Leipfold murmured. "That's a question for the ages. Luckily, I've got an answer. Most murders are committed by someone close to the victim. In this case, the murderer was very close indeed."

"Well, it wasn't me!" Mrs. Thompson shouted.

Leipfold gave her another of his withering looks and shouted right back at her. "I didn't say it was! No, no. It was Jayne Lipton, of course."

Cholmondeley nodded at Groves, and Groves nodded back at him and gestured to Eleanor Thompson. "You take her," she mouthed. "I've got my hands full."

Jack Cholmondeley couldn't lip-read, but he got the gist of it and stepped smartly over to stand behind Jayne Lipton. He rested an arm on the back of her chair so that she'd know he was there. Leipfold was watching her, shrewdly.

"What are you talking about?" she asked, breaking the silence.

"You *knew*," Leipfold said. "You knew Marie did it, but you didn't tell anyone. I wonder how you found out."

"The ring," Cholmondeley murmured.

"What?" Leipfold asked.

"The ring. Our forensic boys found a ring when they looked over the car. We never figured it out."

"It was my ring," Jayne said. "It used to be my mother's. Marie asked if she could borrow it, so I said she could. I never got it back."

"And you'd swear to that in court?"

"If I had to," Jayne said. "Does it help?"

"It puts Marie Rieirson—or at least, your ring, which you say was last seen in her possession—in the back of the car that killed Donna Thompson. And you didn't tell anyone. And then you fought with her. What did you fall out over this time? Tom Townsend? Why? He's not worth the effort."

"You're right, Mr. Leipfold," Jayne said. "He's not."

"Why don't you tell us what happened?"

Jayne said nothing, and Leipfold and Cholmondeley slipped into an old habit, staying silent to make their suspect uncomfortable so they felt the need to plug the gap. This time, it didn't work.

"Fine," Leipfold said. "I'll do it. You see, Jayne and Marie had an argument. And this wasn't just any argument, the usual stuff that two friends bicker about. This was a *real* argument, and one that got out of hand. This was all at Marie's house, of course."

"Of course," Cholmondeley murmured.

"I don't know why you didn't go to the cops," Leipfold said, staring at Jayne across the circle. Her eyes flickered and Leipfold took it as a sign of recognition. "But that doesn't matter. What does matter is that you knew—or at the very least you suspected."

"Knew what?" Mrs. Thompson asked. She was so swept up in the moment that she'd forgotten her own predicament.

"Jayne knew that Marie killed Donna Thompson," Leipfold explained. "In fact, I'm pretty sure it was Jayne who called me after it happened, trying to warn me off the case. Fat chance of that."

Jayne Lipton started to cry, and Leipfold and Cholmondeley tried the silence trick again. This time, it worked. Jayne started to gulp in big breaths of air, smudging her mascara as she wiped her face dry and tried to tell her tale between great heaving gasps that made her look like she was having a seizure.

"She told me about her fling with Tom Townsend and what she'd done to Donna Thompson," Jayne sobbed. "So we fought."

"Yes," Leipfold said. "At the top of the stairs. And you didn't mean to kill her."

"She just slipped." Jayne's torrent of tears intensified, and she held her head in her hands. Then, just as suddenly as she started, she stopped.

"She slipped?" Leipfold asked. "Or did you push her?"

She didn't reply.

***

Constable Groves cautioned and cuffed the two women, scribbled down a few notes and checked the documentation that she'd been working on as the group interview evolved, then stood by for further instructions. Cholmondeley, meanwhile, was waiting for Leipfold to continue, but the detective was almost done. He thanked everyone for coming—Jayne and Eleanor in particular—and then said that everyone else was free to leave. Jowie Frankowska left immediately, but Greg Bateman stayed behind and held out a hand, which Leipfold immediately filled with a fistful of change from the petty cash tin. He was followed out by Mr. Phelps from *The Tribune*, who said he had enough for a dozen stories and that he'd write it all up in the morning.

That left Jayne Lipton and Eleanor Thompson, cuffed and glum and looking more like a mother and daughter than a pair of murderesses, as well as Constable Groves, Detective Inspector Jack Cholmondeley and James Leipfold himself, who watched impassively as his guests left the office.

As soon as they were gone, Leipfold whirled around and punched the wall. It was a solid punch, but it was a solid wall. Plaster crumbled and fell to the floor, but Leipfold's already-damaged fist took the bigger battering. It had never really healed from the last time he'd lost his temper, and the punch popped one of his knuckles. He could feel it starting to swell. He cursed and evaluated the damage. Probably not a break, but damn near close.

Cholmondeley rushed over to him and wrapped an arm around his shoulders. He was surprised to find that the younger man was shaking, so he grabbed the half-empty bottle of Evian from Leipfold's desk and handed it to him. Leipfold drank gratefully from it and then looked at Cholmondeley. His steel grey eyes looked tired, but they didn't betray any emotion.

"Sorry about that," Leipfold said. "It's been a stressful day. And I'm worried, Jack. Tell me you've found my assistant."

Cholmondeley sighed. "Drink up," he replied, gesturing to the bottle that Leipfold was holding. "I wish I could tell you that we have her, but we don't. Not yet, at least. But we've got a team in position and they're ready to go in. I just need to give them the order. You sure about this?"

"I'm sure," Leipfold replied. "Where else would he go? Besides, we can rule out the warehouse. There are too many people there."

"You'd better be right," Cholmondeley grunted. "I had to call in a few favours to make this happen."

"I'm right," Leipfold said. "I always am."

Cholmondeley frowned. "If you say so," he said. "In that case, I'll give the order."

"You do that," Leipfold replied. He scooted over to his desk and grabbed his jacket from the back of his chair. He pulled it on, rifled through his pockets and pulled out a set of keys, which he tossed across the room to Jack Cholmondeley. The policeman caught them and looked back across at him.

"Don't worry," Leipfold said. "I've got a spare set. Just make sure you lock the front door when you're done here."

"Why?" Cholmondeley asked. "Where are you going?"

"I've got a date with Tom Townsend," Leipfold said. "That is, if your men don't beat me to it."

Chapter Twenty-Eight:
On Jermyn Street

TOM TOWNSEND and Maile O'Hara were in a dark room, somewhere beneath street level. Maile was blindfolded, her skinny arms pulled behind her back and tied together with a length of rope, but Townsend had done a bad job of it and she could still see the light and the lack of it.

Wherever they were, the air smelled old and stale. She could make out the distant hum of London traffic from somewhere way up above her. When a tube train passed by as it burrowed beneath the city, it made the walls thrum with movement and rattled thin chips of plaster from the ceiling. They settled on top of her head and made her scalp itch, but she couldn't move enough to deal with it.

She could hear Townsend shuffling around the room. He was talking to himself, alternating between reciting lines from his play and raging at the situation he now found himself in. Sometimes he simply shouted, and other times he came right up close to Maile and talked in a soft, even voice. She wasn't gagged and could have talked or screamed freely, but she didn't want to give him the pleasure.

"He'll drop the case," Townsend was babbling. "He has to. He'll understand. He'll see sense. Every story has to have a happy ending. I don't want to kill you. I don't want to kill anybody. I just want all of this to go away. I want everything to go back to the way it was."

Maile remained silent, although she moved slightly in her restraints and ran a dry tongue across the inside of her mouth. There was a hollow thud as Townsend sat down on something, then silence. It hung thick in the air for a couple of minutes until the man opened his mouth to speak again.

"Maile O'Hara," he murmured. "What a name. You sound like you belong in the theatre. All the world's a stage, Maile O'Hara. You're just playing your part. You can stay silent, if you like. Don't worry. I'm not here to judge you. Your part doesn't come with lines. You just need to sit still and look sharp until Mr. Leipfold drops his case against me."

"Creep," Maile muttered. She didn't know she was saying it until the syllable slipped out, and by then it was too late for her to catch it and to reel it back in.

"She wakes!" Townsend said. He laughed. "Don't worry. You're not in any danger."

Maile held her head up high and said nothing. She'd read books about this, about what to do in a life or death situation. She knew her plan for the zombie apocalypse. And she knew that in a situation like this, her best option was to keep schtum and to hope for the best.

Besides, Tom Townsend liked to talk, and Maile was ready to listen.

"I just want to protect the girls," Tom said, breaking the silence again. "I'm not a monster. Once your boss realises I've got you, he'll drop the case and I can release you."

"He won't stop," Maile murmured.

"What was that?"

"Nothing."

"Yes, well," Townsend said. Maile noticed that there was a slight echo in the room, a warm echo that reminded her of high rafters and polished wood rather than an empty cave with dripping stalactites. "Your boss will drop his case and I'll let you go. Then I'll go and pay a visit to Mary Cholmondeley and see if I can't convince those pesky policemen to drop it, too."

"You're crazy," Maile said.

"No," Townsend said, "I'm totally sane."

Maile laughed.

"I'm serious," Townsend insisted. "I'm perfectly rational."

"You're struggling to tell the difference between life and fiction," Maile replied. "And that plan of yours will never work."

"Why not?"

"It's just a bad plan," Maile said. She was starting to find her voice, her courage. She thought she had a feel for the man. He was weak, squeamish. He threatened to do things and didn't follow through with them. He'd never be anything more than a director in a small, community theatre. He had visions of grandeur, but he didn't have the cojones—or the skills—to follow through with them.

"What's so bad about it?" Townsend asked.

"Someone will figure it out," Maile replied. "You're not some kind of criminal mastermind. You're like a villain from an episode of Scooby Doo, and I know a couple of pesky kids who will stop you from getting away with it."

"Leipfold and Cholmondeley," Townsend murmured.

"Yes," Maile said. "So where are we?"

"We're at the theatre," Townsend said. "On Jermyn Street. Where else?"

"Jesus Christ," Maile said. She laughed, and then she flinched as she felt Tom Townsend's hands on her shoulders. He shook her, an unsettling experience with a blindfold on her eyes.

"Don't laugh at me," Townsend growled. "Don't ever laugh at me. You don't know what I'm capable of."

Maile went quiet for a moment, conscious again of her predicament. She breathed slowly, calmly, bunching both of her hands into fists and practicing some of the mindfulness tricks that she'd read about online. She wished that she could see and that she was holding a weapon in her hand. She wished James Leipfold was there with his cynical stare and his plan for every eventuality. And most of all, she wished Tom Townsend would remove his hands from her shoulders. The latter of these wishes came true, and she relaxed almost immediately.

"Someone will find out what happened," Maile said. "They're probably on the way here right now. What made you choose this place? It's one of the first places they'll look."

"It's the only place I had left," Townsend replied. "And I know this basement like the back of my hand. Only a couple of other people know their way down here, and I'll be gone before they ever think to check."

"You think Jack Cholmondeley and his team don't know how to get hold of the building's schematics?" Maile asked.

"They can do that?" Townsend asked. He sounded uncertain, off balance for the first time since he'd taken her and brought her down there with a rag of chloroform over her mouth. The theatre was theoretically off limits after hours, but Townsend had taken the liberty of making a copy of the key back when *Driven* was running.

"I know they will," Maile said, although she was bluffing. "Let's face it, Townsend. That wasn't your only mistake."

"Damn it," he shouted. His voice echoed again, and Maile got a fuller sense of where she was. She hadn't seen the theatre's cellars during her last visit, but she could picture the echoing space that she found herself in and could remember the floors above her. She wondered if anyone could hear her from Jermyn Street, whether she could call for help from the shoppers at the Tesco Express or the late-night pedestrians whose feet beat the streets of the capital city. But she decided against it. She didn't need to, if Townsend was going to do the work for her.

She could hear his feet pacing back and forth, and she could smell the dust as he disturbed it and sent it whirling through the air in smoky eddies.

"I just wanted what was best for the girls," he said, still walking in little circles like a chicken in the yard. "You have to believe me."

"Let me go," Maile said. "Just let me go and get out of here. Run before they find you. It doesn't have to be like this."

Townsend paused for a moment, collecting himself. Then he started moving again. Maile sensed his presence at the same time as she felt his breath on her neck. She flinched and tensed herself, but Townsend meant no mischief. Instead, he reached behind her head and untied the blindfold, then snatched it aside and tossed it to the floor.

Maile closed her eyes instinctively, trying to protect herself from the onslaught of light, but the theatre's basement was dimly lit. When she opened them, she found that she could see. They were in a circular room with a boiler in it, and Maile was tied to a chair with her hands behind her back. Townsend was on the other side of the room, watching her curiously. He was unshaven and unkempt, looking more like a homeless man than a thespian.

"I loved all three of them," he said. "And then Donna died. It was a confusing time, but I swear I had nothing to do with it."

Maile nodded but kept her mouth shut. She wanted to hear what he had to say.

"Then Marie disappeared and Jayne came to see me. She told me everything. How she'd learned the truth about Marie, and how Marie killed Donna with Bateman's car. How she'd confronted her friend and the fight turned physical. And how she pushed Marie down the stairs and left her to die."

"And you knew all this?" Maile asked.

"Of course," Townsend replied. "Each of those girls told me everything, and I've never known any of them to lie. So when Jayne told me what had happened, I knew I had to protect her."

"By kidnapping me?"

"It was the only thing I could think of," Townsend said.

"I don't get it," Maile replied. "If you loved Marie, why would you try to protect her killer? Weren't you angry?"

"I was at first," he admitted. "But she said it was an accident. And she was all I had left. We were going to try to move past it. We were going to start a new life."

"And then you kidnapped me."

"Exactly," Townsend said. He paused for a moment and took stock of his surroundings. "I'm in trouble, aren't I?"

"Yeah," Maile replied. "You're in trouble. Just let me go and get the hell out of here. Fly away somewhere, go someplace where no one will know you. Anywhere that isn't here."

Townsend dragged a rickety plastic chair across from one of the corners and set it down, then dropped himself delicately into it. Maile noticed—she couldn't help it—that it was the same type of chair that they kept in the office. She was willing to bet it was identical right down to the model and manufacturer. While Townsend spoke, he seemed to sink further and further into the chair, like a cat on the back of a sofa.

"Perhaps you're right, Miss O'Hara," he said. "I've been a fool, an idiot."

"You've acted like a character," Maile said. "Not like a human being. You need to remember what you are, Mr. Townsend."

"You're right," he repeated. "Of course, you're right."

Then he got up and walked towards the exit. Maile, who was still tied to the chair with her hands behind her back, followed him with her eyes. She struggled pointedly with her bonds.

"Well," Townsend said, "so long."

"Wait!" Maile shouted, as his back retreated through the doorway. "Aren't you going to untie me? You can't just leave me to die down here."

Townsend paused on the edge of Maile's line of sight, just on the other side of the doorway. His hand was wrapped around the doorframe. He glanced back at her. She was scowling in his direction and struggling against the bonds that held her to the chair.

"I'm sorry," Townsend said. "I really am. But I can't risk you coming after me. Just hang tight. If you're right about what you said, they'll find you. Good luck."

Maile finally let it all out when he hit the light switch and slammed the door behind him. She could hear the click of a key in the lock, and it hit her head like the sound of breaking glass or a baby's howl. She screamed and screamed and screamed, and the darkness pressed in around her.

***

Maile had lost track of time, and she had no idea how long she'd been beneath the floors of the theatre. The darkness was oppressive, cloying like a bad smell, and the only sound that she could hear was her own laboured breathing.

She was alone, alone beneath the city.

After what felt like half a lifetime, she managed to turn backwards on the chair, which toppled over and splintered when she hit the floor. She worked her hands against the wood, wincing every now and then as it missed the rope and pricked her wrist, and was able to fray it enough to weaken it. After that, she worked the muscles in her arms, tugging at the rope like a Christmas cracker until it popped and she was able to release herself.

She stood up and stretched, then looked keenly around the room. The darkness was less complete than it had been with the blindfold on, and there was just enough residual light for her to make out the light switch. She turned it on and looked around the room, but it had clearly been out of use for some time and there was nothing that might be useful.

Worse still, the door was locked. If Leipfold had been there, he might have been able to jimmy the lock with a hairpin, but Maile wasn't that kind of girl. If the lock had been computerised—and if she still had her mobile phone and an active connection to the Internet—then she might have made it out. As it was, she had no hope.

Well, she thought, sullenly, *I do have* one *hope.*

She waited, and then she waited some more. When she finally heard the voices, she thought she was hallucinating. They were shouting her name from a long way away, from the bottom of a well for all she could tell. But she summoned up a deep breath of air and bellowed, "Help!" at the top of her lungs, then summoned up another and shouted again.

The voices grew closer, and Maile kept on calling to guide them. Her throat felt like she'd swallowed an ashtray, so dry that it hurt to move her tongue around. The voices stopped outside the door and asked what her name was as they tried to open it. When that failed, they started battering against it with some sort of heavy metal rod.

Meanwhile, Maile shouted her name—using the NATO phonetic alphabet—before taking another deep breath and shouting something else.

It was, "Somebody call James Leipfold."

Chapter Twenty-Nine:
A Sudden Hubbub

WHEN LEIPFOLD LEFT, Groves and Cholmondeley were calling for a backup car to transport Thompson and Lipton to the station. Normally, Leipfold would have helped them, but he wanted to see Maile. He needed to know she was safe.

As he ran down the stairs outside his office and through the front door of the building, his hands went automatically to his pockets. But the keys to his bike were no longer there. Greg Bateman had them. Leipfold paused on the threshold, did a quick calculation in his head to figure out whether taking the tube would be quicker and then arrived at a conclusion. Townsend's theatre was just over a mile away, so he set off on foot and made the journey from door to door in about the same amount of time it took him to finish a crossword.

Jermyn Street was a hive of activity. Two police vans and a half-dozen cars were parked haphazardly, like they'd pulled up in a hurry and emptied out without bothering to pay for a permit. Cholmondeley's team ignored him at first, but then there was a scurry of movement.

Sergeant Gary Mogford detached himself from the throng and wandered over to meet Leipfold. He was in uniform, which was unusual, but then he was used to sitting behind a desk or raising his voice in a crowded briefing room. Mogford was out of his natural habitat, and it showed in his worried face.

"Leipfold," Mogford grunted, nodding his head but refusing to shake the man's hand. "I thought you might show up."

"Cholmondeley said you found her."

"Oh, we found her all right." Mogford grinned and glanced over his shoulder at the entrance where his colleagues were gathering as their number swelled. "Don't worry. She'll be fine."

"Let me guess," Leipfold said. "She was in the changing room or locked up backstage somewhere."

"Close," Mogford replied. "She was in the boiler room. He left her there to die. It's a good job we found her."

"Yeah," Leipfold murmured. "It is. And it's a good job I told you where to look. Can I see her?"

"Soon," Mogford said. "We need to clear the scene and ask her a couple of questions. Then you can accompany us back to the station. The boss wants another word with you, too."

"Let me see my assistant. Then I'll help in any way I can."

"We're working on it," Mogford said. "But she—"

There was a sudden hubbub just inside the theatre, and the two men turned to look as the noise intensified and a half-dozen cops emerged through the doorway with Maile in tow. She looked pale but unhurt, her black clothes looking grey beneath the streetlights. Leipfold realised they looked grey because they *were* grey. She'd been coated in a thin film of cobwebs and dust, deep beneath the bowels of the building. But she still looked like an angel of death, at least until she saw Leipfold. Then her whole face lit up and she started to run towards him. She'd only managed a couple of steps before she was yanked back by one of Mogford's cops.

"Calm down, love," the policewoman said. "Let me get a paramedic to check you over. You can talk to your friend in a minute."

Leipfold guessed it was Constable Yates, who he'd never met before but who he'd heard about from Jack Cholmondeley. She was a former army cadet, which was why Leipfold remembered her. He thought she looked more like a PR exec or an air hostess. In her uniform, she probably turned the eyes of the crooks she helped to collar, but Leipfold thought that wasn't necessarily a bad thing. She had an allergy bracelet across one of her wrists, and her only discerning feature was a small mole on her right cheek. Outside the Jermyn Street Theatre, she was working with a quiet self-confidence, and Leipfold thought he wouldn't be surprised if he saw her again sometime, working undercover in a drug sting at the Rose & Crown.

"Boss!" Maile shouted, struggling against the cops who were restraining her. "It was Tom Townsend!"

"I know," Leipfold replied, his voice shaking with a hint of emotion. It was relief and Maile knew it, and she also knew that Jack Cholmondeley was the only other person who would have noticed. It was a tiny tremor, but it was there.

"I told you not to trust him!" Maile shouted. Her words tore at Leipfold's heartstrings, but she was still smiling and so he allowed himself a flash of hope.

Maybe she'll be all right after all, he thought. *As long as that bastard didn't hurt her.*

Leipfold knew that he'd never forgive himself if Maile had come to any harm. But he also thought he knew Tom Townsend. And with Eleanor Thompson and Jayne Lipton behind bars, he could make catching Townsend his top priority.

He allowed himself a smile. Maile was still shouting information across at him as the paramedics started to give her the once over, but Leipfold barely heard her.

He was busy thinking about Tom Townsend.

Chapter Thirty:
To the Future

LATER THAT NIGHT at the police station, Leipfold and Maile sat in the waiting room. They'd both been interviewed—Maile had been interviewed twice—but neither had been ordered to stay behind. They were free to leave whenever they wanted, but they wanted to be at the station. That way, they could keep an eye on developments, and neither had any urge to go back home. Especially with Tom Townsend still out there.

Leipfold felt awkward, out of place. He leaned over towards Maile and murmured, "Are you all right?"

"I'm fine," she said. "Seriously. I mean, I wasn't in any danger."

"How'd you figure that, then?"

"Come on," Maile replied. "It was Tom Townsend. He's all front. After all, he's a frickin' thespian. He tried to play us, that's all. Said he was driven to it."

"Driven to it?" Leipfold murmured. "By whom?"

"No one says 'whom' anymore." Maile looked over at him and laughed when she saw his expression. "That goes right next to 'nerd' in the list of words that make you sound old."

"Whom is used with a preposition," Leipfold said. "I'm right and you're wrong."

"Whatever," Maile said. "Can we get back to Tom Townsend? He said he was driven to desperation, boss. All he ever wanted was to be a polyamorous knobhead, but when you're trying to keep three women happy, something's bound to go wrong."

"Polyamorous knobhead or not," Leipfold said, "he didn't kill anyone."

"I never said he did," Maile replied. "He told me he knew that one of the girls was behind Donna's death, but he didn't know which one. Then, when Marie died, he figured it must've been Jayne Lipton. Crazy thing is, he loved them all, if you can call it that. So he wanted to take the fall for it to protect her. And then, when that didn't work, he thought if he kidnapped me, it'd scare you off the case. Only it didn't work out like that."

"Sure didn't," Leipfold said. His eyes flashed and for a second, they weren't their usual, dull grey but a bright and brilliant blue.

"Anyway," Maile continued, "I figured it was just a gesture, just Townsend being theatric. He didn't even bother to hide his face. At first, I thought it was like something out of a movie, where if they hide their face then it means they don't want to kill you. But once I figured out where his head was, I knew he wasn't a threat. I don't think he realised he was in the wrong. None of this is really real to him."

"It will be," Leipfold said. "Especially when I get hold of him. I already hit him once. Next time, I might not be as friendly."

"You hit him? When?"

Leipfold sighed. "After he posted that bogus review on the Internet," he explained. "I might not be a cop, but I can figure things out when I have to. Stupid little so-and-so was trying to hide out with his arty friends, so I went on over and found him cowering behind a stack of pottery."

"And you hit him?"

"He tried to hit me first," Leipfold protested. "And besides, I needed to get through to him. I told him to sort his life out and to stop pestering people from behind a computer screen."

"I guess he listened," Maile replied. "He came out from behind the screen, all right. How did you know he'd taken me?"

"He left a message," Leipfold said. "Back at the office. I figured it was him from the start. Besides, you told me he attacked you. Whether that's true or not, it stuck in my head and led me to him. I knew Townsend wouldn't take you back to his warehouse space, and he could hardly hide you at his mother's house. Besides…"

"Besides what?" Maile asked.

"It had to be Townsend or Bateman," Leipfold explained, the hint of a smile in his eyes. "They're the only ones who could overpower you. And besides, I just had Bateman at the office."

Maile nodded. "I like your thinking, boss. So where is he now?"

Leipfold glanced gloomily at his watch. "Well," he said, "if I were Tom Townsend, I guess I'd know the game was up. There'd be nothing for it. I'd run the hell away."

***

A grim young man with a scowl that could melt butter was sitting alone at a bar in Gatwick Airport. He paid in cash and ordered two pints and a full English, which he gobbled down with brown sauce while keeping one eye on the departures board.

He'd booked three tickets, each to a different destination, just to be on the safe side. But he wasn't worried. He was the kind of man, with his sallow face and his short brown hair, who could get lost in a crowd. And he had it all planned out. His first stop was Schiphol in Amsterdam, the great European hub from where he could hop across the globe or hitch a ride across mainland Europe. He was travelling under his real name, of course. He just had to hope that his passport wasn't flagged, but there hadn't been any problems so far. As he sat there, drinking Peroni at 8:55 in the morning, he was starting to wonder if his luck was changing.

He smiled sadly, finished his second pint and wiped the foamy residue from his upper lip on a napkin, then scrunched it into a ball and dropped it inside the glass. He looked around, but the place was almost empty. If anyone was watching him, they were doing a good job of hiding it. He scraped backwards on his chair and stood up, then swung his backpack onto his shoulder and headed towards the gate. He was travelling with hand luggage only, partly for convenience and partly because he hadn't wanted to risk going home to fill a suitcase. It was a good job he'd planned ahead and he'd stashed his passport and a change of clothes.

They called his gate number as he approached the labyrinthine maze of terminals, stiles and fast-track lanes. Someone ran over his foot with a trundle case. He cursed and glanced across at them, but they were already twenty feet away and rapidly accelerating. He checked the screens again and made his way towards the gate. He was about halfway there when a heavy hand descended on his shoulder and spun him around where he stood.

"What the hell?" Townsend began, but that was as far as he got. Detective Inspector Jack Cholmondeley cut him off by clicking a cuff around his wrist. He cuffed the other hand and then pushed the man against the wall. The early morning travellers barely noticed, forming a natural conduit around them, but a sleepy-looking little boy lagged behind his family to take a photograph.

"Tom Townsend," Cholmondeley growled, his deep voice barely registering amidst the hubbub of the terminal. "I've been looking for you. You're nicked, sunshine. I'm arresting you for kidnapping, false imprisonment and conspiracy to pervert the course of justice. You do not have to say anything, but it may harm your defence if you do not mention when questioned something which you later rely on in court. Anything you do say may be given in evidence."

***

Later that day, Jayne Lipton sat down with Gary Mogford. They were in one of the station's poky interrogation rooms with Jayne on one side of the table and Mogford and Groves on the other.

Detective Inspector Jack Cholmondeley was on the other side of a two-way mirror, drinking a cup of coffee and watching the interview progress towards its slow but inevitable conclusion. Cholmondeley was a pragmatist. While he had every faith in Leipfold's deductions, actually proving it in a court of law was something else entirely. He needed a confession, and even a confession might not be enough without some proper evidence to accompany it.

But Sergeant Mogford was on the case, and Cholmondeley knew he had the best sixth sense on the force. If anyone was going to get Lipton to talk or to gather enough evidence to make a conviction, it would be Gary Mogford, the tough cop with a burning sense of justice.

Lipton's interview drew slowly to a close, but it was clear from the smile on her face and Mogford's bad mood, as well as from Cholmondeley's own observations, that she'd given nothing away.

She even refused a lawyer, Cholmondeley thought. *Said she didn't need one. But she's guilty, all right.*

Sergeant Mogford led Lipton to the reception area and explained that while they had enough to charge her, they'd struggle to make it stick.

"But make no mistake," Mogford said. "We're keeping an eye on you. This investigation is far from complete. Stick around so we can find you when we need you. And hey, if you're as innocent as you say you are, you won't mind helping us out with our enquiries."

Jayne smiled enigmatically but said nothing, and Mogford handed her over to Groves for processing. Groves, whose shift was officially over, had already changed into a pair of black jeans and a Primark blouse, but she smiled and murmured an acknowledgement before leading Lipton away into custody.

Cholmondeley watched them go and then headed to his office for a private phone call, one that he couldn't risk anyone overhearing. He locked the door after entering the room, then closed the blinds over the big bay windows that looked out on the corridor. With any luck, his colleagues would think he was finally catching up on his paperwork or reading those mythical emails he'd heard so much about.

He picked up his second phone and hit the speed dial. Leipfold answered on the second ring.

***

Leipfold was in his office when the phone rang, with *The Tribune* across his desk and a pen in his hand. He'd already filled out four clues on Alan Phelps's daily puzzle, and he thought he had an answer for the fifth. He answered the call and put the phone on speakerphone, then continued to answer the clues while he spoke to Jack Cholmondeley.

"I'm listening," Leipfold said. "What's up?"

"We've got Tom Townsend," Cholmondeley replied.

"Great," Leipfold said. "And?"

"Jayne Lipton has been released. We didn't have enough to hold her."

"Keep looking," Leipfold said. "The evidence is there, somewhere. You'll find it."

"Maybe," Cholmondeley murmured. "But what if you're wrong?"

"I'm not wrong," Leipfold insisted. Cholmondeley believed him, and he whistled softly to himself. On the other end of the phone line, Leipfold winced and crossed out one of his answers.

"Listen," Cholmondeley said, "you made a convincing argument and I can't fault you for that. But I'm going to need more than just conjecture to get something to stick. If I can't press charges, the case isn't over. Throw me a bone here. Please, for old time's sake. Help me to find some proof so we can prosecute."

"Will you pay me?" Leipfold asked.

Cholmondeley sighed. They'd had this conversation a dozen times throughout the years and always with the same result. "No deal," Cholmondeley said. "I would if I could, but I can't."

"It's not allowed," Leipfold replied. "I get it. And so you want me to work for free, for the common good."

"That's right."

"What's the common good ever done for me?" Leipfold laughed. "Sorry, that's a job for a copper. You're on your own. Besides, business is booming."

"I thought it might be," Cholmondeley said. "I saw the story in *The Tribune*. Thanks for nothing."

"I solved the case," Leipfold reminded him.

"Yeah," Cholmondeley growled. "You solved it, and now it's down to me to prove it. I'd better go. Things to do."

Leipfold grunted and put the phone down, then glanced down again at the crossword. He'd answered a dozen more clues without even noticing. He took a swig of his coffee and checked his timer, then looked over to the right at the clipping he'd pulled from the front page of the newspaper. His own bemused face stared back at him with Maile O'Hara half a step behind him. With the story breaking the night before they went to print, *The Tribune* had neither the time nor the resources to send a photographer, so Maile had snapped a shot on her mobile phone and emailed it over. Now it was on the same front cover that was sitting on kitchen tables and poking through letterboxes all over the city.

His phone rang again, and he stiffened to attention as he answered the call and held the phone to his ear. "Hello?" he said.

"Mr. Leipfold?" the caller replied. "I saw you in the paper. I have a case for you."

"So does half the bloody city," Leipfold said. "You're going to have to wait your turn, I'm afraid. Looks like I'm all booked up for the next three weeks. You'll have to drop me an email and take a place in the queue."

"But this is an emergency!"

"It always is," Leipfold replied. He sighed. "Drop me that email and I'll see what we can do."

Leipfold put the phone down and looked back at his crossword. Eighteen minutes and counting—one of his worst times ever—and he still had a third of the grid left to finish. He stared at the clue for nineteen down and stuck the end of the pen in his mouth. Then the phone rang again.

Leipfold swore. He slammed the pen down and then answered the call.

***

Eleanor Thompson looked terrible. She hadn't slept, she hadn't washed, and she seemed to have aged ten years in a single night. Her face, which still held a few traces of make-up, all smudged and blurred like a Dali painting, looked sagged and worn, like she held the whole world on her shoulders. In many ways, she did.

The old woman was sitting in one of the white-walled detention rooms at the police station. Her spokesperson, a lawyer she'd hired with the last of her dwindling cash reserves, sat to her right, while Detective Inspector Jack Cholmondeley and Sergeant Gary Mogford sat opposite, staring her down across the table. They sat in silence for a moment, looking shrewdly across at each other.

Sergeant Mogford broke the silence. "I'd like to remind you all that this interview is being recorded," he said. "The time is six fifteen p.m. on Thursday, February second. Detective Inspector Jack Cholmondeley and myself, Sergeant Gary Mogford, are present on behalf of the police force. We're joined by the suspect, Ms. Eleanor Thompson, and her legal representative, Mr. Howard Taylor."

Mogford turned to look at Cholmondeley, who nodded his head imperceptibly. He had the ghost of a smile in the corners of his lips, but his eyes were as serious as ever.

"Ms. Thompson," Mogford said, "I'm going to ask you one last time to tell us the truth. Come clean and get yourself a plea deal. Tell us what happened."

"Nothing happened," she snapped. Cholmondeley watched her eyes as they flicked to her left, a tell-tale sign of a lie as she accessed her brain's creative hemisphere. The policeman knew a dozen armchair detectives—one of them called James Leipfold—who swore by the technique, but he wasn't so sure. It was a clue, but not one to be trusted. Nevertheless, it worked more often than not.

"My client has told you everything she can," the lawyer said, holding up a hand to silence her before she said something else, something that could incriminate her if they reviewed the tapes at a later date. "Gentlemen, you know the law. You can't make her stay here forever. Either charge her with something or let us go."

"Very well," Mogford replied. "Then you leave us no choice. We'll see you in court. Eleanor Thompson, you're under arrest for conspiracy to commit murder. You do not have to say anything, but it may harm your defence if you do not mention when questioned something which you later rely on in court. Anything you do say may be given in evidence. Do you understand me?"

Eleanor Thompson whispered something to her lawyer, who nodded in affirmation and whispered something back to her. Then she glared at the two men on the other side of the table and said, "So be it."

***

The following day, after cashing the vital first cheques from some of the agency's new clients, James Leipfold paid a visit to Bateman's Motors. The boss wasn't in when he got there, so Leipfold bullied the staff until they caved and gave him a call.

"I work Saturdays," Leipfold grumbled. "Why the hell doesn't he?"

Leipfold was well aware that Bateman made more money than him, but the idea of a day off was something alien. It turned out that Bateman had been at a restaurant with his wife and kids. His receptionist caught him on his mobile as he was settling up the bill. He agreed, reluctantly, to stop by on his way back home.

He was in a bad mood by the time that he arrived, but he greeted Leipfold politely and led him through to his office in a frosty silence.

"This better be good," he said, sitting down heavily in his leather chair.

Leipfold stayed standing. It gave him a height advantage, and it also gave him a position of power like an animal asserting its dominance.

"I want Camilla back," he said.

Big, bald Greg Bateman stared at him. "Who's Camilla?" he asked.

"My bike," Leipfold growled. "I told you to look after her."

"Gotcha," Bateman said. "Thing is, pal, I've already accepted an offer."

"Cancel the deal," Leipfold said. He shrugged. "She's my bike and I want her back."

"She's not yours anymore."

Leipfold smashed his fist against the desk and then waved it under Bateman's nose. "I don't care what you have to do," he said. "You'll do what it takes. I know things about you, Mr. Bateman."

"Are you threatening me, Mr. Leipfold?"

"Yes," Leipfold said, "I am. I'll pay you back in full, plus ten percent interest. I can give you half now and the remaining payments every month for the next five months. In return, you make a quick profit while helping a friend."

"You're not my friend."

"I will be," Leipfold replied, "if you want me to keep your name out of the press and the police reports. Do we have a deal?"

Leipfold spat in the palm of his hand and held it out, like his father used to do with his crooked friends when they struck up scams over a pint in the Rose & Crown. Greg Bateman stared at him moodily, then shook his head in amazement and took Leipfold's hand. They shook, both men trying to crush the other, and then Bateman wiped his hand against the seat of his trousers.

Bateman called his receptionist on the intercom and asked them to bring Camilla's keys, then hurried Leipfold through the paperwork. Leipfold was happy to sign it, but only after he'd looked it over and arranged to keep a photocopy. Bateman barely noticed when Leipfold handed over the money.

"Will that be all?" he asked, once the deal was done. "Some of us have a life to live. I wouldn't want to keep you any longer."

Leipfold smiled and held the keys up in his hand. "There's just one more thing," he said. "Any chance of a full tank to go with it?"

***

Leipfold allowed himself a grin, knowing no one could see it behind his visor. It felt good to be back on Camilla, like spending the night in the arms of a woman that he'd known, loved, lost and loved again. His senses were alive, and the feel of the bike beneath him as he cruised the streets at random gave him a warm rush of dopamine that tickled his brain's reward centres.

It had only been a couple of weeks since he'd said goodbye to Camilla, but it had taken her loss for him to realise how vital she was to his investigations. No one took him seriously when he arrived on foot or in the back of a taxi, but a motorbike…well, that was one way to leave an impression.

It was raining, but not as badly as it had been on the night that Donna Thompson died, and the weather was already starting to feel a little warmer. Spring was on its way, but Leipfold couldn't shake the feeling that something bad was about to happen.

Leipfold hit a left and then a right, marvelling at the way that the bike gripped the roads, even in the rain. He suspected that Bateman had made a few improvements, and he made a mental note to ask the man what else was new. It was a pleasure to drive, and it let his mind wander.

He was thinking about a quote he'd heard: "A quiet life is just a lie that you buy from the newspapers." He rolled it over in his head and realised it was something Marie Rieirson had said in *Driven*.

"So much for the quiet life," he murmured. "People only want a quiet life when they're driven to it. Give me an adventure anytime."

He hit another left and started whistling a tune to himself. There would be more adventures, and he knew he'd never settle for normal. Life was for living. But that was for another day.

He revved the engine and took a right through an amber light. The rain fell a little harder and bounced off his helmet and his leathers.

He smiled again beneath the visor and drove off into the night.

***

On the following Monday, the sun rose on a different city. Two people were dead, two were behind bars, and Leipfold maintained that Lipton needed locking up, too.

"And they can throw away the bloody key," he snarled, gratefully accepting the stack of papers and the cardboard cup of coffee that Maile was holding out to him.

"Maybe they'd do just that if we helped them to find a little evidence," Maile said, clearing some space on his desk so she could sit down on it.

"Maybe," Leipfold replied, "but we've got bigger fish to fry. The phone's been ringing off the hook."

"I can imagine. I checked the stats on your website. They peaked last night at thirty times the normal rate. I'm getting you out there on social media while people are still talking about the story."

Leipfold frowned. "What do I need with social media?" he asked.

"Clients," Maile replied. "Maybe not now, not while they're still rolling in, but later. In the future."

"Perhaps," he conceded. "I could use the money."

"It'll come."

"It's already coming," Leipfold said. "I'm asking for deposits up front. My diary's filling up fast. I'm going to need a little help."

"I can't work for free forever," Maile replied.

"That's not what I meant," he said, gesturing for her to lean in a little closer. He could smell her perfume, and it seemed alien in his self-confessed shithole of an office.

Leipfold slid a small stack of paper across the desk to her. "Take a look at this," he said. "It's a contract. I want you to join me properly. I want you to make it official."

"Are you serious?" Maile asked. In some ways, the offer surprised her. In others, she'd seen it coming ever since they started work on the Thompson case. "And you're going to pay me?"

Leipfold nodded. "Not a salary," he said. "Not yet, at least. Minimum wage with five days a week guaranteed and time and a half when you work out of hours. If the last few weeks are anything to go by, you'll be doing a lot of that."

"Do I get bonuses for kidnappings?"

"Don't joke about that," Leipfold said. "And keep carrying that pepper spray."

"Why can't I joke about it?" she asked, scowling like a little kid who's been told to turn the TV off and go to bed. "I'm not going to let that creep ruin my life. Besides, he's been arrested. He's not a threat anymore."

"He's not the only creep on the streets, though," Leipfold reminded her.

"So what? Let me help you take some of them down. Let's get them off the streets before they hurt someone."

"We can try," Leipfold said. "But we're not the police, and you need to remember that. We're not working for the common good. We're working to turn a profit."

"They're not mutually exclusive," Maile said. "Minimum wage, huh?"

"To start with," Leipfold replied. "If business goes well—and it looks like it will once I start invoicing—then we'll start you on a salary."

"It's not about the money," Maile said. "I can make plenty of that when I want to."

"How?"

"I'm good with computers." She flashed him a smile and then shrugged, casting her eyes across the contract. "Let's just leave it at that. There's money in it if you're willing to play fast and loose with the law."

"In that case, I don't want to know," Leipfold said. "So what do you reckon? Are you up for it?"

Maile beamed at him, took the pen that he offered and signed on the dotted line. She offered up a mock toast with her coffee cup.

"To the future!" she said.

Acknowledgements

IF YOU ENJOYED *DRIVEN*, it's because of the tireless work of my editor and partner-in-crime Pam Elise Harris. Cheers, Pam. Thanks also to Christoper Wait for the kickass cover design.

Thanks are also due to my friends and family, and to Donna Woodings, Carl Woodings, Heather and Dave Clarke and Alan and Olga Woodings in particular.

Driven is inspired by the works of classic crime writers like Agatha Christie and Sir Arthur Conan Doyle, but all of my books are inspired in part by the works of other authors. This one is dedicated to everyone who's written a book that I've read, from R. L. Stine and Terry Deary to Terry Pratchett, Graham Greene, Charles Bukowski and Ernest Hemingway.

And, as always, a huge, heartfelt thanks is due to you, the reader. Writing a book takes a lot of hard work, but it's all worth it when people take time out of their lives to read it. You guys rock.

About the Author

Dane Cobain is a published author, freelance writer, book blogger, poet and (occasional) musician with a passion for language and learning. When he's not working on his next release, he can be found reading and reviewing books for his award-winning book blog, SocialBookshelves.com.

Join the Conversation

THANKS FOR JOINING James, Jack and Maile for the first instalment of the Leipfold series. Whether you loved the book or you hated it, I want to know what you think. Join the conversation by tweeting @DaneCobain or visiting me on Facebook, and be sure to keep your eyes peeled for more releases in the Leipfold series.

Reviews are important, and they really do help authors to sell their books. Other than buying another copy and giving it to your friend (which you should *totally* do), there's nothing more helpful than leaving a quick review. Hint, hint.

Join me on your social networking site of choice to keep up-to-date with the rest of my adventures.

http://www.danecobain.com
http://www.twitter.com/danecobain
http://www.facebook.com/danecobainmusic
http://www.instagram.com/danecobain
http://www.youtube.com/danecobain

More Great Reads
from Dane Cobain

No Rest for the Wicked (Supernatural Thriller) When the Angels attack, there's *No Rest for the Wicked*. Cobain's debut novella, a supernatural thriller, follows the story of the elderly Father Montgomery as he tries to save the world, or at least, his parishioners, from mysterious, spectral assailants.

Former.ly: The Rise and Fall of a Social Network (Literary Fiction) When Dan Roberts starts his new job at Former.ly, he has no idea what he's getting into. The site deals in death. Its users share their innermost thoughts, which are stored privately until they die. Then, their posts are shared with the world, often with unexpected consequences.

Come On Up to the House (Horror) This horror novella and screenplay tells the story of Darran Jersey, a troubled teenager who moves into a house that's inhabited by the malevolent spirit of his predecessor. As tragedy after tragedy threatens to destroy the family, Darran's mother decides to leave the house and start afresh. But is it too late?

Subject Verb Object (Anthology) Eighteen writers from both sides of the Atlantic come together in this genre-bending collection of new writing. Meet Luís da Silva and get (thickly) settled. Get drunk in Cornwall or lose yourself in the Warren. Find out why Pete's remote control keeps disappearing, how Gary's cat found heaven and what lurks behind Jay's mirror.